Undeniable

CARA DION

Copyright © 2023 by Cara Dion.

All rights reserved. No part of this book may be reproduced or transmitted in any form or by any means, electronic or mechanical, including photocopying, recording, or by any information storage and retrieval system without the written permission of the author, except where permitted by law.

This is a work of fiction. The characters, incidents and dialogue are drawn from the author's imagination and are not to be construed as real. Any resemblance to actual events or persons, living or dead, is entirely coincidental.

Print ISBN: 979-8-9882826-0-0
Imprint: Independently published

First edition

Cover designed by Cover2Cover Services.
Chapter art by J. Laine

For Papa

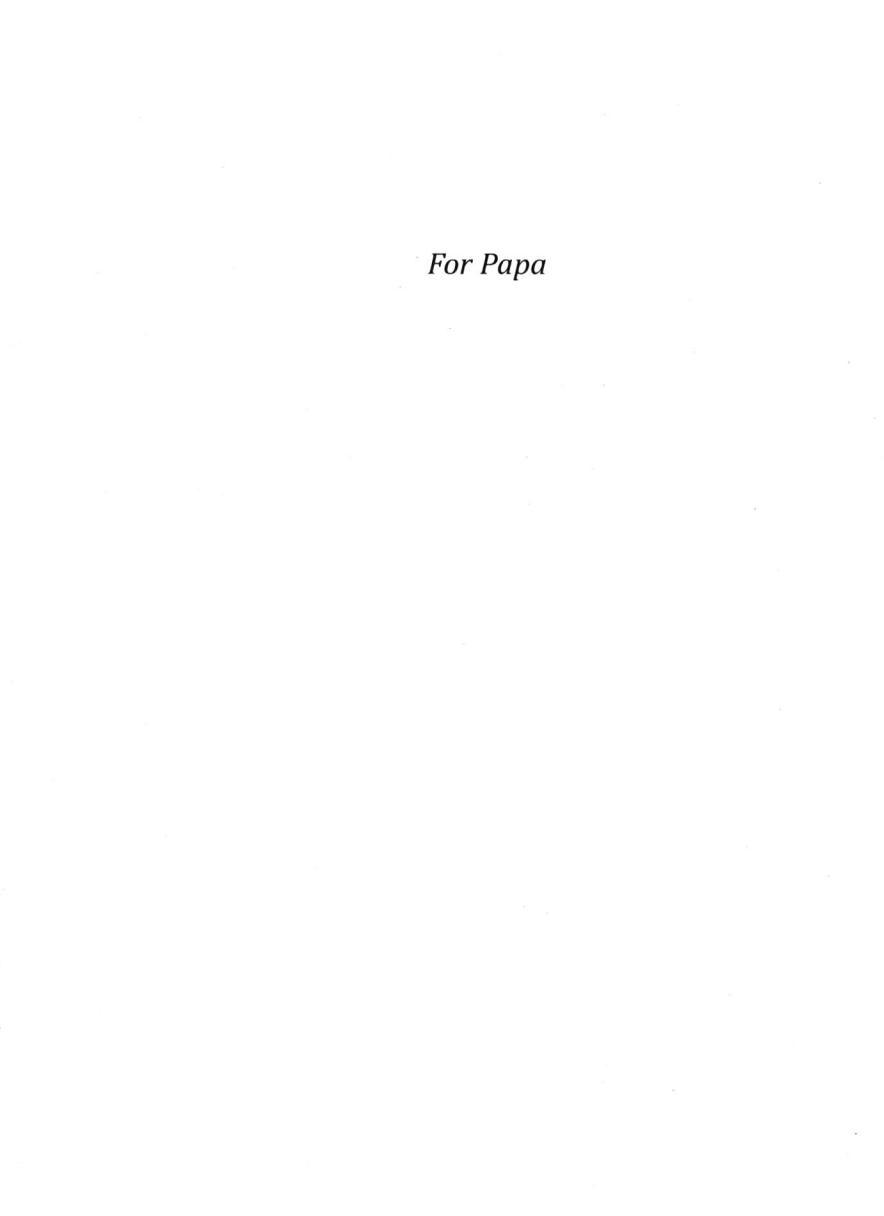

Also by Cara Dion

Love Song Series
Irreplaceable

Indiscreet

Undeniable

Aster Bay
Whisking It All

Visit my website to learn more and download free bonus content:

SENSITIVE MATERIAL WARNING

This book contains a character with a chronic illness (fibromyalgia). It also deals with themes of grief, especially around the loss of a parent. While the death of the parent happens in the past, off page, it may be triggering to some readers.

Prologue

New York City

Noah Van Aller was not going to kiss his little sister's best friend.

Liv had asked him to go, so he was going to make an appearance at this birthday party, have a drink, and then get out of there.

"Who are you supposed to be again?" his best friend Liam asked as they wound their way through the crowded Manhattan bar.

"The Dread Pirate Roberts," he said, sliding on a domino mask to go with his black pants and black button-down shirt. "From *The Princess Bride.*"

Liam shrugged. "Never heard of it."

"At least I have a costume. Who are you dressed as?" Noah asked.

Liam produced a newsboy cap. "Pablo Neruda."

"Nerd."

"You made it!" Liv squealed, pushing through a group of costumed twenty-somethings and throwing her arms around Noah and Liam's necks at the same time. She wore a green high-waisted mini skirt, a purple plastic seashell bra, and a bright red wig.

Born five days apart, Liv and her best friend Callie had been having joint birthday parties their whole lives and they were almost always costume parties. Noah had been unprepared, however, for the day that the costumes transitioned from princess dresses and fairy wings to the kind sold with the word "sexy" emblazoned on the package. Apparently today—their twenty-first birthday party—was that day.

"Happy birthday, Livi," Liam said.

"Where're the rest of your clothes?" Noah grumbled. He scanned the room, trying to look menacing to any guy in the bar getting ideas about his half-dressed little sister.

Liv rolled her eyes and handed them each a name tag sticker and a sharpie. "Make yourselves a name tag—character names only—and grab a drink. We're all at those tables over there," she said, making a vague gesture towards a group of high tops in one corner of the bar.

He was still affixing his name tag when he spotted her: Calandria Cole, Liv's best friend. He'd gotten good at spotting Callie across rooms over the past year, not that she was hard to miss with that riot of red hair. She wore a poofy dress that looked vaguely historical, her cleavage spilling over the top of the low-cut, ruffled neckline. Even at a distance he could see her eyes sparkling as she laughed with her friends, her full lips curved into the most breathtaking smile. She was more beautiful than he remembered, regardless of her ridiculous costume.

Liam disappeared into the crowd as Noah made his way to Callie. She watched him the whole way, her eyes on him like a physical touch. He didn't want to like it. Just as he didn't want to like when she called him late at night to ask for his help with the finer points of music theory. It was never just about music theory.

"Happy birthday," he said, bending close so she could hear him over the music and the laughter.

"Thanks." She smiled, her eyes sparkling. "I wasn't sure you were going to come."

"It's a birthday party for two of my favorite people. Why wouldn't I come?"

His eyes dipped to her lips, to the way her breasts rose and fell with each breath she took. Was she wearing a corset? Did he really want to know?

"Let's get a drink." He snagged her hand and led her through the crowd to the bar.

One drink turned to two turned to three.

"How's your sonata coming?" he asked, his lips almost brushing her ear.

"Better. I think I've figured out the second modulation. Thanks for your help with that," she said, a blush rising in her cheeks.

"Of course."

The first time she'd called him, she was near tears with frustration over her composition professor's comments on the early sketches for her senior capstone project. They'd talked for maybe ten minutes, Noah leaving her with a variety of things to try. He was, after all, a composition professor himself. *I don't make my students cry though.*

When she'd called back a few days later, he'd walked her through an alternate chord progression before the discussion had turned to other things—how much they both missed his sister and were looking forward to her coming home after she graduated, the new reality show starring the front man from one of the 80s hair bands Noah loved so much, and how many marshmallows were acceptable in a cup of hot chocolate. Noah maintained it was three despite Callie's insistence that there was no such thing as too many marshmallows.

By the third call, their conversation had turned flirtatious when Callie casually let slip that she was only wearing underwear because she'd spilled kombucha on her pajamas and the laundry machines in her dorm building were all in use. He hadn't meant to picture it, but how could he not? They'd spent the rest of the call discussing the finer points of fabric choices for women's underwear. He was partial to cotton—soft, simple fabrics without much fuss—which seemed to surprise her. When he'd confessed a preference for going commando himself, she'd simply replied, "Now there's an image."

The next day, he skipped a night out at the bar with his friends to stay home and talk with her. That time they hadn't bothered to discuss music theory at all.

He dragged his fingers through the condensation on his glass. "You haven't called in a while."

"I wasn't sure you wanted me to," she said, avoiding his eyes.

He scooted closer to her, his knees knocking against hers. He shouldn't want her to call. Calandria Cole had lived next door to his family his whole life. When she and Liv were kids, Noah was the one who helped them braid their hair for dance recitals and made chocolate chip pancakes when they were sad. She was little Callie Cole. But suddenly, she didn't seem so little anymore. While he'd been off getting his doctorate and becoming a college professor, she'd grown up. He was having a hard time remembering that he wasn't supposed to kiss her.

He took a sip of his beer, as though his heart wasn't pounding. "I like when you call."

She blushed. He wondered how else he could make her blush.

By their eighth call, he'd been so hard when he hung up that he'd jacked off right there on the couch in his living room, unable to wait even a moment to ease his desire for her. By the eleventh, he'd stroked himself to the sound of her throaty laughter, and thanked every god known to man when she gasped on the other end of the phone and came on her own fingers, pretending they were his.

His eyes swept over the edge of her dress again, this time catching on the name tag stuck to the bodice of her Halloween-store gown. *Hello, My name is: Bernadette Farthingworth.* He ran his fingers over the tag, her breath hitching when his knuckles grazed the top of her breast in the process.

"Who's Bernadette Farthingworth?"

Her cheeks flamed, a pretty pink that traveled down her throat. "She's the heroine in my favorite romance novel," she said. He arched an eyebrow, let his knuckles trail over the swell of her bust as his hand fell away. "*Marrying the Secret Duke,*" she explained. "Noah?"

"Yeah, Calico?" His voice was rough, darker than it should be when speaking to his little sister's best friend. It was the voice he used on their phone calls now, the one he would have used if he were going to kiss her.

"I'm glad you came tonight."

"Me too."

He sipped his beer and thought about leaving it at that. Noah wasn't this guy—he was the guy who would show a woman a good time and then call her a cab. He was the guy who didn't take a woman's phone number because they both knew he'd never use it. He'd never had a girlfriend, never even spent more than one night with the same woman.

He was not the guy who spent three weeks looking forward to the phone calls of a woman eight years younger than him and pretending he wasn't hard as hell just at the sound of her voice.

He was not the guy who thought about breaking his own rules and maybe, just this once, trying the whole relationship thing.

"Callie!" Liv appeared beside them, dropping her head onto her best friend's shoulder. "Come dance with me," she said, pouting.

"You're drunk," Callie laughed.

"So are you!"

"True."

Callie's eyes darted to Noah's, her bottom lip drawn between her teeth. He tilted his head toward the dance floor, encouraging her to go dance with his sister, and returned his attention to his beer.

He was not the guy who was disappointed when a woman he'd known his whole life went off to dance with her friends.

"You ready to go?" Liam asked, appearing at his side.

Noah took another sip of his beer, and watched as Callie pressed a cold glass to her overheated face as she danced. "I'm gonna stay a while longer. Make sure Livi gets back to her hotel okay."

Liam followed Noah's line of sight to where Callie danced with Liv and their friends, her hips swinging, her hair swaying, and her laughter floating across the room even over the music and the noise.

"You're gonna stay for Livi, huh?" Liam said, his eyebrow arched and lips pressed together like he was holding back a laugh. Liam pointed to his mouth, baring his teeth. "Watch out for the braces."

"Fuck you," Noah said, but there was no heat in it, the corner of his lips turning up. "She hasn't had braces for years."

"I'll see you back at your place?" Liam asked, backing away. "Or not? I have an early train back to Boston, so if you're not back by morning, I'll assume you decided to risk the jail time."

"She's twenty-one, asshole," Noah called.

"Just don't wait all night to make your move, old man!" Liam called back.

Around midnight, Noah made his way across the room. Liv was already saying her goodbyes. "How are you getting home?" he asked his sister.

"Jules has a cab waiting," she said, referring to her college roommate.

"You're going straight back to the hotel, right? No stops?"

"Yes, big brother," she laughed, giving him a hug.

Tomorrow morning she and her roommate would fly back to Michigan to finish their last semester of college. He couldn't wait for her to move back to the East Coast after graduation—he missed her like hell.

"You coming with us, Cal?" Liv asked.

Callie shook her head. "No, I'm gonna go back to my dorm. It's not far."

Liv stabbed a finger in the center of Noah's chest. "Make sure she gets in a cab, alright?"

"Scout's honor." He held up three fingers.

Liv snorted. "You were never a Scout."

And then it was just Noah and Callie. He advanced on her, aware that the alcohol had gone to his head—or maybe it was proximity to her making him reckless. Either way, he didn't care. Callie watched him approach, her lips curving into the barest of smiles. She walked backwards as he came closer, her head tipping up to meet his eyes, until her back hit the brick wall of the bar.

He leaned a hand on the wall beside her, bending close until his lips brushed the shell of her ear. "Did you have fun tonight?"

She nodded, her hair brushing against his face. Like silk.

"Do you want me to get you a cab?"

She shook her head and reached up to untie the strings holding his mask in place. She pulled it away, her fingertips ghosting over his cheek as she did. "That's better."

He wasn't sure who leaned in first, but did it really matter? Their lips collided, a hungry tangle of tongues and teeth as if they'd been kissing for ages instead of this being their first time. He pressed her to himself and swallowed her little gasp when his pelvis rocked against her. She fisted the fabric of his shirt, using that grip to pull him closer, and he took that as permission to let his hands wander down the curve of her waist, hook her thigh and pull it up around his hip. He nipped at her bottom lip, smiling when she moaned in response.

She was glorious—everything he'd imagined she'd be and more. And they fit together so perfectly, like they were two parts of the same whole. Maybe it wasn't so crazy to think he could do this. Maybe with Callie he could rewrite the rules that had governed his life since his father's death. Maybe with Callie it could just be this—flirty phone calls, and talking about music, and kissing like they might die if they didn't get another taste of each other's lips.

A bell rang somewhere behind them by the bar. The obnoxious, clanging wrested them apart. "Last call!" someone shouted.

He eased her leg back to the floor, his hand tracing up her side until it cupped her jaw. With a final, lingering kiss, he pulled away, panting. He was so hard he was having trouble concentrating on anything but the way her breasts heaved against his chest as she caught her breath.

"Let's get you that cab," he said, brushing his nose against hers.

"You could come with me," she murmured, her voice breathy and hopeful.

He shook his head, pressing his forehead against hers. "Not tonight."

"Oh." The disappointed sound falling from her lips made him grin.

"Can I call you tomorrow?"

"Yes, please."

He put her in a cab, kissing her soundly before closing the door behind her and ignoring the parts of him that wanted to climb in after her. He would make himself new for her—fashion himself into someone who knew how to take things slow, how to build a relationship and not just a one-night stand. Someone who saw the possibilities of the future, not just the devastation of the end.

The next day, when Noah called Callie, she didn't answer.

Chapter One

Six Years Later

"So, basically I'm fucked," Noah said, staring across the impressive mahogany desk at his uncle.

Stuart Van Aller leaned back in his chair and cast an assessing look over his nephew. But he wasn't acting in the role of uncle at the moment; he was acting in the role of Dean of the College of Performing Arts at Burnett University—Noah's boss.

"This is your second chance, son. Most people don't get more than one shot at their dream. Wolf wants you on this project, but he can't afford to have the family values lobbyist groups banging down his door because you can't keep your pants on."

Noah bit the inside of his cheek to keep from firing back a snarky response. An official meeting in Uncle Stu's office in the ivy-covered brick building, surrounded by more framed diplomas than any one person should hold, was not the time to talk back to his uncle, even if he did take offense at the suggestion that his sex life had anything to do with his ability to compose a documentary film score.

The implication wouldn't have stung so much if it hadn't come from Wolf MacMillan, an award-winning documentary producer and one of his father's oldest friends. He'd have thought that all the years of friendship between his family and Wolf would have earned Noah the benefit of the doubt. Apparently, he'd been mistaken.

"How did he even get a copy of the student newspaper?" Noah grumbled.

He knew it was beside the point. Some college kids had decided to run an article on the "Most Eligible Professors of Burnett" and now he was in danger of losing his chance at breaking into the film industry. He had come in second, thank you very much, beaten only by Liam who was no longer a professor at the university anyway, so it was basically like he'd come in first.

"If I were you, I'd be more concerned with how those students got photos of you wining and dining half the English faculty."

Noah bowed his head, his face hot. It's not that he was ashamed of the photos (they were all sufficiently tame), or of having slept with all those adjuncts—it was, rather, the embarrassment of a child being called on the carpet by a parent. Uncle Stu had practically been a father to Noah and Liv since their actual father, Stu's brother, passed two decades prior. The idea that Noah's sex life was somehow reflecting poorly on his uncle made him feel like he was ten years old again, getting in trouble for trampling the neighbor's flowers with an errant soccer ball.

"I've assured Wolf that the article greatly exaggerated the facts," his uncle said.

It hadn't, though, and Uncle Stu knew it.

"Why does who I sleep with matter? If he likes the music—"

"You're not that naïve. The senator wants this documentary to be airtight. I wouldn't be surprised if it becomes a cornerstone of her presidential bid in four years. Her weak spot is always the family values groups who take issue with the fact that she's a lesbian. You could be the next Vivaldi and she still wouldn't let Wolf put you on this project if she thought you were a liability."

"What am I supposed to do? I can't change what I've done in the past."

"Wolf will be at your sister's wedding next weekend."

"I didn't know mom had invited him," Noah said, surprised.

"Wolf was one of your father's best friends," Uncle Stu scolded, as though Noah hadn't heard all the stories of Wolf, Uncle Stu, and his dad wreaking havoc during their prep school days. "You know, your father wanted to score one of Wolf's films, too, but by the time he got up the nerve to talk to him about it…"

"I know."

Noah knew all about the things his father had left unfinished, the dreams he hadn't had a chance to realize. Over the years, therapists had questioned whether Noah truly wanted to be a film composer, or if he was just checking off the boxes on his father's final to-do list. Most of the time he was certain—he'd dreamt of being a composer for as long as he could remember. He had a niggling suspicion, however, that his father had more to do with his determination to work on this particular project than he'd like to admit.

Uncle Stu cleared his throat, returning their conversation to the present. "The wedding is your chance to prove to Wolf that you're not going to be an albatross for this project. So, no getting caught in broom closets with drunk bridesmaids."

"Not a problem. Liv would murder me if I hooked up with any of her friends."

"Even more reason to keep your nose clean."

"And if I can't change his mind? I've already taken the sabbatical."

"Then I guess you'd better be convincing. Opportunities like this don't come along often. Don't throw it away...again."

His uncle returned to the pile of papers in front of him. Noah knew when he was being dismissed; conversations with his uncle had ended the same way for the last twenty years. Between the August heat and the older man's disapproval hanging thick in the air, the office was stifling, so for once Noah didn't mind the abrupt end to a conversation.

"Are you heading up to Rhode Island tomorrow with Mom?" Noah asked, getting to his feet.

Uncle Stu shook his head. "I'll be there in time for the rehearsal dinner. But I can't afford to spend a whole week lazing about at some hotel just because your sister decided to extend the celebrations." He glanced up at Noah, his face softening. *Slipping into uncle mode,* Noah thought. "The music is good, son. You deserve this job. I'll do whatever I can to help sway Wolf when we see him."

"Thanks, Uncle Stu."

Noah emerged from the office onto the nearly deserted campus, taking off his blazer as he made his way across the quad toward his own office in the music building. A week at a beachfront resort for his little sister's wedding sounded like exactly what he needed. He retrieved his briefcase—and with it, the sample compositions he'd sent to Wolf when he'd first thrown his hat in the ring for this documentary score—and locked his office, ready to head home and pack. He was mid-daydream about going on the road with the film crew and the senator when his phone rang.

"Welcome back to the States," he said when he answered. "When did you get in?"

"We just landed in Boston," his sister replied. "Daemon's renting the car right now."

Liv and her fiancé were both successful musical theater actors. They'd spent the last few months in London, reviving their popular production of *Chess* for a limited engagement on the West End.

"I have a favor to ask," she said.

Noah chuckled. "You usually do."

"It's about Callie," Liv began.

Noah drew up short at the mention of his little sister's best friend. He was not looking forward to a week in close proximity with the woman. She still always seemed to know exactly how to get under Noah's skin. Once upon a time, he'd welcomed her there, but that was before. Now he knew better. It was best for everyone if he and Callie kept their distance.

"Mrs. Cole's in Ohio again. Mom offered to drive Callie to the wedding, but she's been house sitting for us in Brooklyn for the last few nights so she's closer to Long Island than Jersey and she would have such a better time if she drove with you."

"Absolutely not."

Noah Van Aller never said no to his little sister. That is how he wound up proofreading countless high school term papers in between his own schoolwork for his master's program. It was the reason he learned to French braid when he was a teenager and Liv, only in elementary school at the time, begged him to help her get ready for her dance recitals. It was why he learned to make chocolate chip pancakes just right so that the chocolate didn't burn when the pancake flipped. And it was the reason he knew he was about to agree to being trapped in a car for four hours with Calandria Cole, but she couldn't blame a guy for at least pretending to put up a fight.

"Please, Noah? For me?"

Noah scrubbed his hand over his face. "Why can't she drive herself?"

"She just can't," Liv said on the other end of the phone, as if that should be sufficient reason for him to give up his podcast-listening time. "Why are you being difficult? It's just Callie."

Noah took a deep breath in an attempt to calm his rising blood pressure. He hadn't been alone for more than a few minutes with Callie in six years—not since her twenty-first birthday—and for damn good reason.

"Please, Noah. It's my wedding."

"I can't wait until you aren't able to pull the wedding card anymore." On the other end of the phone, his sister laughed. He closed his eyes, his stomach in knots. "Okay. I'll pick her up tomorrow morning."

"You're the best, big brother."

"Don't you forget it."

At nine o'clock sharp on Saturday morning, Noah pulled into a parking space outside the Brooklyn townhouse his sister shared with her fiancé. As he climbed out of his car, Callie appeared in the doorway to the townhouse, her red hair shining in the sunlight and her shoulders weighed down by heavy looking bags. Even struggling with her mismatched luggage, she was stunning. Her hair was pulled back in a long braid that fell over one shoulder—the style she often favored in recent years—and when she smiled, he felt that smile all the way down to his toes.

He scowled, pushing down the warmth that tried to spread through him at the sight of her, and took the steps to the door two at a time.

"Are you trying to hurt yourself?" he asked, lifting the bags from her shoulders and slinging them over his own. Her smile faltered. *Good. This will be easier if we aren't too friendly*, he told himself. It was true, even if he felt anything but *good* about it.

"I can handle it," she said as she pulled a wheeled suitcase through the door behind her.

Noah grumbled and took that from her as well. He would not be responsible for his little sister's maid of honor throwing her back out before she even got to the damn wedding.

"You can handle finding us some good road trip music while I load up the trunk."

"It just so happens I have the perfect playlist," Callie said as she slid into the passenger seat of Noah's Toyota Corolla.

Noah groaned. "Am I going to regret giving you control over the music?"

"Oh, absolutely." Callie connected her phone to the car's sound system. A moment later, the unmistakable opening notes of *Livin' on a Prayer* poured from the speakers. Noah arched an eyebrow at her as he slipped into the seat. "I may have thrown in a few songs for you," she said.

Callie and Liv delighted in mocking Noah about his love for 80s hair bands, so he knew she had likely meant it as a jab, adding a few of the band's greatest hits along with her perplexing mix of folk, alt rock covers, and 90s R&B. It was hard to be annoyed with someone while classic Bon Jovi was playing, though.

"Thanks for giving me a ride," she said.

"No problem." Noah steered the car back into traffic. "Is there a reason you weren't able to drive yourself?"

"My car's in the shop again." Callie sank deeper into her seat and avoided his eyes. "It's fine. It just wasn't up for the drive."

"That's because it's a piece of crap. You need to get a new car."

"We can't all afford to just buy a new car whenever we want. Some of us are on a budget."

"You act like I'm buying new BMWs left and right. I drive a ten-year-old Corolla. But a new car is not a luxury when your current vehicle dies every other day."

There was a long pause while Callie played with the end of her braid. Noah couldn't remember the last time he'd seen Callie with her hair down, but he remembered the way it hung around her face in loose waves, the feel of it between his fingers...

Shut it down.

"Can you lay off with the overbearing thing, please?" Callie finally asked. "If I wanted to spend the entire trip fighting, I would have gone to Ohio with my mom."

"What are you two fighting about now?" He hated that he wanted to know.

"The usual." She looked out the window to avoid his curious glance. "But it's ten times worse since Liv got engaged."

Noah smiled as a memory flashed in his mind. "Do you remember that time you and Liv were playing dress up and you tried on your mom's wedding gown?"

"We didn't just try it on. We took it out of its archival storage box. I thought I was going to be grounded for the rest of my life." Her smile matched his own. "That was all Liv. She wanted to pretend to be Ariel from *The Little Mermaid*, and my mom's dress had those same God-awful puffy sleeves."

Noah laughed. "Your mom takes weddings very seriously."

"She does," Callie said, her smile fading. "She's going to be in fine form. A whole week for her to sigh and fuss about how worried she is that I'll never get married."

Noah's stomach soured at the idea of Callie getting married. He knew she dated—he wasn't naïve enough to think that her childhood crush on him would still be a factor, and anyone with eyes could see that she was gorgeous. All that red hair and big dark eyes and curves you could lose yourself in…

Not that he cared, but Callie tended to date assholes. Each time Liv would mention a new guy in Callie's life, Noah found himself awake at three in the morning with a half empty bottle of Scotch deep down the rabbit hole of the guy's social media profiles. None of the suits she'd dated were good enough for her. He told himself it was nothing more than what a big brother should do, the same as he would do for Liv—only he couldn't remember the last time he'd Facebook stalked someone Liv had dated. He certainly didn't write and delete a thousand texts he never sent asking her what the hell she saw in those guys.

He cleared his throat and stubbornly focused his attention on the bumper of the car in front of him. "Is your date meeting you there?"

She didn't answer at first and he thought he was going to crawl out of his skin. "No date," she said, her voice light in a way that didn't sound totally convincing.

"What happened to what's-his-name? The short finance guy."

"How do you know about Ian?"

Shit. He tried to sound casual, even though he could feel the heat creeping into the tips of his ears. "Liv mentioned something..."

"Oh."

When she didn't offer anything further, he grunted out his impatience. "So, what happened?"

"He got transferred out of state. Not everyone's cut out for long distance relationships, I guess," she said, turning her head to look out the window.

Goddamn it. Now she was sad, and he did not want to have to spend four hours playing therapist while she talked about some guy who'd broken her heart. "At least you're not the only one without a plus one," he offered.

"Yeah, but no one's holding their breath waiting for *you* to get married."

Noah scowled. It was one thing when Wolf MacMillan and Uncle Stu leveled accusations about his love life, but it was another thing entirely coming from Callie, though he didn't want to look too closely at why.

"Come on. When was the last time you were in a serious relationship? Or any relationship for that matter?" she asked. He pressed his lips together and shot her a pointed glare. "That's what I thought."

"I date," he said, not at all liking the direction this conversation was taking. Sad would have been easier.

"I think you need to see the same woman more than once for it to qualify as dating."

"I've never had any complaints," he grumbled.

"I believe that."

He glanced at Callie, his eyes moving over the upturned end of her nose, the dusting of freckles high on her cheek, the hollow of her throat. He refocused on the road before she caught him staring, turning up the music as the song switched to something folksy. *This is going to be a long week.*

Chapter Two

Callie was grateful when Noah pulled the car over at the highway rest stop in Connecticut. The traffic on Rt 95 was intense and they hadn't even hit the worst of it yet, but a distance that should have only taken a little over an hour had instead ballooned to two, and her body was aching in protest.

"I'm going to grab a coffee. Do you want anything?" Noah asked.

"No, thanks. I'm just going to take a minute to stretch before we get back on the road."

He nodded and disappeared into the rest stop. She watched him go, her gaze lingering on the way the breeze ruffled his dark hair, how his jeans clung to his thighs.

"Enough of that," she chastised herself. She made a promise to herself not to spend the entire week lusting after her best friend's older brother, then dropped into a deep squat in the empty parking space next to Noah's car. The stretch burned along her thighs as the tired muscles of her hips relaxed. She winced when the dull ache in her lower back turned sharp.

Exhaling a frustrated breath, she steadied herself with a hand on the car as she came back up to standing. Then she braced her hands on the side of the car and bent forward at the waist, just a little at first, letting the stretch sing along her hamstrings and through her calves. With a baby step backwards, she deepened the stretch again and again until she was bent in half, her hands clasping her ankles and her hips pressing up to the sky like her yoga teacher had taught her. It felt so goddamn good she never wanted to move. But already she could feel the blood rushing to her head and knew she'd have a killer headache if she didn't stand back up soon.

"I got you a—" Noah said behind her, breaking off with a curse.

She shot up to standing at the sound of his voice, turning to look at him over her shoulder. He quickly averted his gaze, but not so fast that Callie couldn't see how dark his eyes had become. *Noah was checking out my ass?* That couldn't be right. There was no way. Noah had made it clear over the last few years that he was not even the slightest bit interested in her anymore, no matter how many times her hopeless romantic heart had wished he would be.

She spun around to face him, but she moved too fast and the vertigo caught up with her, shaking her balance and sending her careening towards the pavement.

Noah reached out an arm to catch her, the jerky motion sending the drinks in the tray he carried sideways. He caught the first cup, but the second fell out of its holder, spilling iced coffee all over his shirt. Noah cursed, shaking his free hand as drips of the milky liquid flowed down his arms in rivulets that drew Callie's attention to the corded muscles of his biceps and forearms.

"I'm so sorry," Callie said, her eyes wandering over the damp fabric clinging to his chest.

"You didn't do anything," Noah grumbled. "Here, take this."

He thrust the sodden cardboard tray at her and, in one swift movement, pulled his soaked t-shirt over his head. Callie's eyes raked over the expanse of tan skin, the lean muscles of his chest and abs, the line of dark hair disappearing into the waistband of the jeans hung low on his hips. It had been a few years since Callie had seen Noah without a shirt on, and in that time he'd sculpted his body into a work of art.

He balled up the t-shirt and tossed it into the back seat of the car, using napkins from his glove box to wipe the last of the coffee from his skin. "I got you one of those disgusting teas you like," he said. Callie raised her eyes to his. His expression was hard, making it clear he'd caught her checking him out, and he was unamused.

"Thank you." She took a sip of the kombucha.

Noah opened his suitcase and pulled on a fresh t-shirt. Though the fabric hid all that defined muscle from view, it couldn't stop her from wondering what it would be like to be the kind of girl Noah spent the night with. Callie knew better than to indulge in the fantasy, of course. One look at the photos Noah was tagged in on social media made it quite clear: Noah Van Aller never spent more than one night with the same woman. Callie's one night had been confined to a single kiss at her twenty-first birthday party. But what a kiss. A kiss to end all kisses. A kiss she had compared every other kiss to for the last six years.

By the time they pulled back out onto the highway, Callie had almost succeeded in putting her inappropriate thoughts about Noah out of her mind. Almost.

To be fair, inappropriate thoughts about Noah had been Callie's constant companion since the summer she turned twelve. Back then, it was Noah, home for a few weeks between semesters at college, who drove Callie and Liv to the mall, Noah who accompanied them to the Shakespeare Festival, Noah who spent his mornings giving her piano lessons. Unlike Mrs. Shabot down the street, Noah didn't chastise Callie when she improvised. Instead, he encouraged her to explore the melodies playing through her mind and helped her channel that music through her fingers as they danced across the keys of the baby grand in the Van Aller family living room. Callie flexed her fingers against the dull ache in her wrists, the constant soreness that left her knuckles swollen and stiff and had put an end to her piano playing.

"You good?" Noah asked, his eyes flicking to her hands.

"Fantastic," she said, her voice too bright even to her own ears. She shoved her hands into the pockets of her hoodie.

"Explain something to me. Why is your mom so hell bent on marrying you off? Is there some secret inheritance or something that you only get access to if you have a husband?"

Callie barked out a laugh. "I wish."

"Then what is it?"

"She's afraid I'll have no one to take care of me."

She braced herself for his follow-up questions. They'd never talked about her illness before, which was odd because Noah was a cards-on-the-table kind of guy and Callie was perfectly happy to answer questions, though she was tired of having to dispel the myth that having fibromyalgia meant she was incapable of taking care of herself. Her mother was insistent that her 'independent streak' was recklessness in disguise. Callie resented the implication that she was careless or cavalier about her health—almost as much as she resented the idea that having a chronic illness meant she needed a husband to take care of her.

Besides, her ex-boyfriend Ian had made it clear that

a life with her was a burden. One that, according to him, had cost him a major promotion. He'd been forced to take a position with a different financial firm out of town, so really, he'd said, it was her fault that they'd been in a long-distance relationship in the first place. Could she really blame him if he'd grown tired of dealing with her flare ups when they had so little time together? She refused to be in a relationship with someone who would resent her for the ways she held him back, or who only cared for her out of a misguided sense of obligation. Maybe she'd read too many romance novels, but she'd have breathless love or nothing at all.

"That's bullshit," Noah said.

Callie smiled in spite of herself. "I agree."

"And she thinks that because Livi is getting married, you should be, too?"

"Well, I am older than Liv."

Noah barked out a laugh. "By five days."

"Tell that to my mother." With her gaze focused straight ahead so she wouldn't see his reaction, she continued. "She wants to move to Ohio to be near my Aunt Shirley."

"She's been talking about that for half our lives," he scoffed, dismissing the idea.

"Yeah."

"What's stopping her?"

"She says she can't go and leave me with no one to take care of me. She's afraid I'll end up…" She stopped herself. Noah didn't need the whole sob story. "Anyway, she says she won't go without me and I refuse to move." Callie shrugged.

"And if you were married, she'd move on her own?"

"Pretty much," Callie said. "She says that if I had a husband—or even the prospect of one—then she'd know I was going to be taken care of. She's been talking about moving back to Ohio for as long as I can remember. Unless something changes, she'll just stay in Jersey forever and blame me for her unhappiness the same way she blames my dad for bringing her to Jersey in the first place."

"That's fucked up," Noah said, his voice hard and his jaw tight.

"That's Mom."

She knew her mother meant well, but Callie was not about to give up her entire life to move halfway across the country because of her mother's fears. So instead she lived with the guilt of being the reason her mother was miserable.

"Let's talk about something else," Callie said. "Liv says you're writing the score for a new documentary."

Noah scowled. "How about we don't talk for a while. Drink your kombucha," he said, gesturing with his chin to the drink in the cupholder.

"Overbearing," she mumbled, but she didn't miss the way the corner of his lips turned up.

Chapter Three

Another hour in bumper-to-bumper traffic and still only halfway to their destination, Noah pulled off at an exit in the middle-of-nowhere Connecticut. He was all too aware of the increasing frequency with which Callie squirmed in her seat, each new position causing a momentary flash of pain to cross her face before she shifted and tried again. He couldn't just ignore her discomfort, even if she was hell bent on trying to hide it from him.

"There's a great diner up ahead," he said.

"Perfect. I'm starving."

The diner was a sprawling maze of mostly empty chrome and cobalt blue vinyl booths. The gray-speckled linoleum squeaked beneath their feet as they followed the hostess to a booth in the back corner of the massive building. The menus were so large they barely fit on the table, their laminated surfaces giving off the smell of lemon disinfectant.

"How did you find this place?" Callie asked.

"I used to stop here when I'd drive to Boston to visit Liam. Now that he and Min are moving to Providence, it'll probably become my regular pit stop again."

Until recently, Noah's best friend Liam had worked with him at Burnett University on Long Island. He'd only lasted a little over a year before he fell in love with Min, who was his student at the time. Min had graduated two months ago, and she and Liam were starting over in her home state of Rhode Island while she pursued her master's degree and he figured out his next move.

It was hard for Noah to imagine wanting the kind of love that Liam and Min had—a love that pushed them both to completely re-evaluate what they wanted out of life, to risk everything for each other. A love that had the power to destroy a person. *Fuck that.* There were enough ways to be destroyed by life without adding another person into the equation.

The waitress appeared and Noah placed his usual diner order: a burger, medium, no onions, no pickles, and a Coke. Safe. Uncomplicated.

"What about you, honey?" the waitress asked Callie.

Callie's eyes lit up as she swept them over the menu, pointing at the items as she ordered. "I'll have the veggie omelet, and can I get an order of curly fries and a side of Thousand Island dressing? Oh, and a strawberry milkshake."

Noah knew he was staring, but he couldn't help it. When the waitress left, Callie called him on it. "What?"

"What you just ordered...that's chaos."

She threw her head back and laughed. "No, that's delicious. I would have thought you'd be over your whole food deal by now."

"My *food deal*?" he asked, incredulous.

"You know." She lowered her voice in an imitation of him. "*No sauce on anything. Foods shouldn't touch. Keep your flavor to yourself.*"

"I don't have a food deal," he said, fighting off a smile.

"I've always wondered what made you hate good food.

Was it that time Liv tried to make pad Thai and we all got food poisoning?"

Noah groaned. "That certainly didn't help. I don't know. It's just the way I eat."

"You can't seriously like a plain burger with nothing on it. There's no way that's enjoyable."

"I don't eat for enjoyment. I eat so I won't be hungry."

"That is blasphemy. Good food is one of life's greatest pleasures. It's right up there with music and sex."

Her smile hit him square in the chest. Just like it had that night six years ago. *Shit.* He needed a distraction, something that wouldn't give his brain space to think about how full her lips were or the adorable dimple in her chin or the fact that now he was wondering what Callie considered good sex— *No.* No good could come from any of it.

He cleared his throat and forced the conversation to a safer topic. "Livi said you've been running more programs at the library lately."

"Yeah. The new director has really let us try all kinds of new things, and the patrons are loving it."

"Like what?"

She twisted up her lips as she thought, a spark flashing in her eyes. "Like last month I ran a workshop on how to build the perfect playlist to listen to while reading a book in any genre. And a few weeks ago, I started a young adult romance novel book club for teenagers where they're going to eventually write their own book. Oh! And I even get to throw a costume party next month to celebrate Fall Into Reading. I'm hoping to make it an annual thing."

Her whole face lit up as she talked, her hands gesturing wildly as she ran him through her plan to teach the kids in her book club how to analyze the story structure so they could write their own novella. "The director even said she'll put a copy of their book into circulation."

"That's amazing," he said.

She shrugged off the compliment. "Libraries aren't just book repositories, you know? They're part community center, part learning annex. If I can help people feel more connected to their community and get them to read a few more books in the process, that's a win."

He was stunned, blindsided by how damn passionate she was about this. It reminded him of all the times they'd talked about music, the late-night phone calls when she was too excited about some snippet of a melody to wait until morning to play it for him. It had been years since he'd heard her talk about music that way, though.

Callie shook her head as if coming out of a trance and leaned back in the booth, taking a long sip of her milkshake. "My mom keeps badgering me to take a job at one of the local colleges. They pay better but I wouldn't be teaching teenagers about the joy of romance novels or helping octogenarians learn how to video chat with their grandchildren."

"You love it."

"I do." She focused her attention on her lunch, cutting her omelet into smaller and smaller bites. "I've just talked your ear off," she said with a self-deprecating smile. "Tell me about your work."

"There's not much to tell," he said, taking a bite of his burger and frowning at the lackluster taste.

"Oh, come on. What are you working on?" She swiped a French fry through her Thousand Island dressing. Her eyes practically rolled back in her head when she took a bite, her face frozen in a moment of pure pleasure. *Nope. Not thinking about what else puts that look on her face.*

"I've got an article in the works for the *American Journal of Score Analysis* examining the way Korngold reuses themes from his film scores in his classical compositions."

"Okay...that sounds very...impressive."

"What about you? Have you written any songs lately?"

"Don't try to change the subject. We're talking about you, not me. Tell me about what you're composing."

Noah took another bite of his burger. He hated this question, which was damn inconvenient considering he was a professional composer. Teaching was always meant to be secondary, a way to support himself while he waited for his big break. He enjoyed teaching and he loved working with his students, helping them discover their own musical voices, but lately he spent more time on the trappings of academia than he spent behind a piano. When Wolf MacMillan had first called him about submitting to be the composer for his new documentary, it had seemed like the job he'd been waiting for—something he could really sink his teeth into. But judging by the things Uncle Stu had said the day before, it was unlikely to ever be more than a dream.

"Mostly exercises for my sight-reading classes," he said.

Callie's brows drew down, her nose wrinkling. "I thought you were working on a documentary."

"I'm in talks with the producer, but he has...reservations."

"About your music? That's insane."

He ignored the flicker of warmth in his chest at her indignation on his behalf and pushed the fries around on his plate just to have something to do with his hands. "Wolf's an old friend of Uncle Stu's and my dad. They went to Williston together and those prep school roots run deep. Deep enough to ask me to submit for the project, but apparently not so deep that he's willing to work with..." He lowered his eyes, dragging his finger through the condensation on the outside of his glass so he wouldn't have to look at her when he said it. "...a 'lothario'—his word, not mine."

"Is he the villain in a historical romance? Who talks like that? *Lothario.*"

"The film is documenting what is apparently going to be a pretty tight race and the senator wants a clean crew that the conservative media won't be able to dig up any dirt on."

"In the film industry? Good luck with that," she snorted.

"Wolf's team found some bullshit article the student newspaper ran a year or so ago that ranked Liam and me as the most eligible professors on campus. It didn't paint me in the most flattering light for the conservative set."

"Ah. The adjuncts," she said, with a knowing nod. How the hell did Callie know about the adjuncts? He wasn't secretive about his love life, but he'd definitely never discussed it with her.

"Wolf will be at the wedding. It's my last chance to prove to him that I'm not a liability on the project. If I don't get this job... I don't know if I'll get another chance like this." He took another bite of his burger, and then threw it down, disgusted with the situation he found himself in and bored by his lunch.

"Give me that." Callie pulled his plate towards her. She ripped off the top bun and slathered it with a thick layer of her Thousand Island dressing.

"What are you doing?"

"You can't expect food to have any flavor when you don't give it any." She shook her head like he was an idiot as she sprinkled the patty with pepper. She dug into her omelet and pulled out a few pieces of mushroom and roasted red pepper, laying them on top of the burger before returning the top bun and sliding it back across the table towards him. She gestured with her eyes to the plate. "Go on."

Noah steeled himself and took a bite, never taking his eyes off Callie. His taste buds exploded with a symphony of flavors—tangy and earthy and acidic.

"How did you do that?" he asked, hungrily taking another bite.

Callie shrugged and took a long sip of her milkshake, her lips curving into a smile around the straw. "Sometimes you have to color outside the lines."

"You're an expert at that."

Suddenly Callie's whole face changed. Her eyes lit up and her grin turned mischievous.

Noah grunted. "I know that look. I've been grounded for not stopping you and Liv from doing the shit that comes after that look."

"When we were kids," she said, the grin still firmly in place. "We're not kids anymore."

"Whatever you're thinking, no," Noah said around a mouthful of burger.

"What if we could solve both of our problems at once?" she asked, pushing her plate to the side and leaning forward. "Noah, we could do this!"

"Do what exactly?"

"You need to convince Wolf that you're not a playboy, and I need my mom to think I've got someone significant in my life. It's perfect!"

His heart pounded. "You cannot be suggesting what I think you're suggesting."

"All we have to do is convince everyone that we're a couple. An honest-to-God, can't live without each other, one step away from buying curtains together couple."

There was a time once when he thought they might actually be that couple someday, no convincing required. The thought of it made him restless, like his blood had gone fizzy and everything was moving in slow motion. He shook his head, forcing the thought from his mind. *A lifetime ago*, he reminded himself.

"You want to pretend to be a couple? At my sister's wedding? You've been reading too many romance novels."

"It's because I've read all those romance novels that I know exactly what to do. It could work! Hold on," she said, digging into her purse. With a squeal of excitement, she pulled out a small teardrop shaped piece of gold hanging from a thin metal chain. "We'll ask the pendulum."

She rested her elbows on the table, took a deep breath, and held the chain suspended over the table, the metal piece swinging side to side. "Thank you," she said, as if she was talking to the metal, and almost immediately the piece began swinging front to back instead.

"What are you doing?"

She shushed him and thanked the object again. This time, it began spinning in a circle. A third time she thanked the object, and the movement stilled. With her free hand, she reached across the table and gripped his hand. Her skin was so damn soft—how could a hand even be that soft?

With her eyes fixed on the pendulum, she spoke softly. "Should we pretend to be a couple?" The pendulum began swinging front to back in larger arcs with each pass. She met his eyes, an irrepressible grin splitting across her face. "See! Even the pendulum thinks it's a good idea."

"That is a hunk of metal. You can't honestly believe it can help you make decisions."

"It hasn't failed me yet." She returned her focus to the pendulum, the teardrop piece now hanging straight down and still. "Will pretending to date help Noah get the job on Wolf's documentary?" Again, the pendulum swung front to back, faster this time. She arched an eyebrow at Noah, as if that had somehow proved her point.

"This is insane. I'm not going to lie to my entire family—and your mother. She already isn't my biggest fan. And what about Liv? She'll know we're lying before we even get a chance to try. We'd have to tell her the truth."

"Liv can't keep a secret to save her life," she said, frowning. "If Liv knows it's fake, everyone will know. We'll just have to be very convincing."

"You're serious about this?"

His mouth went dry. He could not do this. He could not lie to everyone. More than that, he could not spend the next week pretending to date Callie and expect to walk away unscathed. He'd spent the last six years staying as far away from her as he could manage, doing everything he could think of to purge her from his thoughts. A week of acting like her boyfriend was asking for disaster. Surely she knew that?

"The pendulum never lies." She caught the piece of gold in the palm of her hand, murmured a thank you to the inanimate object, and tucked it back in her purse. "But if it would make you feel better, I could also read our cards."

"That definitely would not make me feel better."

He pulled his hand away from hers, needing some distance. He wouldn't have any distance from her all week. Would it actually change anything if he pretended she was his girlfriend? It wasn't like they'd really be together.

"If we do this—"

She squealed, and he shot her a severe look.

"*If* we do this, we have to sell Liv on it first and make sure she's okay with it. I'm not going to be responsible for causing any drama at her wedding."

"Agreed," Callie said, pulling her face into an almost comically serious expression.

"I cannot believe I'm considering this." He shoved his

hands into his hair, adrenaline racing through his blood.

It wouldn't be that hard to put his arm around Callie and call her 'baby' every now and then. *But that's not all it would be. We'd have to kiss at some point. Probably more than once.* He wasn't opposed to the idea. In fact, he wasn't sure he liked how *not* opposed he was.

"It's perfect, Noah. At the end of the week, my mom will be convinced, and Wolf will have no choice but to admit that you are the perfect composer for his film. And once you've got the job and my mom has bought her one-way ticket to Ohio, we'll quietly break up. Tell everyone it was mutual and we decided we're better off as friends. No one ever has to know it wasn't real."

Setting aside the sudden knot in his stomach at the idea of breaking up with her, he couldn't deny there was a certain logic to Callie's plan. It would ease the way with Wolf if he thought Noah was in a committed relationship. *Holy shit, I'm seriously considering this.*

"We'll have to tell Liam and Min the truth. Liam will never believe we've been dating and I didn't tell him before," Noah hedged.

"Then we tell them. But no one else. The more people that know, the more likely it is we'll get found out. We can do this, Noah."

He scrubbed his hand over his face, shaking his head. He had to be out of his mind to think this could work.

Callie flopped back in the booth, fiddling with the straw of her milkshake and avoiding his eyes, that mischievous grin still firmly in place. "Unless of course you don't think you're up to the challenge."

"I know what you're doing."

"Is it working?" She looked up at him through her eyelashes.

Yes. Fuck.

"No cutesy nicknames," he said, using his best professor voice. "I am not calling you pookey or lambkins—"

"Lambkins?" she asked, barely holding back her laughter.

"Or whatever the fuck awful pet names you're thinking about."

"I understand, sugar bear," she said with an exaggerated pout.

"And we keep it simple. No over the top stories about how we got together or crazy dates we've been on. That's just even more lies we'd have to keep track of."

"Got it. Nothing fun."

He shook his head, fighting the traitorous twitch of his lip. "You're a menace." He huffed out a sigh that sounded much more annoyed than he felt. "Okay."

"Really?" She clapped her hands together, pressing them to her chest like she was praying, her eyes sparkling. *Christ, she's beautiful.*

"Really." He looked into her eyes, a smile curling his lips despite himself. "Calandria Cole, will you be my fake girlfriend?"

She laughed. "Noah Van Aller, I thought you'd never ask."

Chapter Four

By the time they arrived at The Barclay, the boutique hotel in Aster Bay on the Rhode Island shore, Callie was ready to burst out of her skin—and not just because she'd spent the last six hours trapped in a car with the guy who starred in all of her alone-time fantasies. She couldn't stop thinking about what it would be like to be Noah's girlfriend. *His fake girlfriend,* she reminded herself.

She'd read enough romance novels to know what usually went wrong in these scenarios. But there was no danger of Noah falling in love with her. Not when he'd spent the last six years avoiding her at every turn. And if after all this time she hadn't stopped caring for him, then what was another week? Besides, any added heartache would be worth it if it meant her mom finally did something for herself and moved back to Ohio.

Despite the adrenaline buzzing through her system at the thought of implementing her brilliant new plan and getting to spend the whole week close to Noah, pain seeped into her joints from the hours-long car ride. Her lower back throbbed with the familiar ache of having stayed in one position for too long, her hips so tight she knew that walking would be painful.

"Are you ready?" Noah asked once the car was in park.

"Operation: Fake Relationship is a go," she said, stepping out of the car. She winced as her muscles stretched but hoped her upbeat tone masked some of her discomfort. Judging by the look on Noah's face, she'd have no such luck.

"You go check in. I'll bring the bags." Noah didn't bother waiting for a reply before he began layering the thick straps of both his and her luggage across his chest and shoulders.

Callie was too sore and stiff to argue. With a stilted step, she walked into the lobby of the hotel and right into the early phases of her best friend's meltdown. After nearly three decades of friendship, Callie knew the signs of an Olivia Van Aller freakout well before even Liv herself could recognize the oncoming storm. Liv stood at the check-in counter, hands gripping the edge like she was in danger of falling if she let go, her shoulders practically under her ears.

"What do you mean there aren't enough rooms?" Liv asked the frazzled looking older man behind the counter.

"Miss, we do apologize, and we are prepared to help your guest find alternate accommodations—"

"There are no alternate accommodations! The next closest hotel is nearly an hour away!"

"I understand, miss." His tone was level in a way that said he had plenty of experience keeping his calm while someone demanded he fix things out of his control.

"What's going on?" Callie asked, coming up alongside her friend.

"Cal!" The tension in Liv's frame dissipated as she pulled Callie in for a hug. Liv's arms wrapped around Callie and held her close without applying any additional pressure to the tender places around her rib cage. "They're short on rooms," Liv said, her cheek pressed against Callie's.

"By how many?"

"Just one, miss," the man behind the counter said.

"What's all this?" Noah asked, coming into the lobby with way too many bags hanging from his muscular frame. *Show off.*

"Apparently there aren't enough rooms," Callie said over Liv's shoulder.

"There's some kind of plumbing issue in one of the rooms so it's unusable and the hotel is completely booked," Liv said into Callie's hair.

"Aster Bay is a very popular tourist destination this time of year," the desk clerk offered.

"It's fine, Livi," Noah said, setting the bags down at his feet. "I'll go to another hotel." Noah disentangled Liv from Callie, pulling his sister against his chest with one arm. Then, to the desk agent, "Where's the next closest hotel?"

"Forty-five minutes north, sir," the man said, typing away on his computer. "I'm told there are two rooms vacant at the Holiday Inn."

"You can't go to a Holiday Inn! We're supposed to all be *here*. All my people together under one roof for a whole week," Liv said against his chest. She lifted her head, a puzzled look on her face. "Why does your chest smell like coffee?"

"Livi, I know it's not what you wanted, but it will be fine. I don't mind driving, and I won't miss any of your activities. You'll hardly know I'm not here."

"You're right. I know you're right," Liv said, standing upright and shaking out her hands, rolling her head on her shoulders the way she did before a performance. Callie watched as a mask slid over Liv's face, the one she used when she needed to be calm but felt anything but. "How was the drive?"

Noah and Callie shared a look over Liv's head, one that clearly communicated that now was *not* the time to drop their little announcement. "Not bad," Noah said.

"A lot of traffic," Callie added.

"Well, I'm glad you're here now. I need to go find Daemon."

"Where is your fiancé?" Noah asked, scanning the lobby.

"He's on the phone with his manager, going over the *Sabrina* contract. We go right into rehearsals when we leave here."

"Some honeymoon," Noah grumbled.

"Rehearsals on Broadway with your husband." Callie was unable to contain her smile. Clearly Noah didn't understand how romantic that was.

"My *husband*," Liv squealed. "It's going to take some time to get used to that."

Once Liv left, Callie leaned against the counter, no longer concerned with hiding the exhaustion and pain pulling at her limbs. Liv had certainly seen her in a worse state than she was just then, but she didn't want to pull any of Liv's focus away from the wedding.

Noah lay his hand low on her back, rubbing in light, soothing circles. The simple touch sent a shiver down her spine. Was he already getting into character, acting the part of the doting boyfriend? There was nothing sexual about the contact, but the intimacy of it threw her off balance. Maybe she hadn't thought this all the way through.

"You okay?" he asked, the concern in his voice evident even if his expression was suspiciously blank.

"Just tired," Callie said, but from the way his eyes narrowed, she knew he didn't believe her. "We need to talk to Liv."

"We will. There's plenty of time before dinner. But right now, you need to lie down." Noah squinted as he read the desk agent's name tag. "Paul? Can you please help my girlfriend check in? Calandria Cole."

Fake girlfriend, Callie reminded herself again, tamping down the giddy pleasure bubbling up in her chest at hearing Noah refer to her as his girlfriend.

He leaned down to speak softly against her ear, his breath on her skin raising goosebumps up and down her arms. "I'll help you get your bags upstairs."

"Thank you," she said, leaning into his side and allowing every solid inch of his six-foot-two frame to support her.

Noah slid his arm around her waist, pulling her even tighter against him, taking more of her weight. Her own arm wound around his waist in return, a stabilizing measure more than anything, though she was momentarily distracted by the solid feel of him beneath her hand.

"Calandria? Who is that handsome—" her mother's voice broke off as Noah turned his head to greet her.

Callie made to stand upright, but Noah kept her tucked against his side. Not that she fought him all that hard. It wasn't every day she got to be held by Noah Van Aller. And she was just so damn sore.

"Hi, Mrs. Cole. Just helping Callie get checked in," Noah said. And there was that smile—the mega-watt, All-American, charms-mothers-and-daughters-alike smile that Callie had seen him use on women of all ages their whole lives.

"Noah! What a surprise!" her mother said, her eyes darting between the two of them with a too-sharp expression that contradicted her pleasant tone. "When did you get here?"

"We just got in," Noah said.

"*We?*" her mother repeated.

"Noah gave me a ride, Mom," Callie said.

"Isn't that nice, that the two of you just happened to be nearby enough for Noah to drive you all the way from New York." Her mother's acerbic tone made it clear she thought it was anything but nice.

Shit. She's going to make a scene. So much for talking to Liv first.

Callie glanced at Noah, waiting for the barely perceptible nod, before she placed her free hand on his chest, smiling at her mother. Her mother's eyes snapped to the spot.

"That's Noah. Always looking out for me."

"Is that what you're calling it?" Her mother's eyes gestured meaningfully to where Noah's hand rested on Callie's waist.

"No. I'd call it dating. Noah's my boyfriend. Isn't that right, lambkins?"

His eyes flared. "That's right, sugar bear," he said, emphasizing the pet name.

No turning back now.

Noah wondered, briefly, if he should be concerned by how natural it felt to hold Callie, but his wondering was interrupted when Mrs. Cole's admonishments continued.

"Darling, you really should have told me," Mrs. Cole scolded. "You know how much I hate surprises."

"Sorry, Mom."

"I thought you'd outgrown this silly crush. She's always pined away for you, Noah. But with your...indifference... towards relationships, I never suspected anything would come of it."

Undeniable

Noah's mind was a mess of static. He'd known Callie had a crush on him as a kid, and there'd been that close call six years ago, but was she still—how did Mrs. Cole phrase it?—pining away? He glanced down at Callie, her face scrunched in a cross between embarrassment and pain.

"Mom, please," Callie said, her voice barely more than an exhausted sigh.

"It's alright." Noah pressed a kiss to the crown of Callie's head. She relaxed against his side. "In for a penny..." he murmured so only she could hear.

"How long did you think you could keep this news a secret? Really, Calandria," Mrs. Cole tutted. "I should have known, what with the way you're always going on and on about Noah."

"Here are your keys, sir," the desk agent said as he handed Noah a small envelope.

Noah accepted it, forcing himself to keep his movements calm, controlled, even though he felt like he was about to burst. *She talks about me with her mother? Why? What does that mean?*

"What's going on?" Noah's mother appeared in the doorway to the lobby, her eyebrow raised as she scanned the tableau before her.

"Well, at least I'm not the only one who's out of the loop. The kids are, apparently, together," Mrs. Cole said, beckoning his mother closer.

"Noah?" his mother asked, a sheen of disbelief coloring the barely restrained hope in her voice, like it was all too good to be true.

That's because it's not true.

Noah swallowed hard. He didn't make a habit of lying to his mother. Sure, there was plenty he didn't tell her, but this was different.

47

Callie's hand bunched in the fabric at his waist, almost like she knew he needed her to take the lead with his mother. "Surprise," she said.

"This *is* a surprise. A wonderful surprise!" his mother exclaimed, clapping her hands together over her heart.

"Shira, I was just saying—"

"I'm sure we have a lot to catch up on, Mrs. Cole," Noah interjected, "but it's been a long day and I'd like to get Callie up to her room so she can rest a bit before dinner."

"*Her* room," his mother said with a sly smile. "No need to be coy. Sue and I are not so old and out of touch that we expect you two aren't sharing a room." His mother either chose to ignore, or didn't see, the shocked expression on Mrs. Cole's face.

Mrs. Cole looked as though she'd bitten into a lemon. "Shira, if the kids don't want to—"

Noah shook his head. "I'm staying at the Holiday Inn. I'm only here to get Callie situated."

"What nonsense!" his mother said. "Of course, you're staying here."

"There aren't enough rooms, Mom. Something about the plumbing."

"Now you two can just drop this charade right now," his mother said. "Oh! Does your sister know?"

"Does his sister know what?" Liv asked, returning to the lobby, her fiancé in tow.

"Apparently your brother and Callie are an item," Mrs. Cole said slowly, her appraising eye still making sweeps over them, lingering for a moment on his hand at Callie's waist, the place where Callie's head rested against his chest. He pressed her closer.

Liv blinked, shook her head like she was clearing away an impossible thought, and blinked again. Her eyes darted between Noah and Callie, then to Mrs. Cole who had spoken the words his sister was struggling to believe.

"Livi, maybe you can help me get Callie up to her room," Noah said, his eyes wide and pleading. *Please don't freak out.*

"I was just telling your brother that it's absolute nonsense for him to trek all the way out to the Holiday Inn. Now that we know he and Callie are together, they should just stay in the same room. Don't you agree?" his mother asked.

He silently pleaded with his sister to suddenly be old-fashioned. He could not share a room with Callie, but if he refused, this whole charade would be over before it even began.

Liv narrowed her eyes at him, just for a moment, and then turned to their mother. "Of course. That makes perfect sense."

Shit.

"There, now. It's settled. Off you go," his mother said with a wave of her hand.

Mrs. Cole started in again as Noah gathered their bags. "Calandria, have you been taking your vitamins? You know you are supposed to—"

"So good to see you, Mrs. Cole," Noah said, cutting her off and guiding Callie towards the elevator. "Livi, are you coming?"

The three of them piled into the elevator, Noah once again laden down with all their luggage. Blood roared through his ears, his heart pounding. How the hell had they lost control of the situation that fast?

As soon as the elevator doors closed, Liv hit his free arm. "What the hell was that?"

Chapter Five

"Start talking," Liv demanded, crossing her arms, her eyebrow raised expectantly as she waited for Noah's answer.

The hotel room was large and airy, decorated with textured wallpaper in soft grays and blues with gauzy white curtains obscuring the ocean view. The room was dominated by a king-size bed made up with more tasseled and braided-edged throw pillows than most home goods stores. Across the room, facing the bed, was an enormous mirror in a gilt frame, giving the illusion that the room was twice as large. At the moment, however, all he could focus on was his sister's furious expression.

"I'm sorry. We wanted to tell you first," Noah said as he dropped their bags in a heap at the foot of the bed.

Oh shit, we're going to be sharing a bed.

He tossed throw pillows aside and helped Callie to a seat at the head of the bed where she could lean back against the tufted headboard. If he focused on making Callie comfortable, he couldn't think too hard about the sour feeling in his stomach from lying to his sister or the sudden rush of blood to his groin at the idea of sleeping next to Callie.

Liv's eyes darted between the two of them, zeroing in on the way Noah fussed over the position of Callie's pillows. "No," she said, shaking her head. "I would have known. You would have told me."

"It was my idea to keep it a secret," Callie said. "We didn't want to make a big deal out of it until we knew it was real."

"Since when do you keep anything a secret from me?" Liv asked Callie. It was impossible to miss the hurt in her voice.

"We didn't want you to find out this way," Noah said.

"So you thought you'd tell me at my wedding?" Liv sank down to sit on the edge of the bed, still eyeing them both suspiciously. "You have never had a serious girlfriend. Ever."

"I know." The words came out sharper than he'd meant for them to.

"And now all of a sudden you're with Callie."

"Yes." He focused on arranging and rearranging their luggage, as if that made any difference. If he looked Liv in the eyes, he was afraid he would crack and tell her the truth.

Callie sank lower on the bed, nestling down amongst the piles of pillows, her shoes discarded somewhere along the line and her feet tucked up under her. Noah was momentarily distracted by how adorable she looked, an oasis of pink cheeks and red hair and curves surrounded by pillows. His hand clenched at his side as he thought of how those curves had felt tucked against him in the lobby, how they would feel beneath him...

No. That is not what this is about. Fake dating does not mean real fucking.

"How long?" Liv demanded.

"Excuse me?" he asked.

"How long have you been keeping this from me?"

The hurt in her voice ricocheted through him, lodging pieces of shrapnel in each of his organs.

Undeniable

"Not long," Callie said, glancing at Noah. "And we were going to tell you. But then we got here, and you were so upset about the rooms—"

"When I called you yesterday and asked you to drive Callie here you were already dating her?" Liv asked him, ignoring Callie's explanation. He grunted an affirmation. "Then why did you try to get out of it?"

"I don't know, Livi," Noah sighed. This conversation was exhausting. This lie was already exhausting. "I panicked. I didn't want you to figure it out before we got a chance to tell you in person."

"So much for that plan," Liv grumbled.

"Are you mad?" Callie asked, her voice small.

"Of course, I'm mad! My brother and my best friend have been lying to me for who knows how long."

Noah dropped to his knees on the rug in front of Liv, taking her hands in his. "I'm sorry. Liv, if I'd thought you would be upset about us dating—"

"Get up." Liv rolled her eyes. "I'm angry that you lied to me, you doof, but you don't need to apologize for finally figuring out that Callie's the best," she said, shoving his shoulder.

He glanced at Callie as he got to his feet. Something flickered in her eyes—something that he couldn't quite read but he was certain had nothing to do with her stiff joints and sore muscles. She tore her gaze away from his.

"So, you're okay with this?" Callie asked.

"If you guys are happy, I'm happy. It's a little weird, but I'm never going to tell someone who they should care about." Liv reached across the bed and squeezed Callie's hand. "I just wish you hadn't felt the need to keep it from me." Liv glanced between the two of them. "I think Callie and I need a minute alone."

He wanted to stay until he had figured out what that

look in Callie's eyes had meant, but he was not about to argue with the bride. "I'll see you both at dinner." He got to his feet and left the two women alone.

Now that Liv had accepted their story—and, thankfully, didn't seem too angry—Noah needed to clue Liam in.

Min opened the door to her and Liam's hotel room after the second knock. "Noah!" She pulled him into a hug.

He was still getting used to being on a first-name-and-hugging basis with his former student, but he knew he had to stop thinking about her that way. The diamond sparkling on her left hand couldn't make that any clearer.

"We were wondering when you'd arrive."

"Traffic was awful," Noah said as he entered the room.

Liam looked up from the book he was reading. He sat on the king-sized bed, shirtless among the rumpled sheets and leaning against the headboard. "About time you got here."

Noah grabbed his friend's discarded Henley from where it lay on the floor and tossed it at him. The shirt hit Liam in the face. He narrowed his eyes at Noah before pulling the shirt over his head. "Scotch?"

"Please."

Liam grabbed a bottle from the top of the dresser, along with the paper cups from the in-room coffee station. He poured them each a glass and gestured for Noah to take a seat on the bed. Noah shot Liam a pointed look—like hell was he going to sit on their post-fuck bed sheets—and sat in the nearby armchair instead. Liam chuckled and sat on the bed, Min coming to perch on the edge of the mattress between his spread legs. Liam's free hand wound around his fiancée's waist, pulling her tight against his body in a move of unabashed possessiveness.

Noah took a slow sip of his drink as he watched his best friend and his former student—the way they moved around the room as though they were one unit, how Min took her place within easy reach of Liam, as though they couldn't bear to go even a few minutes without touching. For a fraction of a second he let himself imagine what it would be like to be in a relationship like that—one where they knew each other so well, relied on each other so completely, wanted each other so fervently. *Recipe for disaster.*

"What's on your mind?" Liam asked.

"You remember Callie?"

"Of course." Liam inclined his head towards Min. "I'm looking forward to Min getting to know her better on this trip. I think they're really going to hit it off."

"I may have just told everyone that she and I are dating," Noah said, focusing his attention on the alcohol in his glass. He downed the rest of his drink in one gulp.

"But you're not. Unless I missed something," Liam said slowly.

Noah shook his head. "We're not."

"Then why do you want people to think you are?" Min asked.

"It's complicated. But basically, we'd both benefit from the appearance of a stable, committed relationship for a little while."

"Callie doesn't strike me as someone who's a very good liar," Liam said.

Noah huffed out a breath that could almost have been a laugh. "I don't think that girl has ever lied a day in her life. Before now." He scrubbed his hands over his face and into his hair. "How hard can it be to pretend to be in love with her for a week? My mom is over the goddamn moon. But Mrs. Cole... she seemed like she knew something was up."

"That's because you're a fucking awful liar," Liam said. "And this is a fucking awful idea."

"I don't have a choice. Callie needs this."

"Oh, *Callie* does?" Liam asked, his eyebrows shooting up. "This is some kind of altruistic endeavor?"

"She's trying to convince her mom to finally bite the bullet and move to Ohio like she's been talking about for years. Mrs. Cole won't go until Callie's in a committed relationship."

Liam barked out a laugh. "So she's pretending to date *you*? Mrs. Cole is never going to buy that. She's always the first one to point out how many *lady friends* you have," he said, imitating Callie's mother.

"One week," Noah repeated. "I can pretend for one week."

"And what do you get out of this?" Noah shot Liam a sheepish look. Liam scowled, shaking his head. "Fuck, this is about the documentary."

"Have you ever considered just actually dating someone?" Min asked. Noah and Liam both laughed. "What? You're a catch, Noah."

Liam stole a kiss from his fiancée. Noah had seen them kiss a thousand times, but this time he had to look away, his muscles tensing uncomfortably beneath his skin.

"No," he said, far too vehemently. "I don't date."

"But you could," Min said with a small shrug.

It was the most ludicrous thing he'd ever heard—even more ludicrous than pretending to date his little sister's best friend to trick Wolf into giving him his dream job. *Jesus fuck, what is my life?*

Some secret look passed between Min and Liam, the kind of maddening conversation they were always having with each other without words.

"You're making a much bigger deal out of this than it actually is," Noah said. If he said it enough times, perhaps he'd believe it. "But you can't tell anyone. You're the only ones who know it's fake."

Undeniable

"What does Livi think?" Liam's measured tone put Noah on edge.

"She was mad we didn't tell her, but she seems to have bought the story that we're together," he said, hating himself all over for lying to his sister. "I need to get out of here for a while before dinner. Callie and Liv are holed up in our room—"

"*Our* room?" Liam asked.

"Something about the plumbing. There aren't enough rooms."

"So you're sharing a hotel room. With Callie. Your fake girlfriend." Liam glared at him. "Do you honestly not see a problem with that? That girl has had a crush on you since—"

"I really don't want to analyze this right now. Can we just get out of here before my mom finds me and tries to set a date for my fake wedding?"

Min shrugged. "There's not a whole lot to do around here." Min and Liam had just moved to Providence, but Min grew up in Rhode Island. They might have settled on the other side of the state, but the state wasn't that big—if anyone knew what to do in Aster Bay, it'd be Min. "There are some shops about a half mile away. But this is a small town. There's not much going on."

Noah cursed under his breath. He could really use a distraction so he could stop thinking about the fact that he'd be sharing a bed all week with Callie, stop wondering what she'd wear to bed, how she'd look with her face relaxed in sleep. He hoped she didn't get nightmares like Livi did, because then he'd have no choice but to hold her, to comfort her, to take her in his arms and—

"Oh!" Min brightened, turning to Liam. "There's that cute second-hand bookstore in town. I wanted to go back there at some point this week anyway."

"Contessa..." Liam said, his voice low and his eyes giving her a quick once-over. Another unspoken conversation, but this one Noah could decipher.

"You have all weekend to have hotel sex," Noah said, getting to his feet. "I'm sure you'll survive if you have to wait a few more hours to defile the room. Again."

Min blushed and Noah immediately regretted saying anything. He and Liam didn't have any secrets, and they talked about their sex lives as easily as if they were making restaurant recommendations, but it still felt new for Min to be present for those conversations. For her last semester at Burnett, they'd maintained at least some boundaries of propriety—he'd still been her professor and he didn't need her blushing every time he walked into a room. But since she'd graduated two months ago, those last vestiges of modesty had fallen away. Now she wasn't his student anymore—she was the woman who would marry his best friend in just a few months.

The new normal was fucking weird.

"I don't understand how this happened. Noah has never had a girlfriend. He might as well have 'commitment-phobe' tattooed across his forehead."

Callie closed her eyes and took a deep breath. Liv was right. This was a batshit plan, but it was her only plan. There was no choice. And pretending to be Noah's girlfriend for the week wouldn't exactly be a hardship. Her blood hummed at the reminder of his hand on her hip, the feel of his lips on her hair. *Definitely not a hardship.*

"Can you get my cream out of the front pocket of my bag?" she asked, pointing to her suitcase and buying herself another minute to figure out how to respond to her best friend's understandable confusion.

Liv retrieved the tube of cream and climbed up onto the giant bed beside Callie. She'd never seen a bed this large. Thank God it came with an overabundance of pillows to match its ludicrous size.

"Where do you want it?" Liv asked, already unscrewing the cap.

"My lower back," Callie said, shifting so she was sitting with her back to Liv. She lifted the hem of her shirt and waited, the pungent medicinal smell of the cream filling her nostrils.

Liv gently rubbed the cream into Callie's skin the same way she'd done so many times before. "When did you two even start talking again? I thought you weren't really in touch anymore now that—" She cut herself off but Callie heard the words anyway: *now that you're not composing.*

"You have to promise me that if my bonehead of a brother fucks this up, that it won't change anything between us," Liv said softly.

"It won't. You're my forever person, babe."

"I don't want to see you get hurt."

"I know. And I won't be."

"You're sure about that?"

No. Callie had never been more unsure about something in her life. They were mere minutes into this scheme and she was already thinking about the next time she'd get to touch him, wondering what it would be like to sleep next to him. But this was her best option. One week and then she could nurse her broken heart while she helped her mother pack.

Liv returned the cap to the cream and set it aside, waiting as Callie repositioned herself in her nest of pillows.

"I'm not seventeen anymore, Liv. I'm well aware of who your brother is, and who he isn't. This isn't like the time he took me to prom." Callie cringed at the memory.

When Callie's jerkwad of a boyfriend—the first of many who could be described that way—had dumped her two days before prom, she'd resigned herself to not attending. Despite being the chair of the prom committee and having spent countless hours picking out the perfect color for the streamers and balloons that would decorate the school gym, clearly, she wasn't meant to go. Then Noah had offered to take her. "You can't miss your own prom," he'd said when he called. It had felt like magic.

Her teenage self had been so certain that if Noah saw her in a prom dress, if he danced with her on that most magical of teenage nights, that he'd suddenly see her as more than his little sister's best friend. That he'd finally see *her*. But Noah had been a perfect gentleman, smiling for all the photos and dancing with her for all the slow dances, and then dropping her off on her doorstep with a horrifyingly polite goodnight and not even the slightest indication that he had even considered kissing her. He'd come to her rescue, but he would never want her. *Just like he's coming to your rescue now.*

"Are you sure you're okay with this?" Callie asked. "We don't want to mess up your big day."

Liv scoffed, waving off Callie's statement. "That wouldn't even be possible. I know I was panicking about the rooms, but that was because I just want us all together. It could hail golf ball-sized chunks of ice, and the caterer could overcook all the fish, and my mom could get so drunk that she sings *Holding Out for A Hero* at the top of her lungs at my reception—"

"That last one could actually happen."

"—and none of it could ruin my wedding. If you want to date my brother, then it's okay with me. You don't need my permission. I just want you to be careful, Cal."

Callie nodded, slashing her index finger over her chest. "Cross my heart."

Another lie.

Chapter Six

Noah returned to an empty hotel room and the sound of the shower running in the adjoining bathroom. He stashed his bag from the bookstore, cursing himself for even buying the damn book in the first place. He wouldn't give it to her. That was the only solution. He couldn't give it to her. Not after Min's eyes had practically popped out of her head and Liam arched his eyebrow so hard Noah thought he might actually hurt himself. It was a stupid impulse buy and no one else ever needed to know about it.

He had ten minutes to make himself decent before the first of what Liv and Daemon were calling "family dinner." Every night for the next week, their families and wedding party would gather to share a meal together. That first night was being held in The Barclay's restaurant so thankfully they didn't need to go far.

After toeing off his sneakers and lining them up beside the door, he pulled off his t-shirt and rummaged through his suitcase for something clean that wasn't too wrinkled. There was no time to unpack properly or iron anything, so the hunter green polo would have to do. He was just about to pull it over his head when the bathroom door opened,

Callie appearing in a cloud of steam.

"Oh!" she gasped, her hand flying to her chest to hold the thin hotel bathrobe closed. "You're back."

He had lost all power of speech, every word he ever knew obliterated by the sight of Callie Cole in a too-small bathrobe. Her skin glistened where water still clung to her, sliding down her chest into that maddening crevice between her breasts. The robe was not meant for a woman as full-figured as Callie, the fabric pulling tightly across her hips and barely held closed by the flimsy tie at her waist. The bottom flared open and revealed her long legs and pillowy soft thighs.

Holy shit.

His eyes finished their too-slow perusal of her body, lingering on her slightly parted lips before meeting her gaze. He cleared his throat and looked away. *Stop staring at your little sister's best friend. She's practically family,* he told himself. But the blood rushing to his groin disagreed. Callie was very much not family. Callie was a wet dream come to life. He pulled his shirt on and turned away.

"Sorry," he mumbled. "Didn't mean to intrude."

"You're not intruding. This is your room, too."

Behind him, he could hear her moving about the room, unzipping parts of her suitcase. "I'll just be a minute," she said to his back. He didn't turn around again until he heard the bathroom door close.

Noah focused intently on tying the laces of his dress shoes. If he worked hard enough at getting the bow perfectly even then he wouldn't have room in his brain to dwell on the image of Callie in his mind. The one where she let the edge of the robe slip, let the fabric spill open at the center. The one where he dropped to his knees and licked away the beads of water still clinging to her skin.

What the fuck is wrong with me?

A few minutes later, Callie re-emerged. Her wet hair was pulled back in one of her signature braids, her cheeks still pink—*from heat or embarrassment?* he wondered. He tried not to notice that beneath her sky-blue sundress she was clearly not wearing a bra, the hard pebbles of her nipples visible through the fabric. Callie rarely wore a bra—and Noah rarely failed to notice.

"Shall we?" she asked, slipping on a pair of nude flats.

They rode the elevator down to the first floor in silence, but Noah's blood was pounding so hard in his ears he could hardly hear anything anyway. As the elevator doors opened, he reached over and took her hand in his. Because that was the way a boyfriend should behave. Not because he wanted to, or because he needed to touch some part of her or he would go out of his mind and her hand seemed like the most innocuous option. No, this was a handhold of convenience, a handhold of deception. Nothing more.

Everyone else was already seated when they entered the dining room, two places next to each other left open for them. "Sorry we're late," Noah said, releasing Callie's hand with a twinge of regret as they took their seats.

"Now that everyone's here, we can make introductions," Liv said.

Most people knew each other, of course, but the three people at the far end of the table were newcomers—Daemon's friends dropped in the middle of the Van Aller extended-family. Aside from Noah and Callie, and Liv and her fiancé Daemon, there was Liam and Min, his mother and Mrs. Cole.

"This is *the* Pattie McDonald," Liv said, gesturing across the table to a petite woman with blonde hair. The woman waved, smiling. "Pattie is an absolute icon, and we were so lucky to share the stage with her for *Chess*, both in New York and in London."

"She also happens to be my oldest friend," Daemon said with a fond smile.

"Not your oldest, chickadee. Just the one who has put up with you the longest," Pattie laughed.

"And next to Pattie is her lovely wife, Maggie," Daemon continued.

"Savior. Saint. And superhero," Pattie said.

"I'm a public defender," Maggie explained.

"That's what I said," Pattie replied.

"And, last but not least, Daemon's brother, Jameson," Liv said, pointing to the man at the end of the table. Not that she really needed to point him out—even in a sea of strangers, there would be no denying the family resemblance between Daemon and the man seated across from him. Same expressive green eyes, same wavy dark hair (though Jameson wore his longer and Daemon's had far more silver streaked throughout), same square jaw and broad shoulders.

"Call me Jamie," the younger man said, lifting his water glass in toast to his brother before taking a sip.

"Jamie's a chef. He has his own restaurant here in town. We'll be having dinner there tomorrow night."

"How long have you lived here?" Noah's mother asked. "I thought your family was from Massachusetts."

"We are," Jamie said. "I went to culinary school in Providence and have been in Aster Bay ever since."

"That's how we found this place," Daemon said. "My little brother couldn't be bothered to take a weekend off to come see us in New York—"

"Weekends are my busiest time," Jamie protested.

"—so we came up here to see him. And Liv fell in love

with the town."

"Can you blame me?" Liv laughed.

A server appeared to take their drink orders. Liv and Daemon had pre-ordered a set menu for the evening. Noah was grateful for one less thing to think about when his mind was whirling with a sea of self-doubt.

Should he be touching Callie? He wanted to, but did that mean he *should*? Would the others think it was odd if he touched her? Or was it weirder if he didn't? With each passing moment—each joke bandied across the table that he registered half a beat too late—he came to the horrifying realization that he had no idea how to behave with a girlfriend. He knew what to do when he wanted to take a woman home with him, when he wanted her to feel like the sole object of his desire for a few hours. And he knew how to be the big brother, the friend. But he was at a loss of how he was supposed to act when he was in love with someone. Even just for pretend.

He glanced at Liam and Min, catching the slow slide of Liam's hand up Min's thigh, his fingers disappearing beneath the hem of her skirt before Min shot him a slightly alarmed look and dropped her napkin over his hand. *Nope. Nope, nope, nope,* he thought, quickly averting his gaze.

Turning to his sister and Daemon—and praying they were not similarly engaged—he found Daemon's hand resting casually on Liv's knee, her arm behind her fiancé's chair and her hand playing with the short hairs at the back of his neck. *Doable.* But a hand on Callie's knee wasn't likely to be seen by anyone else, and the point was to be seen, though he couldn't deny that he liked the idea of putting his hand on her knee. If he was honest, he liked the idea of sliding that hand up her thigh and—*Nope.*

Finally, he settled for laying his arm across the back of

her chair. No actual touching. Just closeness. Just a quiet signal that they went together, like interlocking puzzle pieces. Callie stiffened in her seat—but just for a moment.

"Noah," Mrs. Cole said, her voice sickly sweet. "How long have you been seeing my daughter?"

"Yes, I'd like to know as well," his mother asked, leaning her chin on her hand.

"About a month," Noah replied.

Callie's eyes flared. *What?* Was that the wrong answer?

"Well, that's not long at all," Mrs. Cole clucked.

It isn't? A month of dating the same person seemed like an eternity to him. Then again, he'd never seen the same woman for more than a single night, so what did he know?

"We only made it official about a month ago," Callie said with an easy smile, "but we've been seeing each other since May. You know how Noah is. It took a while for him to be comfortable with the idea."

The table laughed and Noah fought the urge to scowl, forcing his mouth into a half smile that he was certain looked more like a sneer. He didn't like the idea that Callie would put up with anyone not committing to her for months on end, even him.

"I'm glad to hear it," his mother said. "It's about time you settled down. By the time we were your age, your father and I were married with two children."

"Do you want children, Noah?" Mrs. Cole asked.

He nearly choked on his water.

"I think that discussion's a bit premature," Callie said, glaring at her mother.

"You're not getting any younger, dear. If you want children, then you have to ask these questions of the men you date."

They were saved from having to respond when the

server arrived with their salads—a local heirloom tomato and burrata salad with fresh basil and pistachios. Everyone else's salads came drizzled with a dark, syrupy looking dressing, but his dressing arrived in a little cup on the side. Liv winked at him when the server set the dish in front of him.

The salad was delicious, the tomatoes juicy and sweet. But something was missing. He frowned, poking at the cheese that couldn't seem to decide if it was solid or liquid. Callie, mid-conversation with Maggie about a program she was hoping to bring to her library that would help senior citizens register for Medicare, reached over and, without asking, drizzled the thick dressing over his salad. He stared as the brown liquid slid over the tomatoes, sank into the cheese, and pooled on his plate in little sticky drops. With a challenging eyebrow raise, she compelled him to take a bite.

He dragged a tomato through the dressing and warily brought it to his mouth. And just as before, in the diner when she'd fixed his burger, the flavors exploded on his tongue—tart and sweet, acidic and bright.

"Try it with the cheese," she said before returning to her conversation with Maggie.

So he did. He speared a piece of cheese with a tomato this time, wiping up the dressing from his plate and popping it into his mouth. He closed his eyes and hummed in appreciation. It was the most delicious thing he'd ever eaten.

"What is that?" he asked.

"Balsamic reduction," she said.

"Did you just get Noah to put dressing on his salad?" Liam asked at his side, his eyes narrowed in disbelief.

Callie shrugged. "Who wants to live a life without balsamic?"

Noah met her eyes as he chewed his tomato. *Not me,* he thought. *Not anymore.*

Dinner went well into the night, dessert and coffee turning into drinks in the lounge. And the whole time, Noah and Callie touched. His arm over the back of her chair morphed into an arm around her waist when they stood at the bar to collect their drinks, which turned into a hand on her knee as they sat together in the lounge, laughing at his mother's recounting of Liv's impromptu backyard musicals co-starring her stuffed animals. By the time Jamie was telling everyone about the summer Daemon worked as a cabaret singer on a cruise ship, Callie was cuddled up beneath Noah's arm, her head resting on his shoulder so that when she laughed, his body shook. After the first hour or so, Noah was surprised to find it felt natural to be touching her, that this wasn't so different from the way he'd touch a woman he was trying to take home with him. Maybe he knew how to do this after all.

On the elevator ride back to their room, Callie was practically swaying on her feet, leaning against him for support, the long day of travel finally taking its toll. Callie pushed open their hotel room door, kicking off her shoes so that they flew across the room and flopping, arms and legs spread wide, onto the bed. Noah chuckled as he removed his own shoes, setting them in the corner by his sneakers, and gathered hers from where they'd landed to line them up next to his.

"Tired?"

"Mmm," she hummed sleepily. "Lying down was a bad idea. Now I don't want to get up."

"Then don't."

"I need to brush my teeth and wash my face and all that jazz," she replied with a sigh.

Callie grabbed her toiletry bag and a bundle of fabric that he assumed were her pajamas from her suitcase and disappeared into the bathroom. Alone, Noah set about unpacking his things, carefully refolding each item as he placed it in the dresser and tried to determine what the hell he should sleep in. He typically slept naked. Since he hadn't been planning on having a roommate during this trip, he hadn't packed the few pairs of pajamas he kept on hand for times when he went home for the weekend. Boxer briefs and a t-shirt would have to do. He removed his shirt and socks, adding them to the laundry bag he'd packed for the occasion. He had just undone the fly of his jeans when the door to the bathroom flew open.

"Can I borrow—" Callie froze mid-sentence when she saw him, half-naked and with his pants undone. She made a thorough perusal of his body, a blush rising in her cheeks. "Toothpaste?" she squeaked.

He wanted to be annoyed by her interest, to brush it off the way he'd done when she was a kid, but he liked her eyes on him. And she definitely wasn't a kid anymore.

"Of course." Noah retrieved the tube of toothpaste from his suitcase and walked it over to her.

Her fingers lingered on his palm when she took it from him, her bottom lip pulling between her teeth. Had she always had such pouty lips?

Then she was gone, back behind the bathroom door. Which was just as well, because Noah needed a minute to calm the fuck down. This was Callie. Livi's best friend. The wide-eyed redhead from next door who used to bring him the edge pieces whenever she made brownies because she thought the crispy bits weren't as good as the gooey middle. Or maybe it was because she knew he liked those overcooked edges? It didn't matter. Callie was off limits and the sooner his dick got that memo, the better for everyone.

He was half on his way to convincing himself of that very thing when the door opened again and this time it was Callie who appeared half dressed. She wore a simple white cotton tank top and plaid men's boxers, the soft flannel hugging her hips and thighs. The dark circles of her nipples were visible through the thin top. She avoided his eyes as she tucked the wadded-up ball of her sundress back into her suitcase.

He gestured to the bed, forcing himself to look away from her breasts. "Do you have a side you prefer?"

"Oh, no, either side is fine," she said, looking everywhere but at him.

He took the opportunity to slip beneath the blankets so she wouldn't see his body's reaction to her, a reaction that only got worse when she climbed into bed next to him. He lay as still as he could, all too aware of how close she was, that with just the smallest movement, they'd be touching.

He huffed out a breath. "This is awkward as fuck."

Callie laughed. "It really is."

He rolled onto his side, propping his head up on his arm so he could look at her, and she mirrored his posture. "It doesn't need to be, though. Right?"

"Right. We're both adults."

"And we're friends," he said, a hint of a question in his voice.

Were they friends? They didn't spend much time together—something he'd made sure of over the last few years. But they were at least friend-adjacent, surely. Friends through Liv by the transitive property or something, right?

"Definitely," she said, smiling. "Friends can sleep in the same bed and have it not be weird."

But he didn't usually get a hard-on just from looking at

his friends. He didn't wonder what it would be like to touch them.

"Great." He rolled onto his back. "Goodnight, Callie."

"Goodnight, lambkins," she said from the other side of the bed.

He nudged her with his foot, just enough to make her laugh. *Mistake.* Her laugh only made him harder. *What have I gotten myself into?*

Chapter Seven

Callie emerged from sleep disoriented, the morning light filtering in through the blinds and teasing her awake even as the strong arms banded around her from behind urged her to stay in bed a little longer. Half awake, she let herself wiggle against the solid form at her back. It was only when those arms around her body shifted so that one large hand closed over her breast that she fully woke, the realization of exactly who was behind her rioting through her. Those were Noah's legs tangled with her own, Noah's arms holding her tight against his chest. Noah's hand cupping her breast. Noah's erection pressing into her backside.

He squeezed her breast and a bolt of desire shot through her, settling between her thighs. *There's no way he's awake*, she thought. She listened for the rhythmic inhale and exhale behind her in time with the gusts of hot breath on her neck. *Still asleep.* She could extricate herself before he woke up and save them both the embarrassment, because there was no way Noah had intentionally taken up the big spoon position and groped her.

She shifted in his arms in an attempt to begin the process of disentangling herself an inch at a time. It took a moment for her to realize that all that slow shifting was grinding her ample backside against the thick rod of Noah's erection and that—*Holy shit*—he was getting bigger. Harder. He rocked against her in his sleep, the gentle insistence of his length against the crease of her ass sending a fresh wave of wetness rushing between her legs.

She briefly considered not getting out of bed. She could pretend to still be asleep, stay in this moment a little longer and pretend he actually wanted her, not just that he was dreaming and she happened to be the person in his bed. But she knew that if Noah woke up while they were like this—while *he* was like this—then he would pull away and all the ground they'd gained the night before would be lost. By the end of the night, he'd almost seemed comfortable playing the part of her adoring boyfriend. Which made it damn hard to remember it was all for show—especially when she woke up with his morning wood poking her in the ass. But she'd meant it when she told Liv she would try not to get hurt in this mess. And staying in bed was a recipe for heartache.

After several minutes of slow maneuvers, Callie wriggled free of the sleeping Noah's grasp without waking him. Breathing a sigh of relief, she grabbed some clean clothes from her suitcase and shut herself in the bathroom. The night before she'd looked longingly at the soaker tub in one corner of the bathroom and that morning seemed like the perfect time to take advantage of it.

While the tub filled with hot water, she dug through her toiletry kit in search of the one thing she never went on vacation without. She'd practically emptied the entire bag before she found the small pink silicone finger vibe—the perfect size for travel, quiet but powerful enough to get the job done and, even better, waterproof.

Sliding into the hot bath, she let her mind drift back to the man sleeping in the other room. Her hand skated over her small breasts, bobbing at the surface of the water, plucking at her already-hard nipples as she thought of his hands on her. How had she never realized before how big his hands were? A piano player's hands—large and strong with long dexterous fingers. As her hand drifted lower over her body, she thought of all the things he could do with those fingers.

She skated the vibe over her folds. When the toy found her clit, already swollen and aching, she imagined it was Noah touching her instead. His fingers teasing at her entrance, his tongue building her into a frenzy, until her hips rocked against the toy, the water in the bath sloshing around her. And when she couldn't take it anymore, she imagined it was him working her clit until she came with a breathless gasp, the pleasure rocketing through her and curling her toes.

As her orgasm subsided, she knew she should feel guilty—not because she'd masturbated to thoughts of Noah (that was nothing new), but because she'd done it while he was in the next room. But instead, she was just even more turned on than before, knowing that he might have heard her through the thin wall separating them, that he might have woken with a hard cock to the sounds of her getting herself off.

With a mournful glance at her trusty finger vibe, she silently lamented that the few other pieces from her extensive toy collection that she'd thought to pack were in her suitcase in the other room, destined to remain unused on this trip no matter how horny she was. With a sigh, she sank deeper into the tub and resisted the urge to go another round. Because even though the idea of getting herself off while Noah was just on the other side of the door made her incredibly hot, she knew she couldn't do it again. The risk of being caught was too high and, unlike in her fantasies, he wasn't likely to join her if he found her flushed with a toy between her legs—he was more likely to turn tail and run. She couldn't afford to spook him, not when so much was riding on this week together.

"Get dressed. We're going for a run."

Liam stared at Noah through the open crack of his door, his hair a mess of bedhead and sleep still clouding his eyes. "I don't run," he grumbled.

"Tough shit."

"*You* don't run."

"We do today."

Liam gave in surprisingly quickly, but whether it was the way Noah couldn't stand still, pacing the hallway in his gym shorts and sneakers, or the sleepy encouragement from his fiancée, Noah didn't know. Or, frankly, care. He needed to get his blood pumping and he needed to get as far the fuck away from his own hotel room as he could.

Not your own. Yours and Callie's.

Right. That was exactly the problem.

He'd had to get out of there. It had taken all his self-control to leave when what he wanted to do was put his hand on his fucking traitorous dick, hard as steel and far too aware of every sound coming from the bathroom, and join her as she fell over the edge of her pleasure.

Liam emerged in a pair of sweatpants and a t-shirt.

Undeniable

"You owe me."

They made their way out of The Barclay and down the lawn to the private beach in silence. After a few cursory stretches, they were off, jogging through the sand with the hotel at their back.

"You want to tell me why you're suddenly a runner?" Liam asked.

"Nope."

A few more minutes in silence, around another bend of the shoreline. "Did something happen with Callie?"

Noah shot him a look but kept jogging. "The point of going for a run is not to talk."

"How the fuck would I know that? I don't run. But if you didn't want to talk, seems to me you could have gone on this little run by yourself."

Noah slowed his pace, the hotel now far enough behind them that the knot in his chest had loosened. Just a little, but it was better than nothing. "Callie—" he began, cutting himself off. *Am I really going to tell Liam this?*

"Yes, your fake girlfriend—who, up until twenty-four hours ago, was basically our little sister. I'm familiar," Liam said with a nod.

"Callie needed some privacy this morning." Noah shot his friend a meaningful glance before he began running again. "And she's not basically our little sister." He wouldn't have been tempted to stay and listen to what he'd overheard that morning, or—worse yet—to join in, if that was the case.

"What does that mean?" Liam asked, matching Noah's pace.

"When I woke up, she was…in the bath…having some alone time."

"Most people like privacy when they're taking a bath." Liam's eyes widened and realization dawned. "Oh! No

79

shit." He shoved Noah, his brows drawing down into a scowl. "Fuck, I didn't need to know that. That's Callie you're talking about. Little Callie Cole with the braces and the—"

"She's not little Callie Cole anymore. And she hasn't had braces for years."

"Wait," Liam said, slowing until he stopped. "You're not fu—"

"Jesus, fuck, no!" Noah said, driving his hands into his hair. "It's all a show, man. I told you."

"That was before you eavesdropped on her getting off."

"I didn't eavesdrop! I got the fuck out of there as soon as I realized what was going on."

"You know Liv will end you if you do anything to hurt Callie. Shit, *I* will end you. You can't just have a one-night thing with her."

"I'm not having any kind of thing with her," Noah snapped.

"This is terrible fucking idea. You know that, right?"

"It's just a week."

"Oh, come on. This isn't going away when the week is over, even if you two stage some kind of breakup. Your mom is over the fucking moon and Mrs. Cole was asking you about *kids* last night."

"I'm surprised you could even follow the conversation last night with your hand up Min's skirt," Noah grumbled.

Liam flashed a wolfish smile. "She's an exhibitionist. Who am I to deny her? But the point is, you think your mother is just going to let this go because you guys say it's over? Fuck, no. She's going to keep after you to get back together, to find some way to make it work. What happens when you go home for the holidays and you're both there? This can't be truly temporary because Callie's not temporarily in your life."

Noah shook his head, refusing to believe it. "It's just a week."

"Keep telling yourself that," Liam said.

"What am I supposed to do?" Noah dropped to sit on the ground, his legs bent in front of him as he dug his hands into the soft sand. "It's too late to take it back."

"The only way out is through," Liam said, sitting beside Noah.

Noah watched as the thoughts flitted behind his best friend's eyes and knew he wasn't going to like whatever Liam had to say next.

"I know you like to think that none of us are aware of what happened at Liv and Callie's twenty-first birthday—"

"We're not talking about that."

"We have to fucking talk about that. You are sharing a room with her, Noah. Sleeping in the same bed. For a week. While everyone who loves you thinks you're a couple." He arched an eyebrow and waited for Noah to nod his assent. "Do you still have feelings for her?"

Noah blinked, his brain unable to process the question. Did he have feelings for Callie? He'd known her since she was born. He'd been there when she was learning to bake and mixed up the salt and the sugar, when she got her braces and the day she'd had them taken off, the day she learned to ride a bike and the day she passed her driver's test. He'd taught her how to play the piano and how to construct chord progressions, had spent countless hours critiquing her compositions, dreaming with her about the day they were both famous composers. Did he have feelings for Callie? Of course, he did. But those weren't the kinds of feelings Liam was asking about. And he wasn't sure he had an answer to that other question.

"Let me ask it a different way," Liam said in the same tone

he used when a student wasn't grasping a concept in one of his lectures. "If she wasn't Liv's best friend, if she was just some woman you met in a bar, would you pursue her?"

"Yes," he said, his voice low, avoiding Liam's eyes. He hadn't admitted it for years, not even to himself—the attraction he felt to Callie, the times he'd thought about that one night six years ago when he'd ignored his own rules and kissed her. "But she's not some woman I met in a bar."

"You're right. You can't just put her in a cab in the morning and never see her again. And as much as part of me wants to pummel your ass for even thinking about it, there's another part of me that thinks...maybe it's not the worst thing."

Noah couldn't believe what he was hearing.

"What if you and Callie—"

"Don't. It's not an option." Noah threw the handful of sand he'd gathered.

"There was a time you thought it was." Noah didn't respond, throwing another handful of sand. Liam continued, exasperation coloring his tone. "Are you just going to be alone forever?"

Noah glared at his best friend, hating the way his question rankled, how it dug beneath his skin. *Alone is better than half-dead with grief. Better than failing her when she needs me most. Alone is survivable.*

"I'm not trying to talk you into making this thing real with Callie," Liam said.

"You sure about that?"

"It's just odd that you overhear her masturbating—" Noah winced and held up a hand in protest of Liam's insistence on calling the image to mind "—and your instinct is to torture yourself—and me. There was a time when you would have laughed about it."

Was there? He couldn't imagine there ever being a time when he could have heard Callie's soft gasps, the rhythmic sloshing of the water in the bath, her muffled whimper, and *laughed.*

"What's your point?" Noah asked.

"Maybe it's not all fake."

Chapter Eight

Callie had never had a manicure before. Sitting in the salon, surrounded by all the women in Liv's wedding party and breathing in the harsh chemical smell of nail polish and removers, she wasn't sure she'd ever be getting one again. She liked to paint her nails with whatever color caught her eye when she wandered through the drug store to pick up her prescriptions, and she had to admit that the hand massage had been an unexpected treat, but she couldn't see paying for a temporary splash of color on her nails. Not when she was likely going to chip the polish or break a nail when she did arts and crafts with the kids in the children's room at the library anyway. You don't become a championship level friendship bracelet maker without breaking a few nails.

But Liv had wanted a bonding day for all the women that included manicures and pedicures, blow-outs, and makeup before they rejoined the men for dinner. Callie was grateful for an afternoon away from Noah. It had only been twenty-four hours since she'd come up with the ridiculous idea to pretend they were in love and already she needed space to remind herself that none of it was real.

"Have you set a date?" Mrs. Van Aller asked Min. The younger woman's engagement ring shone on her finger as the technician filed her nails into perfect ovals.

"We're not in a rush," Min said. "With the move and starting my master's, and Liam trying to get his summer program off the ground, it might be a while."

"Don't let him put it off too long," Callie's mother cautioned.

"If it were up to him, we'd have eloped already," Min laughed.

"Then why haven't you?" Pattie asked. "Mags and I eloped, didn't we, darling?"

"It was the only way it was ever going to happen between Pattie's performing schedule and my caseload," Maggie explained as she selected a soft shade of pink for her nails.

"We've only been together for... I don't even know how to count it," Min said.

"You know, whenever you hear about the downsides of having a secret relationship with a professor, it's always 'power dynamics this' and 'conflict of interest that' and never 'but how will you determine your anniversary date?'" Liv teased.

"If only someone had warned me," Min joked back.

"What about you, Callie?" Mrs. Van Aller asked. "When might we see a ring on your finger?"

"Oh, I don't think that will be happening any time soon," she said, avoiding making eye contact.

Callie's face was on fire. This was torture, sitting here with these women she loved and lying to them all.

Her mother released a long-suffering sigh. "You're not getting any younger, Calandria. Why you're wasting your time with someone who clearly has no interest in commitment—"

"Go easy on the kids, Sue," Mrs. Van Aller said. "They

haven't been together that long. And dating at all is a big deal for Noah."

"Precisely," her mother said. "If it took them this long to date, imagine how long it will be before she gets him to the altar?"

"He doesn't usually date?" Pattie asked.

"My brother doesn't do relationships. Until now," Liv amended, glancing at Callie. "He's typically been a bit of a rake."

"This is not regency England," Callie muttered to herself.

"That's a polite way of saying he has lots of female friends but nobody he considers special. Until now," Mrs. Van Aller said with a soft smile.

"All the more reason to be proactive. You can't leave these things to chance," her mother said. "A boy like Noah needs someone to insist or he'll never settle down."

"It's not all that, Sue. Clearly, he *is* settling down or he wouldn't be throwing around words like 'girlfriend.' I'm so glad he's finally coming to his senses. I've been so worried about him."

"Worried about what?" Liv asked.

"That he'll end up alone," Mrs. Van Aller replied. "That it will be all my fault."

"Mom..."

"No, I know he carries a heavy heart ever since your father died," the older woman responded, her eyes welling with tears that, Callie knew from years of experience, would not be shed. "He bore the brunt of the burden when he was far too young to have done so." Then, to Pattie and Maggie, "Noah was barely a teenager when my Jerry passed. And he became the glue of our family. Took care of our Livi-bug. Took care of me."

"That must have been hard. On all of you," Maggie replied.

"I fear it was harder on Noah than he'd ever let on," Mrs. Van Aller said.

Callie called up the memory of a thirteen-year-old Noah making her and Liv grilled cheese on Saturday afternoons, teaching them to tie their shoes, making sure Liv's leotard made it in the laundry in time for ballet class. She'd never paused as an adult to consider how hard it must have been on him, how much extra responsibility he took on while his mother drowned in her grief. Because that was the part of the story Mrs. Van Aller had left out—how for over a year after her husband had passed, she could barely function for being so deep in her despair. Callie's parents had helped out where they could, arranging for groceries and meals, giving Liv and Noah rides to school and playdates. But soon enough her parents were embroiled in their divorce and it had been Noah who kept the Van Aller house clean, who remembered when Liv needed something to bring to show and tell at school, who made sure his mother attended those ballet recitals. He never complained, at least not that she'd ever heard.

"He's always taken care of us," Liv said, smiling softly. Then, with a chuckle, "Not that he ever gives us a choice."

"He's delayed his own happiness on our account for far too long," Mrs. Van Aller agreed. "At least he's actually entertaining Wolf's offer to work with him this time."

"This time?" Callie asked.

"About ten years or so ago Wolf asked Noah to submit for his film on the Revolutionary War."

"The one that was featured at Sundance?" Maggie asked.

"That's the one," Mrs. Van Aller confirmed. "He refused to even submit the sample."

"Why?" Pattie asked.

Callie wanted to know as well. Scoring a major film

was all Noah had ever talked about during those summers when he'd taught her to play the piano.

"He said it was pointless since he wasn't going to take the job anyway. He would have had to move to California for a few months to work on the film and he said he couldn't leave while I was still in school," Liv explained.

Callie's heart clenched, imagining a younger Noah turning down his dream job to take care of his sister and mother. It was so like him to put everyone else's needs ahead of his own.

"But enough of this somber conversation! All is well! Wolf has come around with a new project and Noah and Callie... Well, I never thought he'd get his head out of his own backside long enough to see what the rest of us have always known."

"What?" Callie asked, her voice barely a sound.

"I have always thought you two would make a fine couple," Mrs. Van Aller said, shooting a conspiratorial glance Callie's mother, who looked appalled.

"He's eight years older than us," Liv protested.

"Liam's twelve years older than me," Min said with a shrug.

"Of course, I didn't think of it when you were younger," Mrs. Van Aller tutted. "It wasn't until you were all grown that I saw a spark. Don't act so scandalized, Livi. And now you're all adults, what's a few years? Might I remind you that your fiancé is sixteen years older than you, and I myself am seeing a younger man."

"Mom!" Liv gasped.

"Yes, let's hear about that," Pattie said, leaning forward with a wicked gleam in her eye.

Callie only heard pieces of the conversation as the others interrogated Mrs. Van Aller about her mysterious younger man (someone she'd met in her book club apparently). Her mind was stuck in a loop replaying what Mrs. Van Aller had said about seeing a spark between her and Noah years ago, about hoping they'd get together. Mrs. Van Aller was going to be so hurt when she found out it was all a lie. Callie should confess now, put an end to this whole thing.

But...what if Mrs. Van Aller was right? What if she and Noah were meant for each other? What if this week pretending could be the time she needed to stop being just his little sister's best friend and start being...something else? She'd thought she had long ago given up the hope of ever having more with Noah, but now, she couldn't help thinking maybe this was her last chance. If at the end of the week, he still didn't feel anything for her, then she'd know it really was a lost cause and maybe she could finally stop fantasizing about a life where she was his.

Chapter Nine

Callie hummed. All. The. Time.

It wasn't something Noah noticed at first, but by the time they were driving to dinner on that second night and he was doing his best not to stare at the way her hair had been styled in gentle waves around her shoulders, the subtle makeup making her chocolate brown eyes look larger, it was all he could think about. It wasn't in the same way Livi sang snippets of show tunes and car commercials under her breath. Callie hummed entire melodies—meandering, mournful tunes he'd never heard before but that called to mind misty mornings and acoustic guitars. Melodies that got stuck in his own head and drove him to distraction.

Daemon's brother was hosting the second night of "family dinner" at his restaurant and Noah was glad for the opportunity to get out of the hotel. While the women had spent the day at the salon, he had passed the afternoon bent over his laptop putting the finishing touches on a new piece to show Wolf, a snippet of a theme that could work for the main titles if he could convince the producer to hire him. Noah had started out in his hotel room, but everything smelled like Callie. Citrus and rain, which was maddening because, if you'd asked him a week ago, he never would have said that rain *had* a smell. He couldn't focus while engulfed in her scent.

Before long, he had moved to the restaurant just so he could think clearly. It was easier to compose in the restaurant anyway, he supposed, especially since the manager gave him permission to use the largely neglected baby grand piano in the corner of the room when it wasn't in use for any other purpose. The playback feature on his notation software was top notch, but there was nothing like playing the piece himself, feeling the notes flow from his fingers onto the keys to give life to a song that had, until that point, existed solely in his own mind.

Of course, then the tune Callie had been humming while she got ready for the salon had popped into his head and he found himself improvising on her melody instead of working on his own piece. The woman was a distraction he could not afford.

"What is that?" Noah asked, his tone sharper than he'd intended, as he turned the car into the gravel parking lot of Lemon & Thyme.

"Hmm?" Callie asked.

"The song you're humming. What is it?"

"Oh," Callie dropped her eyes to her hands in her lap, stretching her fingers wide before balling them up as if she wanted to hide them. "It's nothing. Just something that's been stuck in my head."

"Who wrote it?" He was confident he already knew the answer. He recognized that melancholic chord progression. He'd been the one to teach her how to add variation to it one summer a million years ago.

"No one. It's just something I've been playing with."

She got out of the car, and he followed her down the

drive towards the entrance. Jamie's restaurant wasn't just on the waterfront; it was constructed on a wharf so that the building appeared to be floating on the water. The gravel drive was lined with glowing lanterns, giving the entire structure an ethereal quality. The raised garden beds on either side of the main entrance were overflowing with herbs, making the humid summer air thick with the scent of dill and thyme. He caught her hand as they approached the large glass doors, interlacing their fingers.

"So *you* wrote it," he said.

"I guess. But it only exists in my head. I haven't written it down."

"Why not?"

"Because it's just a tune I hear in my head," she huffed, obviously annoyed with his persistent questioning. "It's nothing special."

He stopped walking, pulling her up short next to him and turned to face her. "What are you talking about? Of course—"

"I'm not twelve anymore, Noah. You don't have to humor me."

"I'm not. I never humored you." Noah cupped her jaw with his free hand and tilted her face back up to meet his eyes, squeezing her hand still interlaced with his. "You know that, right?"

She looked away, avoiding his eyes, but that wouldn't do. For some reason he couldn't name, it was vitally important she understood how much he enjoyed her song, even if he was being a grumpy asshole. His thumb swept back and forth over her cheekbone, the tender touch prompting her to meet his gaze.

"It's a beautiful song, Callie. You've always written beautiful songs."

"I don't write anymore. My hands..." She flexed and

bunched the hand at her side, a motion she repeated often.

He pressed his thumb into the center of her palm, massaging the tendons and muscles of her hand, their fingers still laced together. "What about your hands?" He had his own suspicions, but he wanted to know for sure, to understand exactly what had taken the music from her.

"They hurt all the time. If they're not swollen, they're stiff. They're slow and clumsy and—" She exhaled a frustrated breath through her nose, the force of it sending a tendril of her hair up into the air. "What's the point of writing songs? I can't play them anymore."

The resigned sadness in her eyes pulled at his chest, as though someone had tied a noose around his heart and was slowly tightening the rope.

"But you still hear them," he said, his voice low.

She nodded.

"You can't play at all?"

"A few notes here and there." She gave a wry smile, the expression all wrong on her soft features. He wanted to wipe it away, along with the crease between her brows. "Guess it's a good thing I had that double major to fall back on. I never finished my composition degree anyway. Looks like only one of us is going to be a famous composer after all," she said with a strangled chuckle.

"You're still composing," he said, his hand sliding around to the back of her neck through the silken waves of her hair.

She rolled her eyes. "I was humming, Noah. I'm not exactly Clara Schumann."

The corner of his mouth tipped up. "No. That song was much more reminiscent of Morricone."

A throat cleared ahead of them, and Noah dropped his hand from Callie's neck, turning to find Liam watching them, his hands shoved in his pockets and his brows furrowed. "Livi's waiting for you," he said. "They're ready to start dinner."

The dining room was sparsely decorated in creams and sage green, three walls of floor to ceiling windows proudly displaying the view of the ocean. Jamie, in his chef's coat, stood to one side of the room, laughing with Pattie and Maggie. At the other end of the long natural wood table, Noah's and Callie's mothers sat, deep in conversation with Liv and Daemon.

"There they are! The love birds have arrived!" Mrs. Van Aller chirruped over the cacophony of conversation and laughter.

"I thought *we* were the love birds," Liv joked, pressing her palm to Daemon's chest.

"Of *course*, you are, darling. Just look at our chickadee. He's positively love sick," Pattie said, gesturing to where Daemon had curled his own hand over Liv's, a look of unchecked adoration on his face.

Noah had to look away, the love burning in his soon-to-be brother-in-law's face too much to take in all at once. He'd always felt sorry for men who looked like that, like their whole world began and ended with someone else. Noah knew the inevitable pain that awaited them—because some day, that world would end, and whoever was left behind to grieve would never be the same. But just then, watching the way his sister glowed under the attention, how in-sync the pair appeared, how helplessly smitten Daemon was... he couldn't identify the feeling twisting in his stomach, making his throat tight.

Instead, he focused on pulling out Callie's chair for her, on the goosebumps springing up on her skin as he tucked the tag peeking out from the top of her dress back behind the fabric, on the softness of that skin beneath his fingertips. He let his hand linger on her back as he took his seat beside her, his fingers gliding over smooth skin and the ends of her hair. Something primal stirred deep inside him when she shot a shy smile his way. He liked making her smile, more than he should. As he watched her, pieces of the conversation surrounding him filtered through his own thoughts.

"How long have you owned this place?" Maggie asked Jamie.

Jamie smiled. "Going on three years."

Mrs. Cole reached across the table and tapped Callie's hand. "Don't slouch."

Liam's laughter rang out over the conversation as he wrapped his arms around Min from behind, his fiancée blushing in response to some joke Noah hadn't caught.

"Oh, you're even more trouble than Daemon!" Pattie said, playfully shoving Liam's shoulder.

Mrs. Van Aller refilled her wine glass from the bottle on the table. "Liv, have you gotten your something blue—"

Beside Noah, a server appeared at the table. "Does anyone have any allergies or dietary restrictions?" she asked, straining to be heard over their raucous group. Noah seemed to be the only one who noticed her question.

"Hey, Liv," Min called across the room, "what time are we meeting tomorrow?"

Liv called back, her response lost in the whirlwind of sound.

"I'm so glad you left your hair down, Calandria," Mrs. Cole said as she dug into the breadbasket on the table.

Noah watched as Callie's smile fell from her face, tension creeping into her shoulders. *What's that about?*

"Allergies?" the server tried again.

Noah glanced around at the rest of their party, few of whom were paying attention to the server. Pattie seemed to shake her head; Daemon shrugged.

"I think we're good," he said with a sympathetic smile. The server, obviously relieved to be able to stop vying for the group's attention, nodded and scurried away.

Mrs. Cole ran a finger through a loose strand of Callie's hair, and her daughter's lips pressed into a flat line. "No one can see that gorgeous hair when it's all tied up in those braids you're always wearing."

"Braids are easier to manage," Callie replied, her smile gone.

Mrs. Cole clucked her tongue in disapproval. "The way you talk, you'd think you were Rapunzel. It's not that difficult to just leave your hair down."

"It is for me. I don't always have the energy to spend on something as insignificant as my hair." Her fingers tightened around the stem of her water glass. Noah caught her other hand where it sat in her lap, squeezing lightly in solidarity.

"Being attentive to your appearance is not insignificant, dear. Your father—"

"—always preferred you wear your hair down. I know, Mom."

"I'm sure Noah expects the young lady on his arm to keep up with her appearance. He has so many *lovely* lady friends, after all," she said, her words venomous.

Noah turned a practiced smile to Mrs. Cole, the same one he'd used all his life to charm his way in or out of something distasteful. The blood was rushing in his ears, part absolute fury that Mrs. Cole would criticize Callie, that she'd suggest he might even consider being with another woman while he was dating her, and part something that demanded he make damn sure Callie knew how wrong her mother was.

"If I was that concerned about your daughter's appearance, then I don't think I would be the kind of person you would want in Callie's life. She's a beautiful woman, and that doesn't change when she wears sweats or her hair is in braids. The way she looks isn't even half of what makes her beautiful."

"Hear, hear!" Liv said, raising her glass.

Noah turned to meet Callie's startled gaze. The fact that his words had come as a surprise, that she didn't *know* that he thought she was beautiful, hit him with an unexpected pang of guilt. He pressed his lips to her shoulder, planting a kiss beside the thin strap of her dress, and murmured against her skin, "You're gorgeous, love. Always."

He hadn't meant to use the endearment, but he liked the way she beamed when the words left his mouth. He liked helping her see how fucking amazing she was. *The same way I like helping Livi to understand that she's a rockstar.* It was exactly the same thing. Right?

Jamie's staff began bringing out plates as he explained to everyone about whatever soup was being placed in front of them. Callie squeezed Noah's hand, and he raised it to his lips, brushing his mouth over her knuckles. He couldn't help himself. He needed to keep touching her—and that was a dangerous impulse.

One he absolutely could not indulge.

It was just a side effect of playing pretend. Of course, he wanted to touch her, to simulate the intimacy they were trying to convince everyone they shared. It was natural. Like actors who fall in love with their co-stars.

He caught her eye, but he couldn't read the look there, and his skin burned under her gaze. It was so much like the way she'd looked at him that night six years ago—the last time he'd had this insane need to taste her lips.

Undeniable

"Oh! It's cold!" Liv's delighted laugh broke through Noah's hazy thoughts. His sister took another bite of her soup, and the rest of their party followed suit. "What did you say this was called again?"

"Vichyssoise," Jamie said.

"That's a fancy word for cold soup," Daemon replied.

"You never did appreciate good food," Jamie said.

"I appreciate *hot* food," his brother shot back.

"Is there shellfish in this?" Callie asked, her hand tightening around Noah's, her other releasing her spoon as though it had burned her.

"Not typically," Jamie replied, his eyes dancing, "but this is my own award-winning recipe. My secret ingredient is lobster stock."

"Shit." Liv dropped her spoon and was on her feet, moving towards Callie.

"Calandria, are you alright?" Mrs. Cole asked, rising from her seat.

"What's going on?" Noah asked.

Callie coughed, like she was trying to clear her throat and couldn't. His heart began to pound and his eyes darted between Callie and the rest of their party, now closing in on them.

"I'm fine," Callie said, coughing again. "It's just a little swelling."

Shit.

"Do you have an epi-pen?" Jamie asked, pulling the contaminated bowl away from her and gesturing for one of his serving staff to take it.

Callie shook her head. "It's never that bad. Just unpleasant."

"You're allergic to lobster?" Noah asked.

"Didn't you know that?" Mrs. Cole asked him, her voice accusatory.

Fuck. Her boyfriend would have known what she was allergic to, and he damn well would have informed the server when they asked. Her boyfriend wouldn't have allowed anything with shellfish to come within ten feet of her.

What were you supposed to do when someone was having an allergic reaction? He tried to remember. He pressed his thumb against her wrist to feel for her pulse, not that he had a clue how to check someone's pulse, or if that was even something he should be doing in this situation.

Callie took a sip of her water. "Does anyone have any Benadryl?"

"Shouldn't we be calling an ambulance?" Noah asked, looking around the table where everyone appeared all together far too calm given that Callie was still coughing. She needed Benadryl and she needed it *now*. How long could someone cough like that with an allergic reaction before they couldn't breathe?

"Don't you have an epi-pen in your first aid kit?" he asked Jamie, aware of the edge of panic creeping into his tone.

"We do," Jamie confirmed before turning his attention back to Callie, "but we only use it if it's absolutely necessary. Callie, do you–"

"This is fucking necessary!" Noah shouted, sweat breaking out along his back. Why did no one else understand that she needed help?

"Let's go." Noah helped Callie to her feet.

Blood rushed in his ears, his breathing coming fast, and he couldn't just sit there and watch her coughing and not *do* something. If she needed Benadryl, he'd get her Benadryl, the fastest way he knew how.

Callie sat on the hospital bed in the emergency room and, for the third time, answered a new nurse's questions. No, she wasn't having any trouble breathing or swallowing. No, her tongue didn't feel swollen. Yes, this had happened before. No, she didn't have an epi-pen because she'd never gone into anaphylaxis. Yes, the antihistamines seemed to be working.

When the nurse left and pulled the curtain on the small bay closed behind her, Callie cast a tired glance at Noah. He sat in the chair next to her hospital bed, his elbows braced on the mattress, a sheepish look on his face.

"You really just needed Benadryl," he said.

"I really did."

He blew out a breath. "I'm sorry, Callie. You were coughing and I got scared—"

"You didn't listen to me."

He nodded, avoiding her gaze, the tips of his ears turning red.

"You need to trust that I know my own body, Noah. I don't need another person in my life who thinks they know better than me about my health."

He met her gaze, looking up at her through thick, dark eyelashes. "I know. I'm sorry."

"I thought you were taking me to a pharmacy."

He winced. "How mad are you right now?"

"I'm not mad. Was it a tad bit dramatic to take me to the ER? Sure, but I know you were trying to look out for me." She mussed his hair, letting her hand linger on the nape of his neck for just a moment. "You've always looked out for me," she said softly.

He met her gaze, his hazel eyes still so full of concern, the slight smile lines at the corners making him look older than his thirty-five years. "Always will. You're family, Callie."

She dropped her hand and looked away. *Right. Family. Because in his mind, I'm just like his kid sister.*

"What I don't understand is why Jamie put seafood in a potato soup in the first place," he continued. It was the thing he kept coming back to, his jaw tightening as though he were angry with Daemon's brother for not magically knowing that Callie had a shellfish allergy, even though Noah himself hadn't known.

"It was just a mistake, Noah," she said for the tenth time. "At least we won't have to deal with my mother for the rest of the night." She dropped her head back on the pillow, hating that her mother's criticism still stung even hours later.

"By the time we get out of here, she'll probably be asleep," Noah said with a grimace.

Callie couldn't help but chuckle. "Next time, just take me to a pharmacy."

"Next time? No, there will be no *next time*. I already bought you a lifetime supply of Benadryl to keep in your purse."

"You did not," she laughed.

"You don't believe me?" He grinned, that same grin he'd had since he was a gangly teenager. The one that always made her want to keep him. He grabbed her purse from the empty chair next to him and tossed it to her, arching an eyebrow at her in challenge.

She unzipped her purse—a purple dinosaur-shaped bag she'd found during a late-night online shopping spree—and burst out laughing at the insane number of travel-sized Benadryl packages shoved inside. "When did you do this?"

Undeniable

"When you were in the bathroom. It only took a minute to go to the gift shop."

"You know these things expire eventually, right?"

"Tell me when they do and I'll buy you more."

"I am capable of buying my own antihistamines," she said, trying to shove all the medication back into her bag.

"I know you can take care of yourself." He took the bag from her hands and zipped it shut so easily it would have been annoying if he wasn't being so damn *good*. "But I will feel better knowing you always have enough Benadryl on your person to knock out a small army."

"Thank you."

He squeezed her hand where it lay next to his on the bed, his thumb sweeping over the back. "Can I ask you something?"

"Of course."

"What you said to your mom earlier, about your hair and not having enough energy... I know you're often sore. But... it's more than that?"

"It is," she said, keeping her eyes locked on their hands. "Fibromyalgia isn't just a single symptom and everyone who has it experiences it differently. Most of the time it's just the soreness. I'm sore all the time, twenty-four-seven—but it's not debilitating unless I sit in one position too long or overextend myself. Sometimes it's also fatigue. I'll fall asleep watching TV at night or nod off at my desk mid-afternoon."

She could stop there. But she didn't want to. She wanted Noah to know, to understand.

"On the bad days it's like someone's tied weights to my arms and legs. They're heavy and clumsy and they ache if I try to lift them. I never know what might trigger a bad day. Some things, like exercising too much or not getting enough sleep, are a given. But other things..."

"Like blow drying your hair?"

She nodded. "Sometimes it's fine. Other days, holding my arms up like that for an extended period of time is enough to trigger a flare. And it's just not worth it. I only have so much energy in any given day. I never want to waste what little I have on styling my hair."

He lifted their clasped hands to his lips. It was such an intimate gesture—the kind of thing a boyfriend would do. But they were alone. There was no one there to see him acting the part. Was it just out of habit that he was treating her like she was precious to him?

"Your mom said something today..."

His brow furrowed in confusion. "What's that?"

"She said Wolf offered you the Revolutionary War score years ago and you turned it down."

His face went blank. "Yeah. Livi was still in school. She and mom needed me close by. And for some reason Wolf always insists on having his composer on set during filming. I couldn't just leave my family to go traipsing around old battlefields."

"That documentary won all kinds of awards. Do you regret turning it down?"

He shook his head, his eyes focused on their interlocked hands. "Not for a second." He looked up at her and smiled, the corners of his eyes crinkling. "It all worked out in the end. And now maybe I'll get to score this film."

"You will. I know it."

The curtain to the bay whipped open. Noah dropped her hand and sat back in the chair, as though they'd been caught doing something much more scandalous than holding hands. A nurse—the friendly blonde one who wore purple socks with cat faces on them—appeared with a stack of paperwork.

"Good news," she said, waving the papers. "Discharge papers."

"You are an angel," Callie said.

"Keep taking the Benadryl every four to six hours until you are completely symptom free," the nurse said. "Do you have Benadryl?"

Noah dropped his head, hiding his laugh, though his shoulders shook.

"Yes, I think I've got more than enough," Callie replied with a smile.

"Alright. Now if you feel any of your symptoms return, or you have any difficulty breathing, you should come right back in and see us again. But I hope you don't have to."

By the time they got back to The Barclay, it was after midnight. Callie and Noah had been texting with both her mother and Liv throughout their time in the ER, so she wasn't surprised that they hadn't waited up. It wasn't until they closed the door to their hotel room that she realized how tired she was. The constant dull ache in her lower back was already growing to a singeing pain, sharp enough to make her suck in a breath when she moved the wrong way. Too many hours sitting in a hospital bed and she'd be paying for it for days.

She reached behind herself to unzip her dress, hissing as the pain tore through her.

Noah was there in an instant, his hand closing around her forearm and gently bringing it back to her side. "Let me," he said as he dragged the zipper down, his fingertips brushing over her spine with each new inch of skin that was exposed.

The touch set all her nerve endings on alert, her skin tingling. His hand lingered, just barely touching the small of her back. Every ounce of her awareness was focused on that single point of contact, on the immense heat of his touch and how badly she wanted more of it.

She held the front of her dress to her chest so it wouldn't fall down and glanced at him over her shoulder. "Thank you."

He hummed an acknowledgment, a low sound that vibrated through her. Their eyes met over her shoulder and for a moment, she thought he might kiss her, their bodies drawing nearer to each other as though they were magnetized. His hazel eyes hooded and darkened to a deep, mossy green, and his jaw tightened in a way that made his already full lips seem so much fuller. He glanced at her mouth and she leaned a fraction of an inch closer.

Kiss me.

But then he blinked, his eyes cleared, and he dropped his hand, stepping back from her. He turned away, shoving his hand roughly through his hair.

"We should get some sleep," he said. Like nothing had happened.

Chapter Ten

Callie nodded off almost as soon as her head hit the pillow. But not Noah. He lay beside her, thinking about what she'd said in the hospital, all the ways she could be hurting and no one else would ever know. He thought about the last time he'd seen her in a hospital bed, the tubes and the beeping machines and the helplessness knowing there was nothing he could do. Knowing that it might have been his fault she was there in the first place. *Just like tonight.*

He didn't want to think about her being in pain. Instead, he shifted his attention to the way the hair around her face fluttered with each of her sleepy exhalations. He couldn't look away—except, of course, when his eyes traced her curves beneath the blanket. Lying beside her and not touching her was a special kind of torture. So when, in her antihistamine-fueled sleep, she exhaled a little whimper and tucked herself against his side, her hand pressing to his chest, it was more than he could take.

He slipped from their bed and, after pulling on a pair of gym shorts, went down to the first floor of the hotel to walk off the need pounding through his veins. *Just lust*, he told himself. *She's a beautiful woman half naked in your bed. It's just lust.*

He swiped a few sheets of paper and a pen from the front desk and took them out to the back patio overlooking the lawn and leading down to the ocean. The moon was bright, making it easy to see even at that late hour. He drew a deep breath of the muggy August air and repeated his lie to himself as he sketched a quick music staff and began jotting the notes that had been playing on repeat in his head all night. He hummed it back to himself, crossed out a note here and there and wrote in the corrections until he had it exactly the way Callie had hummed it in the car.

But he didn't stop there. His pen flew over the paper, marking accents and appoggiaturas, scribbling in a figured bass line. He wrote until he ran out of paper, until every bittersweet note she'd devised had been recorded and highlighted to its fullest. He wrote as he hadn't written in years, like the music was inevitable, irrepressible. When he was done, he took his new score into the restaurant and played it on the baby grand piano, adjusting bits of the accompaniment as he felt the music flow through him. As the last notes floated through the air, he hung his head in his hands, frustrated that putting the music on paper hadn't purged it from his mind.

By the time he returned to their room, the sun was almost up. He slipped back into bed beside Callie. This time, when she pressed herself against him as she slept, he wrapped his arm around her and let his head rest in the curve of her shoulder, his face turned into her neck. That was how he finally drifted off to sleep, cradling Callie in his arms with her song playing through his mind.

He woke up alone.

It was mid-morning, the sun streaming through the

window a too-bright rebuke for sleeping half the day away. Callie was gone, likely down on the beach with his sister and their friends. Noah was in no rush to get up, pressing his face into her pillow and inhaling her citrus and rain scent. *What the fuck am I doing?* he thought with a groan, the scent making him instantly hard. He forced himself from the sheets that smelled like her and into the bathroom. But the bathroom smelled of her, too, and it was too much.

He flipped the lock on the bathroom door in case she should come back to the room and climbed into the ridiculously large shower. The floor was covered in river rock, the walls giant slabs of marble only interrupted by the multiple shower heads placed throughout the enclosure. The warm water slid over him and kicked up the residual scent of her body wash. He thought of her standing in that same spot earlier that morning, the water splashing over her curves, between her breasts. It was too much to ask for a man to be unaffected by that image. If he gave in to the fantasy of it, maybe then it would be easier to remember that none of this was real.

He took himself in hand, his fist sliding over his engorged shaft. He moved slowly at first, up and down from root to tip, squeezing as he neared the swollen head of his cock, and he imagined it was her. Her hand wrapped around his length, working him slowly, methodically. He thought of the way the water would flow over her breasts, how it would gather in the curls at the apex of her thighs. And then all he could think about was that secret place between her legs, the soft heat that waited there and would feel so good wrapped around his cock. The way her pussy would welcome him in, and how she'd rock her hips faster, begging him with her body to make the ache in her core go away.

His strokes quickened, growing rougher with each pass

as the beginnings of his climax gathered at the base of his spine. He pictured how her pussy would look stretched around him as he fucked her, and how she'd writhe when he pressed fast circles to the swollen bud of her clit. He'd make her come at least twice before he let himself go, would want to feel her body grip his before he'd give himself over to the immense pleasure of being inside her.

Noah's breath caught in his chest and he slammed his hand against the wall of the shower, his orgasm ripping through him with the image of Callie's lips parted in her own climax and the scent of her hair all around him. Streams of cum shot from his cock, mingling with the water and washing down the drain, again and again, robbing him of his breath. He imagined filling her, watching his release spill out around himself as he pumped into her and she begged for more.

In his dreams, she always begged for more.

When it was over, he washed his hands and his hair, made sure the shower was spotless, just as he always did. Just as he'd done every time he'd given in to the thoughts of Callie that had plagued him for the last six years. And, as he'd done every time before, he promised himself it would be the last time. But this time, he knew he was lying.

Chapter Eleven

Liv loved a beach day more than anyone Callie had ever met. As teenagers, Callie had tolerated the occasional long weekend in Sag Harbor at her father and stepmother's house only because Liv would go with her and they'd spend the entire day lying out in the sun. Well, Liv would. After a day on the beach, Liv's skin turned a golden bronze, her hair taking on honeyed highlights. But after only an hour or two, Callie's porcelain skin burned bright red. Boiled lobster red. And, unlike the handful of times when Liv's tan had edged into burn territory, Callie's skin didn't settle into a beachy glow after—it just went right back to porcelain. Which was the cosmetic industry's polite way of saying pale. But Liv came alive when the waves crashed around her, so Callie hadn't been surprised when Liv scheduled a beach day smack in the middle of her wedding week extravaganza.

The expansive lawn of The Barclay sloped down to a rocky stretch of ground covered in flat stones smoothed by centuries of waves, before the rocks finally gave way to the sandy shoreline. That morning, after once again carefully extricating herself from Noah's sleeping embrace, Callie had taken her beach bag and met the rest of their party under a cabana on the private beach. Liv and Daemon were already looking sickeningly adorable sharing a lounger with their toes in the sand.

"How're you feeling today?" Liv asked as Callie settled herself on a lounger under the cabana.

"Good as new."

"I'm sorry Noah dragged you to the ER."

Callie waved off the concern with a flick of her wrist. "That's just Noah. Overbearing as always."

"I'm surprised he didn't know about your allergy."

"It just never came up before," Callie said, avoiding Liv's eyes.

She and Noah would need to spend some time getting on the same page if they wanted to avoid raising suspicion any further. Her mother had already intimated over breakfast that she saw Noah's lack of awareness of Callie's allergy as a sign that he wasn't as committed to their relationship as she thought he should be. If her mother didn't believe Noah was in it for the long haul, she'd never move to Ohio.

Liv sat up, bracing herself with a hand on Daemon's chest. His hand closed over hers, his thumb sweeping back and forth over the skin just below where Liv's engagement ring sparkled. Callie's eyes were drawn to the movement and something uncomfortably like envy twisted in her gut.

"Hey, Cal," Liv said with a mischievous smile. "Daemon's never had his cards read."

Daemon groaned at the exact same time Callie gasped. How had this man been dating her best friend for so long and she hadn't read his cards yet?

Liv continued, "Aside from when you read my cards that one time—"

"That I told you about," Callie interjected.

"—and practically forced me to go on a date with him."

"One, I'm pretty sure it was your director who forced you to go on the date. And two, he came up as the *Emperor*. But either way—the cards never lie."

"Mmhmm," Liv said, looking at Daemon adoringly despite his growing scowl. "They told me you were the one for me."

"That's funny. I thought the multiple orgasms did that," Daemon said, the corner of his lips turning up.

Liv rolled her eyes, biting back a smile, and returned her attention to Callie. "But he's never had a reading of his own."

"Well, what are we waiting for, Emperor?" Callie dug in her bag for her tarot deck.

She had several decks, truth be told. One that she only used when she was alone and kept in a carved wooden box with a bundle of sage. One that she kept on her person at all times, the deck held together with several rubber bands and moving from purse to purse as her mood changed. And one that was just too pretty to use: a hand-painted deck that Liv had picked up for her in some new age shop in London's West End that Callie kept in its original packaging until she could figure out how to display them properly.

"We'll start you off slow with a three-card spread," Callie said.

Despite Daemon's grouchy bear routine, he obliged his fiancée—as they all knew he would—shuffling the cards when Callie told him to, cutting the deck and making a gallant effort not to roll his eyes when she tapped the deck to clear the energy. She got lost in the routine of it, the feel of the crisp edges beneath her fingers, the almost meditative repetition of shuffling.

Callie believed in the cards the way some people believed in rosaries or lighting candles. It wasn't that she thought they told the future, exactly—more that it was easier to hear her own intuition when she looked at the images, like the story they told cut through all the noise around her, pulling truth from within herself. Call it spirit guides or the divine or the universe—it didn't matter. When there was so little she had control over, when even her own body was unpredictable, she always had the cards.

Callie shifted so she was straddling the lounger, laying the cards out on the black and white fabric emerging from between her thighs. No surprise that the Emperor made an appearance, and the Queen of Cups—the card that had always signified Liv as her best self, at least in Callie's mind.

She flipped the last card and couldn't help smiling. "Four of wands."

"That's good?" Daemon asked, leaning in to get a better look at the card.

"It's your wedding." Callie traced the image with her fingertip. "A celebration, a gathering of family and friends, a peaceful and happy home."

Daemon's brow drew low as he looked up at Callie, squinting in the sun. "So, your cards just said Liv and I are getting married?"

"Mmhmm."

"What the hell did we need the cards for?" he asked, turning to glance back at Liv who could hardly contain her laughter.

Over the next few hours as more of their party joined them on the beach, Callie did more readings—one for Pattie about a role she was considering (it wasn't a good fit); one for Min to assuage her fears about her new graduate program (no surprise, she was going to be a star); one for Liam about the opera company he hoped to start (he should stay focused on the young artist programs he loved best). She even did a reading for Mrs. Van Aller about her new younger man. The cards were unclear about if there was any real future there, but she would enjoy herself while she found out.

It was nearly noon and Callie was in the middle of doing a reading for Jamie when Noah made an appearance. He jogged down the stone stairs to the beach with a lightness in his step that belied the firm set of his stubbled jaw, the stormy look in his hazel eyes. Callie focused on shuffling the cards. *You're imagining things,* she told herself. He certainly seemed to be his usual affable, charming self as he greeted his mother and hers with kisses on the cheeks and helped himself to a bottle of local lemonade from the ice bucket. He flicked the icy water that lingered on his fingers at Liv, laughing when she shrieked as the water hit her sun-heated skin.

"What's going on here?" Noah asked, dropping onto the lounger next to Callie.

"Callie's been doing everyone's cards," Liam replied. He and Min shared a lounger across the cabana. Min sat between his legs and Liam's arms were wrapped around her so tightly it was a wonder the girl could breathe.

"I see," Noah said.

She felt his eyes on her hands as she shuffled and, for the first time in ages, she bungled the movement. Her cards caught on each other instead of smoothly gliding in and out of the deck as they usually did. She handed the deck to Jamie and instructed him on how to cut and put it back together.

"You ready?" she asked Jamie.

"As I'll ever be," he said.

She laid out the three cards in front of Jamie, grinning at the clear message. "Ace of Wands," she said, pointing to the first card. "That's the card of new beginnings, especially creative projects. Page of Cups is an interesting card to get in conjunction with the Ace of Wands. In this context, it means there is an attractive younger woman with whom you'll share an intense sexual connection."

"Where is this attractive younger woman?" Jamie asked, his eyes sparkling with mischief.

"Not here," Noah grumbled.

Callie bit back a smile, her cheeks warming at Noah's jealous retort. She tapped the last card, The Moon. "I don't know, but whoever she is, she'll be helpful to you in some way—if you can learn to cooperate. And you either already know her or whatever event will bring her into your life has already been set in motion."

"Then I guess I'll have to keep my eye out for her," Jamie said with a wink.

"Your turn, big brother," Liv said, smirking, as Jamie got to his feet and moved away to the other side of the cabana.

"Hard pass," Noah said.

"Surely Calandria's read your cards before now?" Callie's mother lowered her sunglasses to cast an assessing look at Noah and her daughter. Her mother had never been fond of Callie's tendency to read other people's cards wherever they went. But her mother was right—there was no plausible way that Callie and Noah were dating and she didn't regularly read his cards. She read everyone's cards.

"It's okay, Mom. Not everyone likes having a reading in front of other people. I'll just do one for Noah later in private, like we usually do," Callie lied.

"I think you should do it now," Min said, her lips spreading into a grin. "It's only fair. The rest of us already did." Liam planted a kiss on the place where Min's shoulder met her neck, his lips pressed together to suppress his smile.

"I agree," Mrs. Van Aller said. "Don't be a party pooper."

Callie saw the moment Noah caved with a twitch of his

Undeniable

lip. He stuck his bottle of lemonade in the sand at his feet and braced his elbows on his knees, leaning in closer. His eyes danced, his eyebrow quirking up. "Let it never be said that I pooped on any party. Do your worst, Calico."

She held his eyes, the nickname he'd given her six years ago—and rarely used since—seeping into her skin, making her shiny and new.

"You need to ask a question," Liv prompted.

"What?"

"A question. Something you'd like to know."

"Yes, I know what a question is." Noah shot his sister a long-suffering look. "I don't have a question."

Liv rolled her eyes. "Right. Because you already know everything?"

"What should I ask about then?"

"Your relationship, of course," Mrs. Van Aller chimed in. Callie's hands stilled mid-shuffle.

"I don't think that's necessary, Mom." Noah watched Callie with a wariness that set her teeth on edge.

"That's a marvelous idea, Shira!" Callie's mom said, sitting up straighter in her lounger. "This is, after all, such a new development. Perhaps the cards can shed some light on your future together."

"I thought you didn't believe in the cards," Callie said.

"It doesn't matter what *I* believe, darling," her mother said. "It's about what *you* believe."

"It's Noah's reading," Callie insisted. "He has to decide on the question."

She locked eyes with Noah for a moment, trying to read his expression, and found she was unable to. After several long seconds, he gave a slight nod of his head. "Our relationship then."

Callie held his gaze as she tapped the deck, clearing the

117

energy from the last reading. Then she handed the cards to Noah and talked him through shuffling and cutting the deck. When he handed the cards back to her, his fingers lingered against her hand—or did she imagine that? *Focus, Callie.*

For the others, Callie had done a simple three card spread, but for a relationship reading, she preferred five cards. Still a fairly basic reading, the five-card spread was her go-to for quick guidance on matters of the heart.

As she set the last card down, her heart fluttered in her throat. She scanned the cards, then glanced at Noah. He looked at her expectantly, and she forced her gaze back to the five images arranged in front of her.

"Well? What does it say?" Liv asked.

Callie pointed to the first card on the left. "This is you," she told Noah, "The Knight of Cups. He's a dreamer, a romantic at heart, but...he's still learning. He knows how to love—"

"Is *love* a euphemism?" Liam asked. Callie ignored him, but heat rushed to her cheeks.

"—but he doesn't yet know how to be a partner. It's a card that says you need to examine how you really feel, not how you think you *should* feel. What's really deep down in your heart."

"Always good advice," Mrs. Van Aller said.

"And this card," Callie said, moving on to the card on the far right, before she could let her own thoughts dwell on what Noah might feel deep down, "this one represents the other person in the relationship."

"You," Noah said softly, his eyes glued to the image beneath her fingertip.

"Me. The Star. It's about the power of dreaming. Wish fulfillment. Hope and new beginnings."

"Well, that seems appropriate," her mother said.

Undeniable

"This one," Callie said, pointing to the card at the bottom of the spread, "is the foundation of the relationship. The six of cups."

"What's that one mean?" Pattie asked, leaning in to get a better look.

"It's about forming new connections with someone from your past. Someone...unexpected."

"That one looks ominous," Maggie said, indicating the card at the center of the spread.

When had everyone gathered around so closely?

"The Hanged Man." Callie was no longer looking at the cards, her attention focused solely on Noah. "It means you have to leave old pain in the past. It means you have a choice: stay in your suffering or climb down and move forward. It means you want more."

Noah's eyes snapped to hers, their depths stormy in a way that sent a shiver through her body. Callie's gaze never wavered as she tapped the final card at the top of the spread.

"Page of Cups. The likely outcome."

"What does it mean?" Noah asked, his voice a deep rumble.

"An attractive young woman," Jamie said. "Weren't you listening to my reading?"

Callie shook her head. "Yes, but in this context it means that happiness is imminent. That love has arrived and is just waiting for you to notice."

She knew that their friends and family buzzed around her, delighted by the reading, but she hardly heard them over the pounding of her heart, barely saw them with her eyes locked on Noah's. Several long moments passed—or maybe it was no time at all—as they stared into each other's eyes, the expression on Noah's face a mix of wonder and something darker, something she couldn't define but very much wanted to.

Chapter Twelve

Jamie had prepared a picnic lunch for everyone. "No shellfish," he assured Callie with an apologetic smile as he unloaded the coolers, setting out containers.

They ate like kings, the laughter and conversation flowing easily amongst their group, but Noah was only half paying attention. He sat beside Callie and laughed when everyone else laughed, though he hadn't really caught the joke, and ate more food than anyone should eat in one sitting, but his mind was still stuck on the tarot cards.

It means you have a choice.

It means you want more.

He wanted too much.

Callie threw her head back, laughing at something Liv had said—or was it Pattie?—her eyes sparkling. God, she was beautiful when she laughed. Lit from within, like all that joy bubbling within her had nowhere to go so it burst out of her lips.

Before he knew it, lunch was over, the containers packed away as quickly as they had appeared. And then Liv was running down the beach and straight into the surf, laughing and calling for the rest of them to join her.

Daemon and Jamie didn't need much coaxing, and as soon as Min dropped her sarong and began to pick her way across the sand, Liam followed as well. Pattie and Maggie stayed behind in the cabana, keeping Mrs. Cole and his mother enthralled with talk of the cruise they had taken the previous year to the Greek Isles.

Callie shrugged out of the drapey robe-like thing she'd been wearing, revealing an aqua one-piece swimsuit. The cut was scandalously high on her thighs, and a zipper ran from the center of the neckline to just below her full bust. Noah's eyes raked over her, taking in the softness of her thighs and hips, the curve of her ass barely covered by the bathing suit. His brain stuttered over the zipper. The desire to pull it down overwhelmed him, the need to open her up so strong he was half sure he was going to do it.

"Are you coming?" Callie asked.

Love has arrived and is just waiting for you to notice.

But no, this wasn't love. This was lust. He wanted her—there had never been any doubt about that—but wanting her and loving her were not the same thing. And having her without loving her had never been an option, would never be an option. Liv would never forgive him if he broke her best friend's heart. He'd never forgive himself, not when he'd already hurt her in so many other ways. And heartbreak was the only possible conclusion. He knew what happened after the storybooks ended. He only had to look at his parents to know that no one lived happily ever after forever.

Still, he'd be lying if he said his skin didn't buzz with an awareness of her eyes on him when he pulled his t-shirt over his head and discarded it.

"Race you," he said with a grin and then took off down the beach.

He ran just fast enough to stay ahead of her, to keep her laughter nipping at his heels so it could fill him up, make him feel fresh and new, baptized in her joy. As they reached the water's edge, Callie caught his arm, pulling him back so they splashed into the waves at exactly the same time.

"Cheater!" he laughed, wrapping his arms around her waist from behind and tossing her further into the water.

She popped up out of the surf, water flowing off the tip of her nose and over her torso in winding rivulets, and splashed him. "Winner, you mean."

Her body was slick under his hands, her curves sliding against him under the water as they came together, splashing like children, and broke apart laughing. Water dripped from their hair into their eyes. Her leg brushed his as she flitted past him and he reached beneath the water, his hand closing around her thigh and pulling her close. He lifted her leg to wrap around his hip until she was floating in his arms, her legs around his waist and her arms around his neck.

The laughter died on her lips, her eyes holding his, so full of questions he didn't have answers for. He slid his hands over her back beneath the water, savoring the feel of her under his hands, the weightlessness of floating with her in his arms giving everything a dreamlike haze.

It didn't feel real, and if it wasn't real then he didn't need to question what he was doing touching her like she was his to touch. If it wasn't real, then what did it matter if he let his hands drift over the curves of her hips and thighs, if her breathing grew shallow and her nipples, hard points pressing against her swimsuit, were so close to his lips he could practically taste them? If it wasn't real, then no one could get hurt and he could want her without needing to protect her from that want.

Her legs tightened around him and he was certain that she could feel him growing harder by the second. *I should stop this.* The thought came unbidden and unwelcome. He should put her down and make a joke and forget he ever knew what it was to have her legs wrapped around his waist. Instead he slid his hand higher on her leg, his thumb tracing the edge of her swimsuit where it cut across her thigh.

"Admit it," he said, his voice low and rough. Her eyes widened, her pupils blown, dark circles rimmed by a thin border of chocolate brown. "Admit you cheated."

Her lips turned up in a smile so delicious he wanted to know what it tasted like. "There were no rules established. You can't cheat if there aren't any rules." Was her voice huskier?

"I should teach you not to cheat," he said, quietly enough that no one else could hear the low rasp of his voice over the crashing of the waves.

"Maybe you should." Her hand moved into the hair at the back of his neck, nails scraping lightly over his scalp and sending bolts of electricity down his spine.

His thumb slid beneath the seal of her bathing suit, tracing the crease where her thigh met her hip, but his eyes never left hers. How had he never noticed the copper tint in her irises before, the way the sun caught the deep brown and made it gleam?

Water crashed over his head. Callie shrieked and hid her face in his neck as the water broke over them, the splash accompanied by the sound of Liv and Liam laughing. Noah wiped the water from his eyes and looked over to see his sister and best friend high fiving just before a second splash smacked him in the face.

"What the fuck?" he demanded, turning his body to shield Callie from the worst of their assault.

"Get a room!" Liv called.

He set Callie down and took off after their assailants, vowing retribution. It was easier to focus on his return attack than to think about what he'd just done, the way he'd touched her. Easier to leap on Liam's back, to flick water at Liv and Min, than to admit how much he wanted to touch her again.

That night, exhausted from a full day at the beach, they spread blankets on the lawn around a bonfire. Callie felt like a teenager, roasting marshmallows and sharing stories from when they were kids, watching the firelight dance over Noah's face as she'd done during so many bonfires in his mother's backyard over the years.

There had been a moment in the water when she thought he might kiss her, when she could have sworn he wanted to. Since then, it seemed he was never very far from her, his fingers casually brushing against her as they stood together at the fire's edge. They sat beside each other on an old flannel blanket the front desk had provided, their hands so close to each other, they were almost touching.

"Were you always a performer?" Jamie asked Liv when Mrs. Van Aller had finished telling another story about one of Liv's early roles.

"Pretty much. Callie and I were always on stage when we were kids," Liv said, pulling a burned marshmallow off her stick and licking the gooey white stuff from her fingertips.

"You're a performer, too?" Pattie asked.

Callie shook her head. "Not like Liv and Daemon are. My

ambitions for the limelight never went past middle school drama club."

"That's not entirely true," her mother said. "If I remember correctly, you won your high school talent show with that song you wrote."

Callie blinked. Was that pride in her mother's voice? No, it couldn't be. She'd never been all that supportive of Callie's music.

"That's right!" Mrs. Van Aller chimed in. "You were quite the musician."

"It was high school," Callie demurred.

"They're right," Noah said. Then, to the newcomers amongst them, "Callie wrote amazing songs. Every time I'd come home from grad school for the weekend, she'd have piles of new sheet music to show me."

"No kidding," Liv said with a laugh. "Any time you came home, my best friend disappeared into the music cave—"

"Our living room is hardly a cave," Mrs. Van Aller objected.

"—and I wouldn't have her to myself again until you went back to Boston."

"You were always welcome to join us," Noah said.

"To talk about Philip Glass?" Liv wrinkled her nose and shook her head. "No, thank you."

"Do you still write?" Maggie asked.

"No," she said at the same time Noah said, "Yes."

Callie shot him a look, hoping the severity of her gaze conveyed that it was time for him to stop talking.

"No," she repeated. "Noah's the only composer in the group now."

"It's a shame," Mrs. Van Aller said as she assembled another smore. "I remember this one time—oh, it must have been the summer before you started teaching, Noah—I came home from the market and you two were out in the backyard debating chord resolutions. The way you two talked..." She smiled and shook her head, remembering.

Callie remembered that day, too. They'd sat in Adirondack chairs in his mother's yard and discussed the finer points of music theory. Noah swore one day they'd both be famous composers who broke all the rules and new ones would be named after them. It was one of the first times she'd felt like they'd really connected, like he'd noticed her as more than the neighbor girl who was friends with his sister. It was the conversation that had prompted her to start calling him with her music questions when she was in college, the day that had made her think maybe he wouldn't mind those calls. Maybe he'd even welcome them.

"Well, that's when I knew there was something special here," Mrs. Van Aller continued.

"You did?" Noah asked, his brow furrowed.

"Mmhmm. The same way I knew that these two were going to end up together when Liv called to tell me about their first rehearsal," she said, gesturing towards Liv and Daemon.

Liv scoffed. "You did not."

"Of course, I did!" Mrs. Van Aller replied with mock indignation.

As the fire began to wind down and the conversation moved on, a deep ache settled into Callie's back and shoulders. She'd overdone it, stayed too long in the water with the others because she hadn't wanted to call it quits before Noah had. In the weightlessness of the ocean, she could forget all the ways her body betrayed her. But now the tightness in her muscles promised she would pay for that decision. She dropped back to reclining on her elbows, but that only intensified the ache in her shoulders. Before long, she lay flat on her back staring at the stars. The others began to gather their things, ready to call it a night, but she didn't want to move and feel the pain tear through her.

"Are you two coming in?" her mother asked, standing over them as she folded her own blanket into smaller and smaller squares.

"I want to watch the stars for a bit," Callie said.

Noah glanced at her, then back up at her mother. "I think we'll stay out a little while longer."

"Don't stay up too late," her mother cautioned. "You need your sleep, Calandria. And you don't want to catch a chill." Never mind that it was still in the mid-70s even after the sun had set.

"Noah will make sure Callie's alright," Mrs. Van Aller said. She turned to Callie and Noah with a knowing smile as she pulled Callie's mother away. "You two enjoy your evening."

The last of their group disappeared into the hotel and Noah flopped down on his back beside her, his hands folded over his chest. After a moment, he turned to look at her, his attention as hot on her skin as the heat from the fire on her other side. "Seems like I'm not the only composer amongst us after all," he said. She looked at him, confused. "You were humming again."

"Was I? I didn't realize."

"You do it a lot. Always different melodies." He turned back to look at the stars again. "Always beautiful."

She didn't know what to say. The songs that came to her, that apparently she hummed without realizing it, were always there, playing in her head. If she closed her eyes, she could see the piano keys, could almost feel the slight resistance beneath her fingertips as she played. She wondered how long before the songs would be taken from her, too.

"You should write them down," he said.

"I can't play anymore."

"You could write them without playing. You always had a good ear."

In theory he was right. She could notate the melodies in her head without having to touch a piano, but what was the point? Even if she got them down on paper, no one would ever play them. *She* would never play them.

"My mother has certainly bought into the idea of us being together," Noah said.

Callie couldn't decide if this was a better or worse topic, but she appreciated that he knew to change the subject. "Apparently she knew we were meant to be together before we did," she laughed. "Now if only my mother could get on board."

"Do you think she'll come around?"

"I don't know."

"Well, we have a few more days to convince her. He reached over and squeezed her hand where it lay at her side between them. Only, he didn't let go. "Who knows? By the end of the week, maybe we'll both have what we want."

I want you.

She closed her eyes against the impossible thought and reminded herself to stay focused on the goal. Her mother moving, Noah's job—those were the important things. Even if he was still holding her hand.

Callie turned her hand over, lacing her fingers through his, but kept her eyes focused stubbornly on the sky. At the end of the week, they'd go back to how things had always been—with Noah no more than her best friend's older brother, and Callie just another foolish woman who wanted what she couldn't have.

Noah's free hand shot into the sky, pointing at a cluster of stars. "It's a ladybug," he said.

Callie squinted at the place where he pointed. "I'm pretty

sure there aren't any ladybug constellations."

"Not with that attitude." He traced a shape in the air. "See? Definitely a ladybug."

"I guess it kind of looks like—"

"And there." His hand darted to point out another grouping of stars. "That has got to be an otter."

Callie tilted her head to the side. She could almost see it. "Mmm, there's his tail."

He shifted his hand again. "What do you think that is?" he asked, turning his face to hers.

"That is clearly a snowman."

He barked out a laugh. "There's a snowman constellation?"

"If there can be a ladybug constellation, there can be a snowman," she said, tracing the shape in the sky. "See? He even has the top hat."

"And the carrot nose?" he teased.

"Obviously." She let her hand float back down to rest on her stomach.

She turned to meet Noah's eyes, and the look on his face stole her breath away. His eyes were more gold than green in the fading firelight, his stubble thicker at this point in the day. Before she could think better of it, she ran her palm over his jaw, his beard scratchy against her skin. He was so close she could feel the little bursts of hot air he expelled with each breath. So close and yet not nearly close enough.

"Callie…" He said her name like it was something special, something surprising and wondrous. Like he was saying it for the first time and memorizing the taste of it. The deep timbre of his voice vibrated through her.

And then his lips brushed against hers. Warm and soft, barely there. A whisper of a kiss.

She wanted more.

She tipped her chin to meet him, bringing their lips

Undeniable

together again. There and then gone. He pressed his forehead against hers, the tips of their noses skating against each other as they breathed each other's air. She squeezed her eyes closed, tried to focus on each individual sensation, to catalog and memorize them so she could remember them later.

He drew a shuddering breath that reverberated throughout her whole body, and then his free hand was sliding into her hair, angling her just so, and his lips were on hers again. This time, there was nothing soft about it. His kiss was hungry, searching, like he would learn every part of her by learning her lips. He licked over her bottom lip, and she parted for him, meeting his tongue with her own, swallowing his groan.

Callie had spent years imagining what it would be like to kiss Noah again. She'd tried to recall every detail of the last time, but neither her memory nor her imagination could live up to the real thing. This was want and need, power and tenderness all wrapped up in the way he owned her with his kiss. He pressed her back into the blanket and rose up above her, his body caging her in and pressing against her with just the subtlest of shifts in their position, and yet even then he was careful not to give her his full weight.

She gripped the fabric of his shirt, bunching it in her fist and urging him closer as their tongues stroked each other, certain that if she let go, she'd float away. His knee slid between her legs, pressing the hard muscle of his thigh against her where she was already wet and wanting. She moaned at the unexpected friction, grinding down against him.

He broke away, his hand still tangled in her hair and his nose sliding against hers. "What are we doing?" he asked, the gruffness in his tone tempered by something new, something tortured.

She couldn't bear the uncertainty in his voice. All the times she'd imagined kissing him again, she'd never imagined he would be uncertain about it.

"We should stop," she whispered.

She didn't want to stop. She wanted more. But she wouldn't ask him for anything he didn't want to give, and she'd known all along that she could never have this with Noah. It might have been possible once, six years ago... She tried to tamp down the disappointment threatening to strangle her, the old frustration that being with him was yet another thing her illness had stolen from her.

He scraped his hand over his mouth. "Callie, I—"

"It's alright. We've spent the last few days pretending. It was bound to happen at some point."

He glanced away and when he turned his face back to hers, his eyes had become more guarded. "Right." He dropped onto his back at her side and took her hand again, holding it loosely.

For the first time all night, she was cold.

"Will you tell me why we're still out here?" His voice was soft in the growing darkness. She didn't answer, not sure what to say. He squeezed her hand. "Come on, Callie. I know it's not because you wanted to find snowmen in the stars."

"I'm not sure I can get up." She hated the way the words called tears to her eyes. Hated that she even had to say the words at all.

"Alright. Will you be able to get up if we wait a while?" His voice was even, neutral, as though they were discussing the weather and not her inability to move properly.

"Maybe."

He was quiet for a long time before he spoke again. "Would you like me to try to help you up, or would you rather we lay here a little longer?"

Undeniable

"You can go in if you want. You don't need to wait for me."

He shot her a look that said she was out of her mind if she thought that was seriously an option. And he was so damn beautiful it hurt to have him look at her like that, like he would take care of her. Because she didn't need him to take care of her. She could take care of herself. She didn't want to be someone else he needed to take care of. She just wanted him to want *her*.

"I think I'd like to lay here a little longer."

He gave a tight nod and shifted his focus back to the sky.

They lay there for at least another half hour, pointing out constellations that weren't and holding hands like they weren't running out of time.

Slipping out of bed in the middle of the night was becoming a bad habit for Noah. After that kiss, the last thing he wanted to do was leave Callie's side. Which is exactly why he knew he had to. If he could focus on work then maybe he could stop thinking about how soft her lips were, or the little noise she made when he'd slid his thigh between her legs. The problem, of course, was that he couldn't focus on work. He'd been sitting at the baby grand in the hotel restaurant for nearly an hour playing the same four bars of music over and over again and getting nowhere.

"I'd recognize that cadence anywhere."

Noah looked up from the piano to find his sister walking through the darkened room towards him. She wore one of those flimsy hotel bathrobes tied tightly at the waist over her pajamas, her hair piled in a messy bun on the top of her head. It was well after midnight and the rest of the hotel was quiet save for the distant sound of someone running a vacuum.

"I didn't realize anyone could hear me," he said.

"They can't." She sat on the piano bench beside him, nudging him with her shoulder. "The night manager ratted you out."

"What are you doing up?"

She pressed her lips together in a way that made her cheeks puff out and shrugged. "Couldn't sleep."

Noah wrapped an arm around his sister's shoulder and hugged her against him. "Nightmare?"

She nodded. "They don't happen that often anymore. I didn't want to wake Daemon."

"I think I have one of those plastic army men in my suitcase," he said.

He knew he had one. He had several, in fact. Ever since their father died, he'd been planting green plastic army men beside Liv's bed to help her feel brave and keep the nightmares at bay. As they'd gotten older, he'd started giving them to her at other times, too, to remind her that she was unstoppable—like on the first day of rehearsals for her first major production, or when she had to fly to another continent for the first time.

"I'm about to be a married woman," she laughed. "I can't depend on my brother to give me a toy every time I have a bad dream."

"You can if they help you feel better."

"I think I need to learn how to feel better without leaning on you for support."

He rested his head on top of hers. "I'll always be here for you, Livi. Even after you're a married woman."

"I know. But—" She tensed in his arms, rolling her lips

between her teeth to stop herself from speaking.

"But what?"

"Nothing. I just keep thinking about something Mom said. About how you put off being happy yourself so you could make sure she and I were happy."

"That's not true," he said, pulling away from her and not at all liking the way her words made the hairs on the back of his neck stand on end.

"No?" she asked, tilting her head curiously.

"No. Taking care of you and Mom makes me happy, Livi."

"That's not the same as finding out what makes you happy on your own."

"I'm happy," he insisted.

"Are you?"

"Yes!"

She grinned. "Because you're in *looooove* with Callie?"

He scowled, but it only served to make her laugh.

"I'm glad you two are together, you know," she continued. "I think you're good for each other."

He nodded, unsure how to respond. He thought they were good for each other, too, but they weren't really together. It was all a lie, even if he had kissed her only a few hours earlier. Even if he hadn't wanted to stop kissing her.

Liv reached for the sheet music strewn across the lid of the piano. "What are you working on?"

"I'm trying to put together a few more samples for Wolf."

She hummed the melody as her eyes scanned the paper. "These are good," she said. She flipped to the next page, humming again, but this time it wasn't his piece for Wolf—it was Callie's song. She shook her head. "That one's pretty but not the right vibe for politics."

"Yeah," he said, swiping the offending piece of paper. "Probably not."

Liv set down the stack of papers. "You really want this job, huh?"

"Of course. It's my dream job."

"Is it?"

"Yes. What's with the third degree tonight?"

Liv turned around on the piano bench so her back was to the keyboard and stretched her legs out in front of her. "I don't know. You just seem different these last few days. Good different."

They were quiet together for a while in a way that only people who are completely comfortable with each other can be. He'd missed his little sister while she'd been off becoming a musical theater superstar.

"I feel different," he said at last. He couldn't quantify *how* he was different, but he was confident that the cause was currently sleeping in his bed.

"Hey, Noah? Don't fuck it up, okay?"

He huffed out a laugh and ran his fingers through his hair. "I'll try not to."

Chapter Thirteen

"I am not moving to Ohio with you."

"You say that now," her mother said from the other side of the breakfast table.

Callie and her mother had been the first of their party to arrive in the hotel restaurant that morning, choosing a table by the windows so they could enjoy the ocean breeze while they ate their eggs.

"I've been saying it for the past year, Mom," Callie said. "Nothing has changed. You are more than welcome to move to Dayton. I don't want you staying in New Jersey for me. I'll be fine on my own."

"Alright, alright," her mother said, shutting down the conversation. Again. "Now is not the time, Calandria."

"When will it be the time, Mom? First you said not until I was making more money. I was promoted last year. I'm making more than enough to support myself."

"Nonprofits are such a risky venture. It's right there in the name."

"I work for the town. It's a public library."

"With the number of hours you're working, you're going to send yourself right into a flare up."

Callie clenched her teeth and watched as her mother busily buttered her scone for the second time— anything to not look her daughter in the eye as she invoked Callie's pain for her own purposes.

"And then you said you wanted to see me in a committed relationship—which, by the way, is the most insulting requirement—"

"I'm not trying to insult you."

"I am in a committed relationship. With Noah."

"We'll see."

"What does that mean?"

"I'm sure you're having lots of fun together. But that boy has never committed to a relationship in his life. I wouldn't count your chickens."

Callie wanted to scream at how unfair that was, how cruel her mother was being to say that to her... *but he's not committed. It's not real.* Her mother didn't know that.

"That's an awful thing to say."

"I hope I'm wrong," her mother said, squeezing a second lemon wedge into her tea. "But you're still in the early blush of puppy love. When there's a ring on your finger and a date on the calendar—"

"You'd rather stay in Jersey and be miserable than admit I'll be alright on my own," Callie said, leaning back in her chair as the realization rocketed through her. Nothing would ever be enough for her mother. No job or boyfriend would ever convince her that Callie would be alright on her own.

Her mother met her gaze, her lips tightly pursed. When had she started to look so old?

"It is my responsibility to take care of you, Calandria."

"I'm twenty-seven years old."

"You came into this world as my responsibility and you will be my responsibility until the day I die. If you had children of your own, you would understand." Her eyes softened and she reached across the table to squeeze Callie's hand. "I will not leave you without knowing you are going to be taken care of."

"I can take care of myself."

"Oh, can you, now?" Her mother pulled her hand back, her gaze turning hard. "Is that what you were doing when I went away for the weekend only to come home and find you'd been sleeping on the couch for three days because you could not climb the stairs to your bedroom? Three days that you hardly ate because you couldn't stand long enough to prepare yourself a decent meal? You were so dehydrated that you wound up in the hospital."

As if Callie didn't remember every second of that weekend in excruciating detail—including the parts her mother still didn't know after all these years.

Like the fact that Callie couldn't feel her legs for most of that weekend, but she'd convinced herself it was just because she'd overdone it with her new exercise routine. At least until the numbness had turned to burning pain, like millions of tiny paper cuts over every inch of her skin.

That she'd woken the day after her twenty-first birthday party hungover and with the sinking feeling that something was *wrong* so she'd taken the train home, some naïve part of her thinking that if she could sleep in her childhood bed everything would be alright.

That Noah had called, repeatedly, and she'd ignored every call even though she could feel herself losing him with each unanswered ring. What would she have said? *Hey, Noah, so much fun making out with you the other night but now I can't feel my legs and, I know you didn't sign on for this, but I think something is seriously wrong with me.*

Her mother sucked her teeth and shook her head,

returning her attention to her breakfast. "If that's what you call taking care of yourself, Calandria, then clearly you're not as independent as you think you are."

Her face was hot, her hands shaking as she struggled to calm the anger and shame rising within her. The nerve of her mother to call up the memory of that weekend, of that first horrible flare up before Callie even had a diagnosis.

"That was six years ago." She hated the way her voice trembled, the stinging in her nose that warned of frustrated tears to come. "I know how to deal with the fibro now and it never gets that bad anymore."

"But it could," her mother said, throwing down her butter knife. The clang as it hit her breakfast plate rang out in the mostly empty hotel restaurant, making Callie jump at the harshness of the sound. "I will not leave you all by yourself!" Her mother's hands shook as she reached for her tea, her chest rising and falling with her too-quick breaths. Her voice was low and ragged, like the words were being pulled from her very soul. "Aunt Donna lay on the ground at the foot of her back steps for two days before someone found her. Two days before the *mailman* heard my baby sister calling for help. She never should have been alone, not in her condition. If her good-for-nothing husband hadn't been so busy diddling his secretary—Who leaves a woman with a heart condition? I warned her not to marry him. He was a skirt chaser, just like—" She squeezed her eyes shut, shaking her head.

Just like Noah, Callie filled in, the lump in her throat becoming almost too much to breathe around.

"I'll never forgive her for not telling me he'd moved out, for not letting me help her. She was furious that I'd moved to New Jersey with your father and left her behind. She was as stubborn as you are."

"I'm not Aunt Donna." The first tear rolled down her cheek, her throat choked by an unspeakable sadness for her mother.

"No, she was only alone for two days. You had three. I chose my own silly dreams over the people who should have been the most important in my life once before when I took up with your father and left my sisters. And look where that got me? Halfway across the country and traded in for a younger, shinier model with perfect hair and perfect makeup and—" Her mother stopped herself and took a deep breath. When she spoke again, her voice was strangely calm. "I've found a lovely condo just outside of Dayton, not far from Aunt Shirley. You and I will be very happy there."

Callie shook her head. "I'm not going."

"Really, Calandria, this is tiresome."

She fought against the wave of overwhelming grief that swept over her for her mother. She'd let herself be controlled by that grief for too long, though. "I'm not going, but you should. And if you don't, that's on you. You don't get to blame me for your unhappiness."

Her mother's eyes grew wide and her neck flushed. "I'm not unhappy."

"I hope that's true."

"I don't know why you're getting so worked up about this. You'll find another job. There are libraries everywhere."

"It's not about finding a job! New Jersey is my home. It's where my friends are. It's where I grew up. It's where I want my kids to grow up." She stopped short, realizing what she'd just said.

She hadn't put much thought into having children—certainly had no immediate plans or prospects to become a mother—but she knew in her bones that it was true. She could picture it: a chubby little boy learning to walk, hazel eyes gleaming and a laugh just like his father's...

Her mother arched an eyebrow. "And Noah wants this, too? He's going to walk away from a tenured professorship and settle down in New Jersey?"

"We haven't—it's still too early for us to be talking about things like that."

"Things like what?" Noah asked as he dropped into the empty seat next to Callie, Liam and Min joining them as well.

"It's not important." Callie forced a smile and dashed away the tears that lingered at the corners of her eyes.

His eyes narrowed, searching her face, until she looked away, turning her attention to her uneaten breakfast. She was too raw from the conversation with her mother to put up her usual cheery front, and she couldn't handle letting him in any closer than she already had. Thankfully her mother didn't seem inclined to fill him in either.

"Melynda, I really must thank you for that wonderful book recommendation," her mother said, turning to Min as though she hadn't been engaged in emotional warfare with her daughter a moment before. "My book club has not stopped talking about it."

"Hey," Noah said, leaning close so only she could hear as the others continued their conversation. "You okay?"

Callie gave a tight nod. "Fine."

Callie barely met Noah's eyes all through breakfast, and each time he tried to touch her, she stiffened beneath his hand. What had happened between the night before and when he arrived at breakfast to make her pull away? Not that he should care. It was all just for show. Except for that kiss under the stars, and when she'd held his hand. There had been no one around to see those things. He had no one to blame but himself for the bright flash of anxiety in his chest that he was somehow losing her, because really, it was a ridiculous thought. You can't lose something that you never had.

They rode the elevator in silence, but the second their hotel room door closed behind them, she ripped off her shoe and flung it across the room with a violent cry.

"What the—" The words died in his throat at the sight of the tears spilling down her cheeks, her fists balled so tightly she was shaking. "Callie, come here." He pulled her into his arms. She didn't return the hug, just stood in the circle of his embrace vibrating with the intensity of her emotion. He stroked her hair and kissed her temple. "What is it, love?"

All at once she clasped him to her, her shoulders shuddering as silent tears turned to great gulping sobs. She buried her face in his chest, tears soaking his shirt. He crooned nonsense into her hair, desperate to comfort her and not entirely sure how.

"What happened?" he asked when her sobs had slowed to intermittent shuddering breaths.

She shook her head against him, her fingers digging into the back of his shirt.

"Calico," he murmured, sliding his hands into her hair and tilting her face up to him. He brushed his lips over her tear-stained cheeks. "Are you in pain?"

She winced—just barely, but enough that he caught it— and shook her head.

"Did I do something?" he asked, the question a knot in his throat.

Her eyes flew to his, those hands at his back flexing and bunching, tugging him even closer. "No! My mother..." She broke off, tears welling in her eyes again.

A growl rose in his throat. The ferocity of his desire to protect Callie—even from her own mother—took him by surprise. "What can I do?"

She shook her head again, swallowing down the last of the tears. "You're already doing enough."

"Let me help you. Tell me how."

She placed her hands over his own where they cupped her face. Turning her face into his palm, she planted a kiss there, and then stepped out of his hold. "I have to get ready. Liv will be waiting for me."

As she stepped back, he caught her arm, his hand trailing down until he grasped her hand in his. "Don't shut me out, Callie." He hated the plea in his tone.

She stared at their hands for a moment before pulling away. "I'll see you at dinner," she said as she disappeared into the bathroom.

It didn't matter that the adrenaline coursing through his veins demanded he take care of her; she didn't want him to. Which was for the best. They both knew how spectacularly he'd failed the last time he'd tried to take care of her in any meaningful way. This restless need to go after her, to hold her until she told him everything, to fix it so nothing and no one ever made her cry again—it was untenable. She wasn't his girlfriend. She was barely his friend. None of it was real.

So why did it feel like it was?

Noah found himself at Liam and Min's room, uncertain when he'd made the decision to go there. He had just raised his fist to knock when the door swung open.

"I am not going for another run," Liam said.

Noah didn't say anything, just stared at his friend, until

Liam nodded, then stepped aside and ushered Noah in. He paced the room, glancing in the open door to the bathroom to confirm they were alone.

"Min's not here. She had plans with Liv and Callie," Liam said.

"How do I make it stop?"

"Make what stop?"

"This! Whatever this *thing* is."

"You're going to need to be more specific," Liam said, taking a seat in the armchair in the corner of the room and crossing his ankle over his knee. Like he had all the time in the world. Like Noah wasn't losing his shit right in front of him.

"She was crying. And I couldn't make it stop. She won't even tell me what's wrong. If she would just let me *fix it* then she wouldn't be crying."

"Callie isn't the type to want someone else to fix her problems."

"She was crying," he repeated helplessly.

"I know."

"And I have all these..." He waved his hand around in front of his chest as if that explained what he meant.

"Feelings?" Liam asked, arching his eyebrow.

Noah scowled. "How do I make it stop?"

"You think I know?" Liam laughed. "Do you even remember what I was like when I first met Min?"

"This isn't that," Noah said, shaking his head and sitting on the edge of the bed. "I don't know what this is, but it isn't that. Callie's basically family."

Except when you're kissing her, or inhaling her scent while jerking off...

"Oh yeah? When was the last time you thought about Livi the way you've been thinking about Callie?"

Heat flared in Noah's chest, working its way up his neck

to his face. He would never think about Livi the way he thought about Callie—the two didn't compare. Livi was his little sister, the baby-faced kid whose skinned knees he used to bandage. And Callie was...not.

"Face it, Noah. You like her."

"Don't."

"You're falling for her."

"Don't," he repeated, more sternly this time. Not that his stern voice did fuck all to deter Liam.

"It's not a bad thing. Fuck, it's the only thing that matters at all. Falling in love with Min... it's the only thing I've ever done right. And I'm so fucking grateful that woman loves me back. If you and Callie could have what we have—"

"I have no interest in what you have. I'm so goddamn happy that you're happy, but you lost *everything*. Your career and—fuck, everything."

Liam sighed, pity bleeding into his eyes. *Fucking perfect.*

"I lost my career. But what I have with Min—*that's* everything."

"I've seen what it's like when a love like that ends," Noah said, fighting against the lump in his throat and the memories that threatened to drown him. "I promised myself a long time ago that I would never go through that, or put someone else through it."

His chest tightened just thinking about losing Callie. How much worse would it be if she were actually his? He wouldn't survive it.

"You can't live your life in fear of the end. That's no way to live."

"I can't do it." He pressed the heels of his hands into his eyes to blot out the images of his mother, unable to get out of bed, a shell of her former self. "I won't do it."

Liam sighed. "Then I guess it's a good thing this whole

thing is fake."

Noah's stomach twisted at the words. An illogical reaction. His relationship with Callie *was* fake. She wasn't his girlfriend, and she never would be. But then he'd kissed her on a blanket under the stars, and spent half the night writing accompaniments for her songs, songs she didn't even know she was humming but that he felt like a brand on his skin...

No number of knots in his stomach could change the fact that he meant what he'd said, though. He was not interested in falling in love. More than that, he wouldn't allow it to happen. It had never been a problem before. He'd never even been tempted to let someone close enough to have there be any real threat of breaking his rule against relationships. *Except Callie. I almost broke my rules for her once before.*

It was like she'd buried a landmine in his heart all those years ago and was just now coming back to claim it, digging it out of the place where it had scabbed over, scar tissue giving way to the explosive beneath. One wrong move and it would detonate. If only there was some way he could neutralize the threat, scoop out the weakened flesh and let himself heal anew.

"What if I've been going about this all wrong?" he asked, an idea beginning to take shape. It was insane—a hail Mary if he'd ever heard one—but it just might work. "What if I shouldn't be trying to keep her away?"

"That's what I've been saying," Liam said.

"What if the only reason she's under my skin like this is because we've never given in to the attraction?"

"Wait a minute—"

"It makes sense." His thoughts raced ahead as he tried to chase down the trail of logic that was already starting to sound shaky at best to his own ears. "I've never been tempted to get serious with a woman before. So, what's different about Callie? She's the only woman I've ever wanted and stayed away from. Maybe if we just fu—"

"Woah, that's not... you can't really think sleeping with her will make you care about her less."

Noah wasn't sure he'd ever seen Liam look so flabbergasted.

"Not less, just...differently. Maybe the only reason I'm even thinking about her like this at all is because we haven't gotten it out of our system."

"Yeah," Liam snorted, "because that always works."

"We're already pretending to be a couple in public. What if we just acted like it in private, too. Just until the wedding is over. Then we could go back home and leave this whole thing here—the lying and the sexual tension and—"

"The feelings?"

"All of it."

He knew he sounded like a mad man, but what other option did he have? If he didn't do something, this landmine would be in his chest forever and one day it would blow him apart, and Callie with him. He couldn't let that happen.

"This is the worst fucking idea you've ever had," Liam said. "Every time you have an uncomfortable feeling, you try to fuck it away."

"That's not even remotely accurate." *Is it?*

"You can't have meaningless sex with Callie."

"Not meaningless. Cathartic. A time-limited arrangement to purge us both of this goddamn chokehold we've had on each other for six fucking years."

"I knew it!" Liam said, the smug son-of-a-bitch. "I *knew* you weren't over it."

"Of course I'm not over it!" Noah roared, shooting to his

feet and pacing again. "She needed me and I wasn't fucking there!"

"Noah...you didn't know. None of us knew."

But he couldn't hear it. Some dim part of his brain knew what Liam said made sense. It was exactly what he'd been telling himself all this time, but no matter how many times he repeated it, he still didn't believe it. He could still hear Mrs. Cole's voice, see the accusation in her eyes, as they'd stood in that hospital waiting room.

"Maybe we both just need some closure," he said quietly.

"And you think that sleeping with her will do that?"

"Fuck if I know," he said, exhausted. "But I have to try something."

Chapter Fourteen

Callie lay in corpse pose, barely hearing the guided meditation the yoga teacher was leading them through. All she could focus on was the god-awful ambient "music" piped into the room through the tinny speakers, a repetitive tinkling cadence over a deep bass warble. *That has to be a didgeridoo,* she thought as the bass vibrated through the floor.

Finally, the teacher brought the class to a close. Liv and Min sat up at her sides, both looking dewy and fresh-faced while she was certain she was giving off more of a sweaty tomato vibe.

"That was such a good class," Liv said. "Thanks for finding it for us, Min."

"It was nice to have someone to go with for a change," Min said, getting to her feet and rolling up her yoga mat. "My sister-in-law used to go with me but lately she's so busy between work and my niece that she just doesn't have the time."

Liv reached out a hand to Callie, helping her to her feet. For now, Callie's limbs were light, her muscles loose and warm from the hour-long class, but she knew that might not last. She'd have to be extra careful not to push herself too hard while she was still feeling good.

"What's next on the agenda?" she asked.

"First, showers. Then you both are going to help me pick out my something blue," Liv said with a mischievous smile.

After quick showers in the yoga studio locker room and a stop at their juice bar for something called a Zen Zinger smoothie (Callie was pretty sure it was just coconut water, strawberries, and yogurt, but it tasted fine, so whatever), the three women strolled out into the August heat. The yoga studio was in the heart of downtown, not far from The Barclay. The main street was a bustling two-lane road lined with trees and historic buildings, most converted into shops and restaurants.

Callie could see why Liv and Daemon had wanted to get married here. The salt air blew up from the beach just a few blocks away and baskets of flowers hung from the decorative lamp posts that ran along each sidewalk. It was quaint and charming but turn a corner and you'd be just as likely to find a boudoir photo studio as you were to find a seashell-themed gift shop.

They rounded one such corner and Liv led them to a small brick storefront. The windows were draped with heavy pink and purple curtains and a single word was written on the door: Desire.

"Please tell me your something blue isn't a vibrator," Callie said. "I mean, I'll help you find the perfect one, babe, but that's really more something Daemon should help you shop for."

"It's not a sex toy store," Liv laughed. "Though I guess they might have sex toys, too. It's a lingerie shop."

They entered the shop, the bell above the door announcing their arrival to the stunning woman behind the counter. She was probably in her forties, tall with an hourglass figure, her dark hair sporting a single streak of gray on one side like that character from X-Men. "Good morning, ladies," she said, setting aside her oversized coffee mug and greeting them with a wide, genuine smile. "Welcome to Desire. Are you looking for anything in particular today?"

"She's getting married," Min said, hooking her arm through Liv's.

"Congratulations!"

"We're on the hunt for her something blue," Callie added.

"You came to the right place," the woman said, rounding the corner. "I'm Natalia. Let me show you some of our customers' favorites."

Natalia led them around the shop pointing out corsets and crotchless jumpsuits alongside tasteful bra and panty sets. After a full tour of the shop, she left them to peruse on their own, returning to her place behind the counter and assuring them she'd love to help them if they had any questions.

Liv fingered the lace on the edge of a short chemise. "I have something similar," Min confessed quietly, her cheeks bright red. "The lace gets itchy when it's wet."

Liv laughed and moved on to the next rack. "I need something that I can wear under my dress. And I want it to be surprising, you know?"

"Surprising how?" Min asked.

"I'm going to be in this frilly white gown all day, all prim and proper and *virginal*-looking—" Callie snorted, but Liv continued on, shooting her friend an amused look, "—and when I take off the dress, I want to feel the opposite of that. Not precious or porcelain, or any of those other ways my mom will try to describe me when I'm wearing my wedding dress."

Callie considered a corset and returned it to the rack. "You want to feel strong. Powerful."

"Yes."

"Unbreakable," Min said with a knowing smirk.

"Exactly!"

"How about this?" Callie reached to the back of a rack and pulled out a bodysuit that was little more than thin strips of lace forming a giant v shape for the main body with satin straps wrapping around the sides.

"Definite possibility," Liv said, taking the hanger. "These shoulder straps are thin enough that they should fit under the straps of my dress."

"What about something like this?" Min held up a sheer corset, the boning visible through the aqua mesh, garters dangling from the side.

"Gorgeous!"

"Babe," Callie said, pulling one more hanger out to show her friend. "This one." It was a one-piece teddy, high cut, sheer mesh forming the panty attached to a strapless corset covered in intricate floral embroidery. The corset curved at the top, rising to a high point in the middle, and then swooping down on each side before rising at the back again.

Min frowned. "That top looks like it'll be too short for Liv."

"It's an under-bust corset," Callie explained. She held it flush to her chest, demonstrating the way the boning would sit beneath the bust. "All the support and none of the coverage."

"That's the one," Liv said, taking it from Callie's hands.

"I think I might get this one myself," Min said, biting her lip as she surveyed the corset and garter set she'd held up to Liv as an option.

"That color will be stunning on you," Liv said, holding the hanger back out to Min. "It'll really make your eyes pop."

"You should get the one you picked out, Callie," Min said.

Undeniable

"Oh! In the green! It'll be so perfect with your hair!" Liv said, diving back into the rack and producing the barely-there teddy in a deep emerald green. Her nose wrinkled. "Did I just tell you to buy lingerie for my brother?"

Callie snatched the hanger from Liv's hands and placed it back on the rack. "No, because I don't need any lingerie."

"Everyone needs lingerie," Liv said. "You should get it. I'm just going to pretend it's not my brother who's going to see you in it."

Min found Callie's eyes across the store. *She knows it's not real,* Callie thought. *Noah will never see me in this.*

"You should get it because it's beautiful and you'll feel beautiful when you wear it," Min said softly. "Get it for yourself."

Callie smiled at Min, grateful for her deft handling of the situation.

"My treat," Liv said, plucking the hangers from both Min and Callie's hands. "We are going to be smoke shows, ladies."

Each with a tiny silver gift bag overflowing with tissue paper that concealed the wisps of fabric Liv had purchased for them, they left the shop and began their walk back to the public parking lot a few blocks away. Callie's feet were already sore, but more than that, she could feel the tension creeping into her hips. All this walking combined with the yoga class had probably been too much in the middle of a week that was pushing her physical limits each day, but she couldn't bear to break up the fun they were having. She didn't want Liv to spend even a second of her wedding worried about Callie's comfort.

"Do you have your something old?" Min asked as they walked.

"Noah's taking care of the something old and something new. Not that he'll tell me what they are," Liv said. "Oh! Cal, you can tell me!"

Callie shook her head. "Sorry. I don't know what he's got planned."

"He didn't tell you?"

No, because we're not really a couple. "He was afraid I wouldn't be able to keep it a secret," she lied.

Liv huffed. "If he gives me something embarrassing, I will kill him. First degree murder right there while I'm standing at the altar."

Min shook her head. "I'm sure it'll be fine. He's not going to try to embarrass you."

"Oh shit," Liv said, stopping in the middle of the sidewalk. "Now that you're dating him, does this mean that if my brother and I are fighting, you have to take his side?"

Callie barked out a laugh. "Absolutely not. You're my person."

"Damn straight I am." She hooked her arm through Callie's on one side and Min's on the other. They continued walking in silence for a minute before Liv spoke again. "Can I say something mushy for a minute?"

"It's your wedding, Liv. Be as mushy as you want," Min said.

Liv kept them moving, her eyes focused straight ahead and Callie knew that whatever she was about to say was going to hurt.

"I've never seen my brother so happy," Liv said quietly, her voice almost drowned out by the sound of their footsteps on the pavement. "You're really good for him. I hope he's good for you, too."

"He is," Callie said around the lump in her throat.

"I hope he knows how lucky he is to have you. That's all."

Tell her. Tell her now.

"Noah's a smart guy," Min said. "If he doesn't realize it yet, he'll figure it out soon enough."

"I don't know whether to hope he gets this job with Wolf or not," Liv said, her tone lightening. "I don't know how I feel about him leaving my best friend for months on end while he galivants around some flyover state with a film crew."

"What are you talking about?"

Liv glanced at her, concern etched into her features. "If Noah gets this commission, Wolf wants him to go on the road with the film crew. Three months. They leave the Monday after next. He must have told you about it."

"Right," Callie said, blinking and forcing a weak smile on this face. "Sorry, the way you said it sounded like you thought he was going to be gone for longer."

"Three months is long enough. Who is going to make me chocolate chip pancakes at two in the morning?"

"I'm pretty sure that's Daemon's job now," Min said.

Liv's smile stretched across her face. "That's right. Because I'm getting married in two days!"

Min and Liv continued to chatter about the wedding, but Callie hardly heard. He was leaving for three months. Was he even going to tell her? Was he just going to leave?

Why would he tell me? He's not really my boyfriend.

The thought made her want to cry, because Noah Van Aller might not really be her boyfriend but he had really kissed her like she meant something to him. He had really held her while he slept and called her 'love.' Was any of it real? And if he left for three months, would she ever get the chance to find out?

Chapter Fifteen

Callie was exhausted, physically and emotionally, her mind repeating the words *three months* on an endless loop. She was also out of time. She should have been dressed by now, her hair dried and makeup in place. But no. Instead she was still standing in the shower, staring at the pink plastic razor in her hand like she could make it magically shave her legs on its own if she looked at it long enough.

"Are you alright in there?" Noah called through the closed bathroom door over the sound of the shower.

"Fine!" Callie called back. Her voice was bright—too bright, almost brittle.

"You've been in there a long time."

That was an understatement. She'd been in the shower so long it was sporadically shooting out bursts of cold water, unable to keep up with her demand for water hot enough to fog up the glass shower doors and mirror.

You can do this.

She braced her right foot on the ledge in the corner of the shower and steadied her left hand against the wall. Slowly she bent over, little by little. Before she even made it halfway, her back screamed with pain, a sharp bolt down her spine and through her hip. She cursed and jolted upright, knocking over the bottles of body wash and shampoo precariously balanced on the narrow shelf along the shower wall.

Noah was through the door before she'd even fully registered how loud the crashing bottles were, their impact with the river rock floor echoing against the marble walls.

"What happened?"

"Noah!" Callie hugged her arms around her body in an attempt to cover herself from his view.

On the other side of the steamed-up glass door, Noah's eyes swept over her. The panic on his face faded, a restrained heat taking its place.

"Sorry." He turned his back, covering his eyes when they locked with hers in the mirror. "I heard a crash. I thought you fell."

"No, I just dropped...everything. I just wanted to shave my legs," she muttered to herself.

"Is something preventing you?"

"I can't...bend like that right now. It's too painful." She could feel the tears building again, but she refused to cry over something as stupid as shaving her legs. It wouldn't be the first time she couldn't do it, nor would it be the last.

"What do you need to make the pain go away?"

She blew out a frustrated breath. "It doesn't work like that. Nothing makes the pain go away. There are things that help—"

"Tell me what you need and I'll get it for you."

"I already took ibuprofen and I'll put on my cream when I'm done in here. There's nothing to do but ride it out. I thought the heat would've loosened things up enough by now, but..." She sniffled.

"Callie." His voice was full of concern. He dropped his hand from his eyes and met her gaze in the mirror.

She waved it away. "It's stupid. No one will even care if my legs are shaved or not. I just wanted to, I don't know, feel a little like I used to before—"

Noah, fully dressed in a white button-down and dark dress slacks, threw open the shower door, the spray from the shower's multiple heads hitting him with a fine mist that left dark spots on his clothing.

"What are you doing?" she squeaked, pulling a towel off the nearby towel bar and holding it over herself. It was immediately soaked through, the fabric plastering itself to her body.

He stepped into the shower, closed the door behind himself, and dropped to one knee at her feet.

Of all the ways she'd imagined being in a shower with Noah Van Aller, this was never it. Despite that, the flush creeping over her face was much less about being embarrassed and much more about the fact that Noah was only a few inches from her naked body. He kept his gazed fixed on the floor, but if he were to raise his head, he'd be eye level with her most intimate place. She could hardly breathe at the thought.

He took her foot in his hand with a firm but gentle touch and placed it on his knee, her toes resting on the soaked fabric of his dress pants. He retrieved the fallen bottle of body wash and squirted a generous amount into his hand. And then he touched her. His hands skated over her calf, her knee, massaging the slippery liquid into her skin. As he did, his thumbs pressed into the tense muscles of her calf.

"What are you doing?" she asked again, softer this time.

"I can't take away the pain, but I can shave your legs for you."

Callie's breath hitched as his hands traveled over her thigh, massaging the body wash into her skin. His knuckles brushed against the edge of the towel that barely concealed her nakedness from him as he worked. She fought the urge to squeeze her thighs together as desire pulsed deep in her core. Not that she could have anyway, with one of her feet still propped on Noah's knee.

"Razor?" He held out his hand.

"You don't need to do this."

He lifted his head to meet her eyes. "Let me take care of you, love. Just this once."

There it was again—*love.* Like she meant something to him. Like she was more than just his little sister's best friend. Surely the fact that he was about to shave her legs meant she was more?

She handed him the pink, plastic razor and watched as he dragged it slowly, carefully over her skin in long, even strokes. His movements were methodical, precise. He kept one hand wrapped around her calf to steady her and made a thorough job of shaving her leg, unfazed by the shower pouring down on him and soaking through his clothing, pushing his hair into his eyes in streaming wet tendrils.

When he was done, he set her foot back on the floor and began again on the other leg. Callie tried to focus on the rhythm of it, the softness of his hands on her skin. She did her best not to think about how labored her breathing had become, or how much she ached for his touch to move higher. For so long she'd wondered what it would be like to have him touch her—she'd never thought she'd find out.

As he moved to her thigh, his hand slid higher, holding her knee tight against his chest. Even with the water crashing down around them, the weight of his breathing hung between them, the harsh exhales and shaky inhales as he went about his work.

Callie glanced down at the man at her feet, pressing

her hand to the shower wall to steady herself as the sight sent a new wave of desire flooding through her. His shirt was plastered to his body, displaying the hard planes of his chest and abdomen, the corded muscle of his arms. Lower, his pants were soaked through, the wet fabric clinging to the obscene outline of the most intimidating erection she'd ever seen. She'd felt him before, when she'd woken to his morning hard-on pressed against her, but seeing it was another thing entirely, even through the layers of cloth and at this odd angle. She exhaled a curse and brushed his dripping hair out of his eyes, needing to touch him back somehow.

Noah finished the final stroke of the razor and set it down on the floor beside him, his other hand still gripping her thigh. He looked up at her as she continued to run her fingers through his hair, but he made no move to release her or get up.

"Thank you," she said, her voice a raw whisper.

He turned his head to the side and pressed his lips to the inside of her thigh. A slow, lingering kiss, heat blooming beneath his mouth. She gasped, her free hand tangled in his hair, holding him against her skin, like she could keep him if she could hold him closer.

He wrapped his free hand around the upper thigh of her other leg, fingers brushing against the curve of her ass, and he kissed her again, half an inch higher. Her hips bucked of their own accord, straining to get his kiss closer to where she wanted it. The things she wanted him to do to her... He grinned against her skin as if he had heard her thoughts.

On the counter, her phone vibrated, buzzing loudly against the marble and pulling them both back to their senses. He released her and fell back on his heels, his hands planted on the floor. She stumbled back and clutched the towel to herself tighter.

When had the shower turned cold? She hadn't even noticed. Noah scrubbed his hands over his face, brushing the water out of his eyes, before getting to his feet. Callie reached around him and turned off the water. Then, without a word, she stepped out of the shower and wrapped herself in one of those tiny hotel bathrobes. She caught his eye in the mirror and gave him a shaky smile.

"I'm sorry," he said.

Her smile faltered. "They're waiting for us."

I'm sorry?

Jesus, what was he thinking? And what had he even apologized for? For nearly putting his mouth between her legs? For being interrupted before he could? Worse still, all he could think about was taking her back up to their room and finishing what they'd started, dinner be damned.

What the fuck is happening to me? It had to be all the pretending, like Callie had said the other night. His body was confusing their fake relationship with a real one. And he dared anyone with eyes to see Callie naked in the shower and not go half mad with want. The water had wrapped around her curves as though outlining all the paths his tongue could take, daring him to do it.

But he hadn't just wanted her. He'd wanted to take care of her. He'd heard the tremor in her voice, and it was such a simple thing to help her shave if it meant that tremor would go away. And if it meant he had an excuse to touch her, to for a moment feel her bare skin on his... *Fucking hell.*

Everyone else was already assembled in the dining room when they arrived. "Arriving late is becoming a habit," his mother said with a raised eyebrow as he pulled out Callie's chair for her.

"It's my fault, Mrs. V. I was daydreaming in the shower and lost track of time," Callie said.

"I bet you did," Jamie said, his eyes laughing as he raised his water glass in a silent toast to them both.

Shit. We both have wet hair. They think we were fucking in the shower. Noah shifted in his seat, willing himself to stop picturing it before his dick got any bright ideas. Again.

Callie caught his eye for a moment but looked away, fussing with her napkin in her lap. *Fuck. Why the hell did I say I was sorry?* He took her hand where it lay in her lap. He didn't understand this need to be constantly touching her, nor did he want to examine it too closely.

What if Liam is right? What if I'm falling for her? For the first time, he didn't immediately reject the thought. He let it linger in his mind, tried it on for size. Ridiculous. Impossible. Noah Van Aller didn't do relationships. He certainly didn't fall for people. But Callie wasn't just *people*...

"Room for one more?"

All eyes turned to the entrance to the dining room. Uncle Stu, suitcase still in hand, did an impressive job of filling the doorway, light reflecting off his snow-white hair.

"Uncle Stu!" Livi shot to her feet and met him in the doorway, wrapping him in a fierce hug. "I thought you weren't coming until tomorrow!"

The older man dropped a kiss on her forehead, setting his bag to the side. "I moved some things around. I'm only sorry I couldn't get here earlier."

"We're glad you're here now," Daemon said, shaking his hand. "Please, come, sit."

Uncle Stu made his way around the table, pausing to greet everyone in turn. When he reached Noah and Callie, his eyes lingered on their clasped hands, an eyebrow arching.

"Stu, you remember Callie," his mother said.

"Of course. So nice to see you again, young lady," he said with a smile. "Noah." Was he imagining it or was his uncle's voice already full of disappointment before Noah had even opened his mouth?

"Good to see you, sir," Liam said, shaking his former boss' hand.

Uncle Stu clapped him on the shoulder. "You too, son. And you, Ms. Taylor," he said to Min, who blushed under his gaze. "Or is it Mrs. Jacobs now?"

"Not yet, sir," she said with a shy smile.

Stu gave a tight nod of acknowledgement. He still sometimes looked at Liam and Min with that institutional disapproval that came from years of having to deal with professors' impropriety with students, but he was working on accepting their relationship, for the sake of the family.

Throughout dinner, Noah felt his uncle's eyes on him—when he rested his hand on Callie's knee, when she leaned her head against his shoulder and he pulled her close, when she laughed and wiped a smudge of chocolate sauce off his lower lip. As dessert was cleared, Liv tapped her spoon against her water glass to get everyone's attention, rising to her feet.

"Aren't we supposed to do that for you?" Pattie teased, clanging her spoon against her own glass and staring down Daemon with a challenging quirk of her bright red lip.

Daemon huffed out a sigh as though he were terribly put out, but the smirk on his face gave him away. He rose to his feet and swept Liv up against him, planting a thorough kiss on her lips.

"No one needs to see that," Jamie grumbled, tossing a balled-up napkin at the couple.

Liv laughed as she pulled away, her happiness overflowing around her. Noah couldn't help his own smile at his little sister's joy, though there was something bittersweet about it that he couldn't put his finger on. A melancholy longing he couldn't define.

"Alright, alright," Liv said to quiet the hooting encouragement rising from the table. "Daem and I just wanted to thank everyone again for spending this week with us. Tomorrow evening is the rehearsal dinner, but my fiancé and I will be spending the morning doing press calls for *Sabrina* so you are all off the hook until the afternoon."

"I think I know how Liam and Min will be spending their morning off," Callie whispered to Noah, her breath tickling his ear. She inclined her head towards the couple. Min's bottom lip was drawn between her teeth, her chest rising and falling rapidly. If Noah were a betting man, he'd wager good money that Liam had his hand up her skirt.

Noah wondered if Callie would be as discreet if he were to slip his hand beneath her skirt. Would she be able to maintain her control when his fingers sank into her, or would she let loose one of those delicious gasps she'd given him in the shower? He wrapped his arm around her shoulder to hold her against him as the others began to gather their things and leave the dining room. *Just for another minute*, he thought, though he couldn't help but ask, "And how do you want to spend your morning off?"

Heat flared in her gaze, her eyes darkening, only a moment and then it was gone. She turned her face away from him. But it was too late. He was on fire, his fingers tightening on her shoulder.

"Use your words, love," he whispered into her hair, his

voice rough with the promise of sin.

She lay her hand on his leg, just a little too high up his thigh to be polite. "You first," she said.

Could he have real sex with his fake girlfriend? All the reasons he knew it was a horrible idea escaped him as her hand inched higher on his leg, her thumb drawing ever widening circles that were dangerously close to brushing against the place where he was already half-hard.

"Noah, have a drink with me," Uncle Stu boomed from across the table, shaking Noah from the sex-filled haze of his thoughts.

Fuck.

She pressed a kiss to his cheek. "I'll see you upstairs," she said, getting to her feet and joining the others on their way to the elevator.

He watched her go, sure that she was swinging her hips like that just to drive him out of his mind. The skirt of her dress swished about her legs, revealing tantalizing glimpses of her plush thighs—thighs he had pressed his lips against mere hours earlier. Some distant part of his brain blared a danger signal, warning him that he was approaching an uncharted precipice with her, one from which they would not be able to easily return. He wasn't sure he'd want to.

Stu took Noah by the shoulder and led him over to the bar in the corner of The Barclay's restaurant. They made small talk about Stu's drive while they waited for the bartender to bring their drinks, all the while his uncle cast that too-keen eye on him, like he could see beneath the layers of his skin.

Uncle Stu took a deep drink of his Scotch. Keeping his eyes trained on their reflection in the mirrored backsplash behind the bar, he finally spoke. "When I told you not to get caught with your pants down in a broom closet, I didn't

Undeniable

mean you should move the display out in the open."

Noah bristled. "I'm not—"

"That girl. Liv's friend. Wolf will be here the day after next. You're meant to be proving to him that you have some self-restraint."

Noah took a long sip of his drink, steeling himself to repeat the lie. "She's my girlfriend." Funny, it didn't feel like as much of a lie as before.

Uncle Stu snorted. "You've never had a girlfriend in your life. Not that you've lacked opportunity."

"Callie's different. I'm—" He stopped short. *I'm different.* Did he mean that?

"Why didn't you tell me about her when we talked a few days ago?"

A reasonable question, and one he definitely couldn't answer honestly. He shrugged, too nonchalant. "We hadn't decided whether or not to tell people yet."

Uncle Stu narrowed his eyes at his nephew. "What game are you playing?"

"No game."

His uncle was too good at sniffing out a lie. Noah would need to lean into the truth if he wanted to convince him. But what was the truth?

"I've never felt this way before," he began tentatively, testing the veracity of the words. He took a breath and kept going, trying not to think too hard about what he was saying, or the implications of meaning every word. "She's chaos," he said with a chuckle, "but she's also sunshine and laughter and she looks at me like maybe I could be too." He took another sip of his drink, an excuse to swallow down the lump in his throat.

Uncle Stu clinked his rocks glass against Noah's, but the look on his face made it clear he still wasn't convinced.

"Then here's to Callie."

They drank, but the cool liquor did nothing to calm the blood racing through Noah's veins. Admitting to himself that he had feelings for Callie was terrifying because it would never last. It couldn't. One way or another, love never did. Not that he loved her. Not yet, at least. There was still time to stop it from getting that out of hand.

But what if he didn't stop it? What if it didn't need to be all or nothing—casual sex or devastating love? If he were honest with Callie from the start, told her that he wasn't capable of forever... It wasn't what she deserved—Christ, how he knew it was nowhere near what she deserved—but maybe she'd want him anyway?

Chapter Sixteen

Callie paced in their hotel room. She'd been on edge since Noah had stepped into the shower with her earlier that evening, but after a dinner full of little touches and heated glances, the implication in his voice when he'd asked how she wanted to spend the morning, she was so turned on she could hardly stand it. There was no mistaking the hard-on he had sported while he shaved her legs, or the path his lips had taken up her thigh before they were interrupted. He wanted her. The knowledge was a high all by itself.

And so what if it was tempered by her absolute certainty that he would never be hers—not really, not the way she wanted him to be. Not in the lazy-Sunday-mornings way she'd fantasized about. But what if they could have something else? What if she could find out, once and for all, what it was like to be the object of Noah Van Aller's desire? What if she could share that part of him, even for a little while? He was going to get this job and he was going to leave whether she wanted him to or not. What if they could spend these last few days together for real before she had to let him go? Wasn't having him for a short time better than never having him at all?

When the week was over and everything went back to normal, she was going to be heartbroken. She already knew she'd miss holding his hand, sleeping wrapped in his heat. How much worse could it be if they crossed this final barrier? More to the point, did she care if it destroyed her?

No. She'd gladly make that trade.

Callie didn't know how long she had before Noah would come back to the room, but she resolved to make it as hard as possible for him to turn her down. She unbraided her hair, brushing the auburn strands until they only held soft waves. Then she stripped off her clothes, tossing them into the growing pile spilling out of her open suitcase and slipped beneath the sheets of their bed. She buried her nose in his pillow, breathing in the smell of him—sage and leather-bound books.

Her hands skated over her breasts, pulling at her nipples until they hardened to stiff peaks, each twist sending bolts of pleasure arrowing down between her legs. She took her time winding her hand down her body until her fingers brushed the neat patch of hair covering her mound. She didn't need to touch herself to know she was wet, but she did it anyway, moaning when her finger lightly brushed over her clit. If she lingered on that swollen bud she'd come too quickly, and she needed to draw it out so she could be sure he'd find her like this—wet and aching for him. The idea of it, of him coming into their room and discovering her touching herself, was nearly enough to make her come all by itself.

Callie rolled to the edge of the bed and threw open her suitcase—the only one she always kept zipped— revealing the small stash of toys she'd brought with her. Just the basics, the quietest and most reliable pieces from the large collection she'd curated over the years. She selected one of her favorites: a stainless steel, double-ended G-spot wand.

Settling back amongst the pillows, the thin sheet still draped over her body, she guided the smooth, curved piece of metal over her skin. It was cool to the touch. That was part of what she loved about this particular piece, the way it simulated ice on her skin. At each end of the curved metal bar was a round knob, one larger than the other. She'd start with the smallest side, she decided, dragging it through her slit to warm the end of the toy and get it wet and ready for her.

When she slipped it inside her pussy, her walls contracted around it, her body shuddering in anticipation of the relief to come. Slowly she worked the toy in and out, the curve ensuring it brushed against that tender spot on her front wall with each pass. Callie wanted to go slow, to take her time and stoke her pleasure to its highest point, but the more she moved the toy, the harder it was to restrain herself. She arched off the bed, moving the toy faster, deeper, a cry falling from her lips.

She didn't realize she wasn't alone until she heard the door close.

Callie's eyes flew open, snapping to Noah's. He stood just inside the door, frozen, his eyes dark and hard, jaw tight. For a moment, she thought she'd miscalculated, that he didn't want her after all, but then he closed the distance between them in three strides. He sat on the edge of the bed at her side and took the sheet between his fingers. He waited for her to nod, her breath coming too quickly for her to speak, and pulled the sheet back to reveal her. He growled, a low sound in the back of his throat, as his eyes raked over her nakedness, latching onto the place where that shiny metal toy disappeared inside her.

She began to move it again, in and out in a slow tortuous

rhythm. She didn't trust herself to last, not now that Noah's eyes were on her. How many times had she imagined this exact thing? How many times had she ridden a toy to a breathtaking orgasm while pretending he was watching her? Her thighs shook as she neared her climax and he cursed under his breath, his large hand clasping her thigh and pinning it to the bed, holding her open so he could watch.

"Look at you," he said, his gaze focused on her pussy. "So goddamn pretty."

His voice was so low and husky she hardly recognized it, but it sent shivers over her skin just the same. She kept her eyes locked on him, even as her hand moved faster between her legs. She was so close, but no matter how fast she worked herself, she wasn't falling over the edge.

With a frustrated grunt, she withdrew the toy and flipped it around, this time pressing the larger ball into her opening. She was so wet and ready she hardly felt the stretch as it slid inside her, and she whimpered with relief when it moved against her G-spot.

"You needed more?" he asked. She moaned and nodded, the weight of the toy making her deliciously full. "Good. Let me give you more."

"God, yes."

He wrapped his free hand around hers, the one holding the toy in place, and began to move it, forcing her to take it harder and deeper. His forearm flexed as he pumped the toy between her thighs, his fingers brushing the curls at her entrance, but he kept his rhythm maddeningly slow.

"Faster," she gasped.

"No."

They locked eyes as he continued to fuck her with her toy, keeping her balanced on that knife's edge but never quite letting her tip over into release. She whined, bucking her hips in search of the friction she needed.

"I'm not done watching you, love," Noah said. He leaned forward and pressed a sucking kiss to the underside of her breast, withdrawing with a nip to the sensitive skin there, his pace steady. "That's what you wanted, right? For me to watch you?"

"Yes," she gasped.

She shifted, pressing the sole of her foot flat against the erection straining his pants. He chuckled darkly and let her stroke him through the fabric. "You're not ready for me yet, sweet girl," he said. "This little toy has hardly stretched your pussy at all."

"I have others."

His eyes hooded and he released his grip on the wand. "Show me."

Callie once again leaned over and flipped open the lid of her suitcase, the toy shifting within her as she moved. Noah sucked his teeth as he took in her stash.

"Which one is your favorite?"

She pointed to a yellow vibrator, slightly curved and covered in a web of ridges. It was the largest dildo she owned, and at its head, a series of small beads beneath the surface of the silicone did exquisite things to her most sensitive places. He grabbed the toy and switched it on, then he knelt between her thighs, his knees holding her open for his inspection.

"You've been holding out on me, Calico," he said, withdrawing the wand from inside her.

He raised it to his lips and sucked her taste off the end, and she thought she might die on the spot. She was still watching his mouth, wondering how it would feel to have it buried in her cunt, when he pressed the head of the vibe against her opening. It was significantly larger than the other toy, but judging by the outline in his slacks, still not as large as Noah. He slid it into her slowly, working it in and out in slow thrusts. Her pussy stretched to accommodate it, and when it was fully seated, he bent over her and pressed his lips to hers. His hand pumped between her legs as their tongues tangled, every part of her hot and wet and aching for more and terrified that she would wake up at any moment and realize this was all a dream.

"More. Noah, I need…"

"What, love?" He dragged his lips down her neck and to her breasts. He bit down on her nipple, and she cried out, arching into the sharp sting and hoping he'd do it again.

She fumbled with his belt, his zipper. His cock jutted from the placket of his pants, hard and rude and glistening with precum. Her fingers skated over the swollen crown, massaging that glistening bead into his velvet skin. He took her hand and placed it on the toy between her legs, urging her to keep fucking herself with it.

"Do not come yet. You come with me," he said.

He made quick work of removing his clothes, and then he was back on the bed beside her. He ran his thumb over her jaw, across her lower lip, the touch so tender it took her by surprise.

"Do you think you can take me here?"

She sucked his thumb into her mouth and scraped her teeth over it, releasing him with a pop. "God, yes."

"If it gets to be too much, you tap on my leg. Do you understand?"

"Yes. Noah, please. I want to taste you."

He spun around and straddled her, lining himself up so his head was between her legs and his cock dangled over her waiting mouth. With a steadying hand at the base of his shaft, he drew the tip over her lips, painting them with precum, then slipped himself into her mouth. He only gave her the tip, just enough for her to lap at the ridge of his crown.

She didn't know this version of Noah—all quiet power and commands, an effortless authority that had turned the tables on her so quickly and thoroughly that she hadn't even realized she was no longer the one in control. She never could have imagined that there was a side of him she'd want even more than his easy charm and unassuming care. But if the Noah who carried her bags and bought her a purse full of Benadryl was attractive, this version of him was magnetic, impossible to resist. Not that she would want to even if she could.

As she explored the ridges of his cock with her tongue, he took over working the toy between her legs, releasing her hands to explore his naked body. Her nails scratched over his back and hips. She wanted to memorize the contours of the muscles beneath his skin, the scrape of the coarse hair on his legs, the salt and musk taste of him. She needed to remember it all.

He slid further into her mouth, giving her the weight of him on her tongue, and she lifted her head in an attempt to take more of his length. She wasn't foolish enough to think she could take it all, but fuck if she wasn't going to try. The intensity of the vibe between her legs increased, the hum of the motor growing louder. All the sensations in her body converged, coiling tight low in her belly as he fucked her with her toy. And still she needed more. She whimpered around his cock, digging her nails into his ass and urging him deeper into her mouth as she canted her hips, seeking. She dropped one hand between her legs to grip the toy, to make him move it faster, but he batted her away.

"Let me take care of you, love," he said.

When his tongue hit her clit she thought she might cry

in relief. As he licked her, he finally thrust the vibe between her legs harder, faster, driving her towards her climax. Tongue and lips and teeth and heat and one sensation blurring into the other, her hips rising up to meet each thrust of the toy and flick of his tongue. She moaned as his cock hit the back of her throat, swallowing him down as her legs shook uncontrollably.

Noah pulled himself from her mouth as she broke apart beneath his tongue, coming so hard she arched against his weight, her hips bucking violently, pleasure tearing through her like a firework. Ropes of hot cum jetted from Noah's cock across her chest, spurring on her own climax. Her thighs clamped around Noah's head as he continued to suck on her clit until the wave finally crested and broke, the force of her climax so strong it forced the toy from within her and soaked the sheets beneath them.

Noah dropped the toy and swung off of her, his eyes raking over her as she lay exhausted on the bed, coated in his cum and surrounded by a puddle of her own. He dipped his head between her legs again and gave her a long lick, from the pleated rim of her back entrance all the way to her pulsing clit. Her body jolted beneath the touch.

"You're so fucking beautiful," he said, dragging his mouth up her body, planting kisses along the flare of her hips, the swell of her belly.

When he reached her breasts, he drew his fingers through the cum there, painting her nipples with it, before drawing a stiff peak into his mouth and sucking her clean. It was filthy and depraved, every part of it, and she loved it. She wanted more.

He cupped her between her legs, the heel of his hand pressing into her sensitive clit, and said against her lips, "This pussy is mine now, Callie. From now on, you don't come unless I say so."

"Overbearing," she whispered through her tired smile before she succumbed to sleep.

Chapter Seventeen

Noah was not accustomed to fucking up. He was the guy who sailed through high school, college, and grad school. He was the guy who always kept his nose clean and was ten minutes early to every appointment. He was scrupulously honest (this week notwithstanding), even when that honesty wasn't what someone wanted to hear. It was how he made sure that every woman he took to bed was absolutely clear on what he was—and was not—offering them: a night of fun, as many orgasms as they could handle, and then he'd order them a cab to take them home. No spending the night. No cuddling. No flirty texts the next day. No chance of falling in love.

As he lay in bed with Callie—a woman he'd been sleeping next to for the past three nights, a woman who would be in his life indefinitely, the woman he was pretending to date—he was wholly unprepared for the sudden and crystal-clear feeling that he had fucked up. Royally.

He had intended to talk to her, to propose that they took their fake relationship to the next level. A temporary friends-with-benefits arrangement. One where neither of them could get hurt because their only promises to each other would be pleasure and discretion, both things at which he was eminently talented. But he hadn't counted on walking into their hotel room, finding her naked with a toy between her legs, and losing his damn mind. He hadn't counted on how raw he would feel after they'd both come, like his skin was all tender and new, the pink flesh that forms over a wound.

And I haven't even been inside her yet.

He wasn't sure when they'd fallen asleep, but it was still dark out when he woke so they hadn't slept for long. Callie's back was pressed to his front, the ripe curve of her ass nestled against his half-hard dick. He had one hand banded across her chest, clasped around her breast, and the other buried between her thighs, cupping her pussy.

Does it count as cuddling if it's so overtly sexual?

He untangled himself from her, lying on his back at her side, and dragged his hands through his hair. Soon she would wake up and they would have to talk about what they'd done. Where to start? *Well, Callie, I know you've had feelings for me since you were a teenager, but I'm only looking for a sexual arrangement. I'm a heartless bastard, you remember.*

"Noah," she said, rolling over and nuzzling her cheek against his chest, "you're thinking too hard."

"I'm sorry. I fucked up." She lifted her face to look at him, her eyebrows high on her forehead, eyes wide. *Shit.* He hurried to reassure her, skating his hand over her arm. "I mean, we should have talked before we..."

"Got naked?"

He exhaled a laugh. "Yeah." He turned to look at her—she deserved eye contact at least after she'd had his cock in her mouth—and instantly realized his mistake. She was still naked, her breasts red from his facial hair and her hair tousled in that just-fucked way that made him want to ravage her all over again. "Shit, I suck at this."

She sat up, pulling a sheet around her chest to partially cover herself, though her nipples were still visible through the thin fabric. Somehow the sight of her half concealed was even more distracting. He cursed under his breath as his cock twitched, preparing for round two.

"Then I'll start," she said. "I'm not naive, Noah. I don't think that my magic pussy—" He nearly choked at the phrase. "—has suddenly turned you into a relationship guy. So maybe we just don't think so much."

He scanned her eyes, trying to get a read on if she meant it. It seemed too good to be true. "Just to be clear, you're proposing that we...?"

"Keep having sex. Yes."

"I can't give you more than sex." He hated each word as they left his lips.

"I'm not asking for more," she said, settling back on her side next to him. "We have a few days left here. I say we enjoy ourselves while it lasts."

"And when we go back home?"

Something flashed in her eyes—there and then gone before he could identify it. "You won't be home for long."

He winced. "*If* I get the job."

"*When* you get the job." She trailed her fingers through his chest hair, her touch too light, and yet he felt it everywhere. "We leave it here, in this room. What happens in Aster Bay, stays in Aster Bay."

"I don't know." He brushed a lock of hair behind her ear, let his hand fall away, dancing over the perfect curve of her waist until it settled on her hip. "We're already pretending to be a couple, lying to everyone. This keeps getting more complicated."

"Maybe this uncomplicates things, at least a little. It makes the lie a little more truthful."

He didn't know how to respond to that, or why he was arguing at all. Wasn't this the exact arrangement he had been hoping for when he'd come up to their hotel room? It was hard to think clearly when her fingers were drifting lower, following the trail of hair over his abs.

"Unless you don't want to do it again." She pulled her hand away before it reached his cock, her eyes narrowing.

His dick kicked in protest, and he resisted the impulse to grab her hand and place it on his shaft, his chest tightening uncomfortably at the thought that he had put that look of insecurity on her face. Instead, he reached for her, cupping her face and pulling her towards him. The sheet fell away as she leaned closer and neither of them made a move to right it.

"There has never been a question that I want you," he said. She sucked in a breath, her eyes darting back and forth between his. "Jesus Christ, Callie, you have to have known."

She closed her eyes and took a slow, deep breath. When she opened her eyes again, they were glistening, the evidence of her emotion like a knife to his gut.

"I can't be the guy who hurts you," he said, his thumbs stroking her cheeks.

"I'm not made of glass, Noah. I can decide what I can handle, what I want. And I want this. With you. For however long I can have it."

He wanted it, too. He wanted every second with her. Every sigh, every moan, every sweaty, frantic moment. He'd never thought of himself as the possessive type but lying there with her, skin to skin with the scent of their sex still hanging in the air, the idea that anyone else might ever touch her like this was enough to drive him insane.

He should tell her no, put an end to this before that feeling had a chance to grow, to consume him. He'd been an idiot to think he could sleep with Callie, that he could know the taste of her and the way his name fell from her lips when she came, and not want it again and again. That he wouldn't let this thing destroy him in exchange for a chance to be with her again.

But he was tired of trying not to want her. He'd spent six years trying not to want her. Six years of losing himself in his work and the beds of women he would never see again, but nothing had worked. Maybe nothing ever would.

In two days, Wolf would be there and Noah would convince the producer to hire him. And then in a little more than a week, he would join the film crew for three months. He wouldn't ask her to wait for him. This thing with Callie had an expiration date. And while he was absolutely certain now that he would never dig her landmine out of his chest completely, that there would always be shrapnel embedded in him, maybe he could at least give her the closure she deserved. A few days to get her out of his system, and then the rest of his life to live without her.

"Come here," he said, his voice low and rough, before he claimed her mouth, swallowing her moan and reveling in the taste of her. He dragged his lips over the column of her throat, his hands already tearing at the sheets to get to her.

He lost himself in the salt of her skin, in the little whimpers and moans that slipped from her lips as he slid his hand between her thighs. He worked her hard and fast, her hand wrapped around his shaft giving as good as she got. It wasn't long before she arched beneath him, crying out his name as her heat contracted around his fingers. She was still coming when he grunted out his own pleasure, his sticky release spilling over her hand.

After he'd washed them both with a warm washcloth, he gathered her to his chest and pressed a kiss to her hair. He held her close as she drifted off to sleep, as though he could hold her close enough to calm the fear clawing its way through his chest.

Callie tossed aside her romance novel and looked at Noah where he sat next to her in bed, the sheet pooling around his hips. He scribbled on a piece of staff paper, occasionally pausing to conduct for a few bars with his pencil before furiously erasing and scribbling again. The fine bits from the pencil's eraser had mixed with the dusting of hair across his chest and he absent-mindedly scratched at it between bursts of writing. Dark frame glasses, like Clark Kent's, perched on the bridge of his nose. She never knew he wore glasses before.

"You're staring at me again," he said without looking up from his work.

She sank down into the pillows, letting the sheet fall lower on her chest, the tiniest bit of areola peeking out. His eyes snapped to the spot. He shook his head, exhaling hard through his nose as he tried to hide his smile, and returned to his work.

"When did you get glasses?" she asked.

"A few years ago. I mostly wear contacts, but I forgot to clean them last night."

"I like them. They're sexy."

The flicker of heat in his gaze made her squirm. "I

thought you were reading."

"I finished my book and I didn't bring another one."

He set down his work. "I can fix that," he said, climbing out of bed.

He was a thing of beauty, the perfect curve of his ass, the muscles moving and shifting beneath his skin. Would she ever get used to seeing him naked? *No. You won't have time to get used to it before it's over.* She shook the thought away, focused on watching him rummage in his suitcase. When he climbed back into bed, he handed her a small brown paper gift bag.

"What's this?"

He shrugged. "Just something I picked up a few days ago. I thought you might like it."

Her chest warmed, a bright glowing ball of something that had nothing to do with the fact that Noah Van Aller was sitting naked a few inches from her and everything to do with him buying her a gift just because he thought she'd like it. Inside the bag was a small paperback. It was fairly beat-up, the spine cracked and bowed, one corner of the cover dog-eared. She ran her fingers over the raised lettering of the title, *Marrying the Secret Duke* in swooping gold script.

She blinked, tracing the letters over and over, her eyes suddenly stinging.

"It's signed." He reached over and opened the front cover. Sure enough, the author's signature was scrawled in black marker across the lower corner of the stunning step back, the ink carefully avoiding the couple and only slightly obscuring the field of wildflowers in the image. "I know you probably already have a copy, but—"

"Thank you," she said, her voice small. "It's my favorite book."

"I know."

"How did you know?" she asked. Her heart was beating wildly as she clutched the book to her chest.

He looked away, returning his attention to his composition. "You know how."

He remembered the name of a book she mentioned to him once. Did he also remember the costume she'd worn that night? The way he'd kissed her like he couldn't stand not to touch her? Had he worked out what happened after, why she hadn't answered his call the next day, or the day after that?

They'd never talked about it. She'd lain in a hospital bed, woozy with pain killers and wishing she didn't have to pee again from the multiple bags of fluids they'd been giving her all day, and she'd wanted to call him so badly to tell him what had happened. But she didn't have words for it then. She was scared and her mother was making her crazy and all she wanted was to hear his voice, but she hadn't wanted to come to him like that—needy and broken and not knowing if she'd ever be fixed. So she hadn't called him back. It had only taken a week before he stopped calling her.

"Noah..." she began, not sure what exactly she wanted to say. *I'm sorry. I was sick and scared and so young.*

"What do you think of this?" he asked, tilting his pad of sheet music towards her so she could see what he'd written.

She blinked, unable to switch gears so quickly when her mind was still in that hospital room. She refocused her attention on the notes on the page and hummed the melody as she went, pausing when she hit the end of the second stave. Frowning, she returned to the top of the page, humming more slowly, her fingers tapping absent-mindedly as though she were playing the piece. Again, she stumbled on the same note.

She tapped the offending note. "I think you're missing an accidental."

"Good catch."

He scribbled in a sharp symbol next to the note and tilted the paper back towards her. She hummed through it again, this time all the way through.

"I like it. Much more *West Wing* theme song than John Phillips Sousa march."

Noah smirked, making a few other adjustments to the piece. "I was going for Copland, but I'll take it."

"I'm pretty sure the theme song was influenced by Copland. All those perfect fourths."

"Does it sound *too much* like Copland," he asked, frowning at the notes on the page.

She considered the piece for a minute, humming through it again. "Can I try something?" she asked, taking his pencil. She wrote a handful of notes on a clean line of the staff paper, just a few bars, then handed the pencil back to Noah. "What if you do something like that at the end of the second phrase before you resolve the chord?" Noah hummed through the piece with her addition. "Just something a little unexpected, you know?"

"It's perfect. Thank you," he said, smiling.

"We make a good team," she said more casually than she felt. Composing with him again, even just a few notes, was such a high. She hadn't realized quite how much she'd missed it.

Noah set aside his staff paper and his pencil. "What do you want to do today? We could head into town. See if there's anything interesting to do."

Callie thought of the lingerie shop, of the strappy lace contraption in her suitcase.

"We could stay here." She let the sheet slip a little further and dragged her hand up his arm.

Noah smirked. He leaned in and dropped a kiss on the tip of her nose. "Get dressed, Calico. We're not spending the whole day in bed."

"Who are you and what have you done with Noah Van Aller?" She laughed, giving him an appreciative once over when he stood up, all tan skin and coarse hair.

He chuckled, the sound dark and full of promises she hoped he intended to make good on. He leaned close, and traced one finger around her nipple until it hardened beneath his too-gentle touch.

"If we spend all day in this bed, then you're not going to be able to walk down that aisle tomorrow." He pinched the stiff peak, a sudden bolt of electricity blooming from the spot, making her yelp in surprise. He grinned. "So let's go find something to do with our clothes *on* before I forget that I'm a goddamn gentleman."

Chapter Eighteen

Callie buried her nose in the spine of the old book and inhaled deeply, the smell of the yellowed paper familiar and comforting.

"What are you doing?" Noah asked, the corner of his mouth tipped up.

"Smell this." She held the book out to him.

"I'm good." He put up a hand to hold her at bay.

"Come on. Just a little whiff."

His brows drew low, but he leaned forward and took a quick sniff of the book. "It smells like old paper."

"Isn't it great?" Callie beamed.

"No. It smells like old paper."

She sighed, adding the book to the stack tucked under her arm. "Philistine."

"What did you just call me?" he asked, his eyes wide, sparkling with restrained laughter.

"Philistine," she repeated slowly. "It means—"

"I know what it means."

He followed her around the corner of the small used bookstore as she continued browsing their extensive romance section, her fingertips dragging over the spines as she went. The bookshelves stretched nearly to the ceiling; sliding rickety-looking ladders were placed periodically throughout the too-narrow aisles. In the back corner of the store, a wisp of sheer fabric had been hung like a canopy over a half-height bookshelf stuffed with children's books, the floor beneath strewn with mismatched pillows and cushions. At the center of the pillow pile, an elderly orange tabby cat slept, casting disdainful glances at any customer who dared get too close to his nest—not that Callie was deterred. She cooed at the cat as they passed before returning her attention to the numerous shelves of romance novels.

"You are aware that I make my living in the arts," he said, leaning against the shelf at her side.

Callie shrugged. "And yet you have no appreciation for the smell of old books."

"I also don't want to stick my nose in a container of old vegetables. What does *that* make me?"

She shot him a pointed look. "Not the same thing. Oh! I love this one!" She pulled a well-loved paperback from the shelf.

"*Nine Rules to Break When Romancing a Rake?*"

"It's one of my favorites." She ran her hand over the cover before adding it to her stack. "You better get me out of here before I spend all my money on books."

"Hold on. We haven't even gotten to the music section yet," he said, moving further down the aisle as he scanned the signs overhead.

Callie watched him go, her skin cooling as all the excitement left her. She trailed after Noah until she found him crouched down to look at the bottom shelf of a bookcase overstuffed with sheet music. He glanced up as she approached.

"They have a whole American composers section." He

pulled a score off the shelf. "John Adams," he said, dropping the score on the floor at his side and pulling another, "Samuel Barber," and another, "Corigliano, Glass, Copland." He smiled up at her, his smile so bright and boyish that it drew a smile of her own, despite the itch in her fingers and the urge to get as far away from his growing pile of scores as possible.

"That's quite a selection."

"What crazy person gave away all their sheet music to a used bookstore?" he asked, pulling more scores off the shelf.

"Maybe they had no use for them anymore."

"Why wouldn't they have a use for them?" He huffed out a laugh, continuing to add to his stack. "It's not like sheet music has an expiration date on it?"

"If they can't play them anymore..."

"What—" He froze, sliding the score beneath his fingers back into its place on the shelf. He closed his eyes and scrubbed his hand over his face. "Shit. I'm sorry, Callie."

"It's fine."

She hoped her voice sounded light and easy and not like she was slowly suffocating on her own frustrations. It was one thing to watch Noah create a new piece, even to offer suggestions to him about that piece, and entirely another to stare at all those pages of music. Music she had learned seated at his side, melodies she would never play again but could still feel in her fingertips when she closed her eyes.

"Let's get out of here," he said, standing and leaving his stack of music on the floor.

"What about your scores?"

"I don't need them."

"Noah, you're a composer. Buy the scores."

He took her chin between his thumb and forefinger, tilting her head up so her eyes met his. Before he could say anything, she pulled out of his grasp, taking a step back.

"I'm not so fragile that I can't handle the sight of some sheet music." She hated the defensive edge in her voice—almost as much as she hated that she was dangerously close to tears. *Of all the stupid things to make me cry.*

"I didn't say you were," he said, crossing his arms over his chest. "It was still insensitive of me. The Americans are your favorite."

"Not all the Americans." Her heart clenched at the idea that he remembered the detail even after all this time. "I don't love—"

"Bernstein."

She nodded, a quick bob of the head. "Buy the scores, Noah. Someone should play them."

Then she turned on her heel, deposited her stack of books on a nearby armchair, and left the shop. She took a deep breath, filling her lungs with the salty ocean air, and shook out her hands, stretching and clenching her fingers as if that could somehow make them work the way they once had. As if she hadn't tried everything she could think of already. She couldn't say why she had been so affected by Noah shopping for sheet music when she'd lain in bed beside him as he composed just that morning and only felt an overwhelming attraction to him.

Maybe because this was the very thing she had fantasized about all those years ago during their late night phone calls: filling their arms with scores that they would spend the rest of the day playing side by side on the piano bench until one of them made a move, brushed a hand over the other's, or nudged a knee. Music would be their own kind of foreplay, as it had been during those long phone calls. He might be in her bed—for now—but she would never again sit beside him and coax a song into life with him. She hadn't realized how badly she still wanted to.

The ringing of the bell over the door announced Noah's arrival beside her on the sidewalk. He carried two bags, one full of scores and the other holding the romance novels she'd left behind. "You didn't need to get them for me," she said.

"I'm starving. Let's grab lunch," he said, as though she hadn't just behaved irrationally in a bookstore.

"I think Jamie's restaurant is just around the corner."

Noah narrowed his eyes. "Alright, but we are making sure they know you're allergic to shellfish before we order a damn thing."

She laughed. "Don't worry. I've got a purse full of Benadryl just in case."

Noah watched Callie over the top of his menu and fought the urge to kiss her. The sun streaming in through the large windows glinted off her hair as she screwed her lips up to the side and considered her options. How should he behave with the woman he was pretending to date now that they were also sleeping together? Casual kissing over lunch didn't seem quite right, even if he had already had his face between her legs.

"What are you guys doing here?" Jamie asked, appearing at their table. He wore his chef's coat and his hair was tousled like he'd been pulling at it.

"Just having lunch," Callie said, smiling up at him. "I didn't get to try much of your food last time I was here."

Jamie winced. "Again, I'm so sorry."

Callie waved the apology away. "Don't even start

with that. I won't take another apology. I *will* take your recommendation for the best thing on the menu, however."

Jamie smiled, a dimple popping out on his cheek, and Noah had the irrational impulse to punch him. He clutched the edges of his menu instead. *What the hell was that?* Noah had never thought of himself as the jealous or possessive type. Then again, it was hard to be jealous or possessive about women he only saw once.

"Tell you what," Jamie said, plucking their menus from their hands, that stupid dimple still fixed in place. "Let me make you something special. Something off-menu. My treat."

"You don't have to do that," Noah said.

"I'd like to. My last apology," Jamie said, with a deferential head tilt towards Callie. "No shellfish involved. Any other allergies I should be aware of?" They both confirmed that they had none. "Great. Hold tight and I'll send something out in just a minute."

"That was nice of him," Callie said, arranging her napkin in her lap.

"He was flirting with you."

Callie paused, her eyes twinkling. "Why, Noah, are you jealous?" He clenched his jaw and reached for his water glass. Callie laughed. "He wasn't flirting. He was being friendly. A man can have a friendly conversation with a woman without it being about sex, you know."

"If you say so."

"And it's not like I'm really your girlfriend," she said, lowering her voice.

A growl rose up in the back of his throat. "He doesn't know that."

Callie shrugged.

Infuriating woman.

He reached beneath the table and grasped her leg, high

up on her thigh, his hand hidden by the tablecloth. He tightened his grip, just enough to make her eyes snap to his, her pupils already dilating. He slid his hand higher, dragged his thumb over the seam at the apex of her thighs.

"You're mine now, remember?"

She let out a shaky breath. "For now."

One more slow drag of his thumb, pressing harder just to see the surprise in her eyes when he hit the right spot. Then he dropped his hand, returned it to his water glass and took a sip before he said something stupid—like how she would always be his.

She was right; she was only his *for now*. He had nothing more than *now* to offer, even if the idea that someone else might someday touch her made him want to flip the damn table. She watched him like she was waiting for his next move, but he had no idea what that next move should be. It wasn't like he had planned on sticking his hand between her legs in the middle of a restaurant.

"Here we go. A little something to get you started," Jamie said, returning to their table with a pristine white dish containing two pieces of what looked like very fancy, very small toast. "Waygu beef tenderloin crostini with horseradish chimichurri and a caramelized onion cream." Noah didn't understand half the words the man had just said.

"Caramelized onion cream?" Callie gasped, her face lighting up in a mix of surprise and delight.

Jamie leaned in, that fucking dimple popping out again. "It's my secret weapon."

"I thought your secret weapon was lobster stock," Noah grumbled. Jamie's smile faltered.

Callie shot Noah a pointed look and picked up one of the tiny toasts. She inspected it, her eyes sparkling. "And you put the horseradish *in* the chimichurri?"

"We like to play fast and loose with the classic recipes around here," he said with a wink, his hand brushing against her shoulder.

"This looks amazing, Jamie. Thank you," Callie said, flashing a smile.

Noah mumbled his thanks as Jamie excused himself.

"Be nice," Callie chided. "He feels bad enough as it is."

"Then he should stop flirting with my girlfriend," Noah replied, leaning on the title.

Noah took a bite and immediately hated that the tiny toast was so fucking delicious. The most tender beef he'd ever eaten—it practically melted on his tongue—and a green sauce with lots of herbs in it, something sharp and spicy at the back of his throat, and something creamy and sweet. Who thought of putting these things together? And why had he never known food could taste like this?

"Oh, God, that's good." Callie closed her eyes as she swallowed her bite and just like that Noah was hard as a rock, thinking about the last time he'd heard her say those words and how she'd bloomed beneath his touch.

He cleared his throat. "My uncle is suspicious," he said, moving the conversation back to something safer. A reminder he needed that they were not in fact a couple.

"Why's that?" Callie asked, her tongue darting out to swipe a speck of cream from her upper lip.

"He's a curmudgeonly old man," Noah said, looking away to resist the temptation to lick her lips clean himself. "We need him to believe this thing is real if he's going to help convince Wolf to hire me. Uncle Stu can be very persuasive—he might even be able to help convince your mom it's time she finally moved."

"Okay. Then let's clean up our story," she said. "We told our mothers that we started dating in May. How did that happen?"

"I don't know. We were both at the same bar—"

"Nope. I don't go to bars."

"Okay, then the same club."

"You think I don't go to bars, but I go to clubs?" She chuckled, shaking her head.

"Didn't I see you at karaoke with Liv in May?"

He knew he'd seen her. She'd worn a green blouse with a high neck and jeans that made her ass look amazing. Back then she'd been using a purse shaped like a pair of lips—hot pink—and that night she'd worn matching earrings.

"Oh yeah," she said, smiling. "When Liv and I did our tribute to Poison."

Noah groaned. "You two are savage."

Callie laughed, a full-throated laugh that made her whole face glow. "Okay, so we reconnected at karaoke because you loved my rendition of *Every Rose Has Its Thorn*."

"No one who was there will believe that," he said, grinning.

"Now who's savage?"

"We reconnected at karaoke, in spite of your massacring of an 80s classic, and I texted you the next day to invite you to dinner."

She arched an eyebrow. "Just like that? After a lifetime of knowing each other, all it takes is one Poison song?"

"It was a very convincing performance. Especially in that blouse."

Her smile wavered.

Shit. Is it creepy that I remember what she was wearing?

"Where did we go to dinner?" she asked, her voice low, her expression unreadable.

"I cooked for you." He dropped his tone to match hers and her eyes flickered to his. "I make a mean grilled cheese."

"I remember." Then, "Is that your move?"

"My move?"

"Do you make all your women grilled cheese?"

He felt like he'd been sucker punched. He didn't want to think about any other women. And none of them had been *his*.

"No," he said tightly.

"Just kid sisters then?"

Something hot and dangerous flashed low in his belly. "You were never my kid sister."

"Close enough."

"No." She made that huff/laugh sound again and he gripped her chin, turned her face to look at his. "You haven't been a kid for a long time, Calico. And the way I feel when I'm around you is anything but brotherly."

"Prove it," she breathed.

He crushed his lips to hers in a bruising kiss, deep and commanding and over too soon. He released her chin and sat back in his seat, hating the way that landmine in his chest shifted, just enough to remind him that it was there.

Callie wasn't sure why she had pushed him, why she couldn't stop needling him. Noah had always treated her well. This whole week he'd gone out of his way to take care of her. But that was the problem. She didn't want his gentleness and his caretaking. She wanted the heat he'd only let her glimpse, the animal he kept caged somewhere out of her reach. She'd only have him for another few days and she wanted each one to leave scars, to brand them both in ways they couldn't take back, even after he was no longer hers.

Jamie reappeared, setting down two plates in front of them and explaining about the poached peaches and the perfectly seared chicken breast, the wine and the figs and the fresh pasta to soak up the sauce, and all she wanted to do was kiss Noah again. After Jamie left, they each took a bite of their lunch. She watched Noah chew, watched his throat work as he swallowed, the way he cut into his chicken as if it had done something to offend him.

She set aside her fork and knife. "Did I stay over that first night?"

He glanced up from his food, cut off another bite. "My uncle won't ask that."

"Liv might."

He glanced up again, chewed the bite slowly, and swallowed. When he spoke, his voice was sandpaper and broken glass, dark and sharp and just dangerous enough to catch her by surprise. "Yeah. You stayed over."

She nodded, picked up her utensils and began cutting her food as if her hands weren't shaking. That edge in his voice was turning her inside out with every word. Is that what it would have been like? If she hadn't gotten sick all those years ago, if she'd answered when he called—would he have made her grilled cheese and she'd have spent the night in his apartment, and they'd be the ones who were getting married now?

Stop. Just stop.

Noah dropped his fork and knife, scrubbed his hand over his face, and leaned back in his chair. He watched her as she ate, every move that she made infused with the awareness of his eyes on her. After what felt like an inordinate amount of time, he picked up his utensils and began eating again.

"What did Jamie say this purple thing is?" he asked, poking at the offending item on his plate.

"A fig."

"Huh. It's good."

She bit the inside of her cheeks to keep from smiling. "Mmhmm. It's really good with the feta cheese."

He stabbed a bit of each and took a bite, grunting in approval as he dove in for a second taste. "How have I not been eating stuff like this my whole life?" he asked, shoveling more into his mouth like he'd only just realized he was hungry.

"Stick with me and I'll show you all kinds of things you'll love eating."

Her heart stopped as he turned an almost feral look on her. She'd meant she'd introduce him to pickled red onions and tzatziki and Indian food but, *holy shit*, did she like him looking at her like he might eat her alive. She squeezed her thighs together to soothe the insistent pulse that had settled there.

He blinked, the wild look in his eyes disappearing. He held her gaze for another half a second and then burst out laughing, his shoulders shaking, and before she knew it, she was laughing, too.

"You should have seen your face," he said between bouts of laughter.

"You should have seen yours!"

How could he be both of these people—the man who laughed with her and pointed out ladybug constellations, *and* the guy who had just kissed her like he wanted to devour her? How could she want both parts of him equally?

"Okay, so we have our origin story," Noah said, still grinning. "What else?"

Callie thought for a moment. "Has anything significant happened for you in the last six months? Anything a girlfriend would know?"

"I've really just been working. Senator Thorne announced her re-election bid right before the holidays and Wolf contacted me in January to put together a package for the documentary. Between writing my submission pieces and teaching my classes, there hasn't been much time for anything else."

"I didn't realize you'd been working on this for that long."

Noah nodded, speaking around a bite of peach. "I beat out the competition through three rounds of submission. I'm the last man standing. I just have to convince Wolf that having me on the project isn't going to cause trouble for the senator."

"You really want this job."

"Big films like this have always been the goal," he said, shrugging.

"I know. But I thought you liked teaching?"

"I love teaching. But it was never the plan."

Right. Noah always had a plan, a defined set of rules that he lived by. If those rules said that he needed to score major films, then that was what he would do. *And if the rules said he didn't do relationships...*

"You're going to get it. You deserve it."

"The world doesn't work that way, Callie."

"I know. But we're going to get you that job." Even if she hated the idea of him leaving to go on the road with the film crew.

"What about you? Anything significant?"

She sat back in her chair, pushing her now mostly empty plate away from her. "I went to Florida in March—West Palm Beach area—for a librarians' conference. I had a bad flare up when I got back."

He stilled, eyes locked on her. She hated this part, when the pity and concern overtook the conversation and she wasn't Callie anymore, just a conglomeration of symptoms and maladies.

"How bad?" he asked.

She shrugged.

How could you quantify pain? How did you describe it to someone who'd never experienced the terror of sitting down in a chair and realizing you couldn't stand back up? Would he understand how her legs were on fire some days, and others they were numb? Or how she felt like her body was collapsing under its own weight? Would he listen when she explained that every day was a horrible mystery, and she never knew when her body would betray her next?

"Thankfully it only lasted a few days."

"I spent them with you."

"No."

"Callie, if you needed me—"

"No, Noah. I wouldn't have let you."

He pressed his fingers into his eyes, shaking his head, like he couldn't believe what he was hearing. "You can't even let me be there for you when it's pretend," he muttered.

"I don't need you to take care of me," she said, her voice louder than she'd realized as the flash of anger shot through her, hot and stinging.

It was one thing to let him carry her bag or even help her shave her legs, but if he ever saw her when she was in a full-on flare, when she couldn't walk, when she did nothing but sleep for days on end, curled around a heating pad next to a jumbo-size bottle of ibuprofen... No. Being in that much pain was frightening, even after all these years, and she couldn't manage anyone else's fear when she already had to work twice as hard to manage her own. Besides, if she let Noah take care of her—*really* take care of her—then how long would it be before he was just like her ex-boyfriend, tired of being tied to someone who was always sick, resentful of the ways loving her would hold him back? She couldn't bear it if Noah ever looked at her that way.

"Why does everyone think I can't take care of myself?"

"Because you shouldn't have to," he shot back. "Because there are people who care about you—"

"Like you?"

"Yeah. Like me."

"My health is *my* problem. No one else's. And I don't need people to care about me because they think they have to."

She looked away, unable to see the intensity in his eyes without wanting to believe it. And she couldn't afford to believe it because it was all temporary. A brief indulgence built on a lie and all of it would be over soon. If she looked at him, she'd think about how she'd lost him six years ago—just another thing fibromyalgia had stolen from her. She dashed away a tear before it could slide down her cheek.

"Callie..." His voice pulled at her, but she didn't want him to see how much this wasn't temporary for her. "Love..." It was the *love* that broke her, tears sliding down her face faster.

He grabbed the underside of her chair and pulled it closer to him, wrapping his arms around her, and holding her against him, her head in the crook of his neck.

"Caring for you is not an obligation," he said, his cheek pressed to her hair. "It's a privilege."

She wanted to believe him, but she'd had years of evidence to the contrary—boyfriend after boyfriend who couldn't handle the flares, friends who eventually disappeared without a word, a mother who used her illness like a weapon. Caring for her was a burden, one she knew he'd come to resent eventually.

Not that he'll be around that long.

Chapter Nineteen

The rest of their meal was quiet, both Callie and Noah lost in thought. Noah had always been the one who fixed things—for his mother, for his sister. He was the guy who took care of the people in his life. It was how he showed them they were important, how he made sure they all got from one day to the next. But Liv was getting married, his mother was moving on with her life, and Callie absolutely refused to let him in. *Just like she wouldn't let me in all those years ago.*

They thanked Jamie for their meal (he wouldn't let them pay) and walked back to Noah's car in silence. It bothered him more than it should that Callie wouldn't let him care for her when she was sick, even in a lie. And yet he'd seen cracks in that armor over the last few days, moments when she'd accepted his help, when caring for her had been something that brought them closer.

They had a few hours before they were due at the rehearsal dinner, so Callie went back to their room to take a nap. Noah dropped her off at the hotel and then drove back into town to the unassuming shop with the nondescript sign that he'd clocked when they were walking earlier, a plan forming.

It was selfish to want her to invite him into the most vulnerable part of her life, but he couldn't help it. He couldn't stand by while someone he cared about suffered and do nothing. The helplessness would destroy him. He would prove to her that he could carry the weight of it, that his desire to take care of her had nothing to do with obligation. And he would start by proving she could trust him with her pleasure, so then she'd know she could also trust him with her pain.

Noah returned to the hotel room a half hour before the rehearsal dinner to find Callie stretched out on the bed reading *Marrying the Secret Duke*. She'd changed into a knee-length black wrap dress, her hair braided and wound up in a bun on the top of her head. He had the most intense desire to undo her hair, to have it fall around her shoulders and bury his face in it.

She looked up when he entered the room, her face lighting up. "You're just in time for the best part," she said, waving the book. "Bernadette is about to go to the masquerade ball where she realizes the pleasure club owner is really a duke."

He toed off his shoes and tossed the small paper shopping bag on the end of the bed. "Oh yeah? And how does she realize that?"

Callie smiled, a mischievous glint in her eye. "By kissing him of course."

"Like this?" Noah asked, kneeling on the bed beside her and capturing her mouth. He moved slowly, tasting her, and licking at her lips until she parted to let him in. His tongue stroked hers and she went soft in his arms, her breathing coming faster. He kissed her neck, dragged his lips over her collarbone.

"Mmm, just like that."

His hands found the tie for her dress, undoing the knot and peeling back the fabric to reveal her body as if he were opening a present. Like most days, she hadn't worn a bra, the small globes of her breasts laid bare for him, tipped by soft pink nipples already pulling into tight peaks. He ran his hands over each breast, across her stomach, hooking his fingers in the waist of her simple cotton panties.

She groaned. "Noah, we have to go to dinner."

"We have time." He pressed a kiss to the low curve of her belly and dragged her panties down her legs, his lips following in their wake. Once he'd tossed the wisp of fabric aside, he planted a kiss on the inside of her ankle. "I'm going to fuck you tonight, Callie."

She drew a shaky breath, her eyes growing darker, hooding with desire. "Now?" she breathed.

He chuckled, his lips pressed to her calf. "No, love. This is just the opening act."

She shivered as his mouth moved higher, and he promised himself he'd remember every reaction—the way she sucked in a breath when he dragged his stubble across her skin, the needy tilt of her hips when he rolled her nipple between his fingers.

He slid a finger inside her, his thumb working her clit in slow circles as he teased her from within with long, languid strokes like he had all the time in the world, like he wasn't interested in making her come. He drew her nipple into his mouth, sucking on it in long pulls that had her arching against him.

She reached for his belt, but he shifted his hips out of her reach, sliding a second finger into her.

"Let me touch you," she said.

"No. This is just for you."

"Why?"

"Because the next time I come, I'm going to be deep in your pussy." He added a third finger and she gasped at the intrusion.

"Do it now."

He increased the pressure on her clit, loving the way she lifted her hips to meet his touch. He was so fucking hard it took all his restraint not to grind himself against her. But he meant what he'd said—this was just for her.

"Do you trust me?"

"Yes," she gasped, her pelvis shuddering as he moved his fingers faster.

"That's all you have to do, love. Just let go and trust me."

She caught his eye, a question posed there, but before she could ask it, she threw her head back and came, her hips rocketing up to grind against the hand working between her legs and his name on her lips. Callie was always beautiful, but when she came she was transcendent. He'd never seen anything so magnificent as Callie with her back bowed in pleasure, her pussy clamping down on his fingers with each wave of her orgasm. He almost came himself just from watching her.

When she stopped shaking, he withdrew his fingers and reached for the bag, producing a shiny silver plug with a jeweled end. He held it up for her, making sure she got a good look.

"Tell me again, Callie," he commanded. He held his breath, waiting for her answer, watching as her eyes flicked between the toy in his hand and his face.

"I trust you."

He lowered himself between her legs, lifting her feet over his shoulders and licked a long stripe from her opening to her clit. As his tongue flicked against that beautiful, swollen bud, he slid the plug into her pussy. He held it in place with two fingers, using a third to stroke the pleated rim of her asshole. Softly he circled her back entrance, his tongue moving faster now over her clit. She began muttering low curses, her body tightening beneath him, and just before she climaxed a second time, he slipped his finger inside that tight little hole. She gasped, as though her orgasm was a surprise, her clit pulsing on his tongue. She was still coming when he removed his finger and pressed the tapered tip of the plug to her back entrance.

"Oh, God," she moaned, her hand digging into his hair and holding his mouth against her as another stronger wave washed over her.

He continued tonguing her clit without reprieve as he slid the plug into her ass, slowly working the toy deeper until it was fully seated, the jeweled end peeking out between her cheeks. When her climax abated, he sat back on his heels, wiping her release from his chin and admiring his work, the way her pussy shuddered with the aftershocks, wetness dripping down over the shiny toy buried in her ass.

"Come on," he said, his voice rough. "We don't want to be late for dinner."

She looked at him like he'd gone insane, a brief moment of panic in her eyes before understanding dawned and settled into something deeper, something like excitement and lust and even a touch of shame.

"You want me to go to dinner like this?" she asked, arching an eyebrow at him.

He retrieved her panties from where he'd dropped them and slid them back on her legs, pulling them up.

"That's right. I want you to wear my plug while we make small talk and toast my sister's marriage. I want you to feel it inside you every time you move, knowing I put it there. I want you desperate for my cock to stretch your pussy the same way my plug is stretching your ass. And I want you to trust me that before the night is over, I'm going to make it feel better." He cupped her mound through her panties, his fingers pressing lightly on the end of the toy concealed beneath the cotton. "Unless this is too much," he said, suddenly unsure. Was he pushing her too hard?

"It's a lot." She wiggled her hips as she adjusted to the toy. "But I like it."

"Yeah?" he breathed, relief and arousal flooding him—as if he wasn't already hard as a rock.

"Yeah." She sat up and kissed him lightly. "Let's go to dinner."

For once, Noah and Callie weren't the last to arrive. Walking with the plug in her ass was a new experience, strange sensations moving through her with each step, an ever-present reminder of the secret beneath her clothing. She loved it, sharing this moment with Noah without even touching him. Each shift of the plug was like he was caressing her from across the room. Callie wasn't a stranger to backdoor play, but she'd never worn a toy in public, never been asked to do so by a lover. She wondered if others could tell that she was so turned on she had soaked through her panties and the night had only just begun. And while she knew she should be appalled by the idea that anyone could tell, it just made her wetter.

"Alright?" Noah asked, his lips close to her ear.

She squeezed his hand. "Perfect."

"Bridal party over here!" Liv called, gesturing for them to join her under the tent that had been erected on The

Barclay's lawn. "You okay, Cal? You're flushed."

"I'm fine," Callie said, blushing. "I just got too much sun today."

Liv walked them through the motions of the ceremony—who entered with whom and where to stand. The whole thing took ten, maybe fifteen minutes, before they returned to the hotel's dining room for dinner.

Callie took her seat next to Noah and gasped when her ass hit the chair, the toy shifting and driving itself deeper into her.

"Are you sure you're alright, Calandria?" her mother asked from across the table.

"It's nothing, Mom. I just bit my tongue," she lied, kicking Noah under the table when he smirked in response.

Once dinner was served, Jamie got to his feet, clinking his spoon against his water glass to get everyone's attention. "The time has come for me to embarrass my big brother," he declared.

"We said no speeches," Daemon grumbled.

"You said no speeches at the wedding. You didn't say anything about the rehearsal." Daemon grunted in response, his brother grinning as he continued. "You're a grumpy fucker—"

"That's the pot calling the kettle black," Daemon interjected.

"—and I can't believe Liv wants to put up with you for the rest of your lives."

"Aren't toasts supposed to be complimentary?" Daemon asked.

"I'm getting there," Jamie said. "I can't believe Liv wants to put up with you, but I'm grateful that she does, because it means I won't have to take care of you when you're old and gray. Well, gray-er."

"You're not that far behind me," Daemon said, a grin

peeking through his scowl. "Give it another year or two and you'll be gray, too."

"Don't listen to him, chickadee. Women love a silver fox," Pattie said.

"Damn right!" Liv laughed and took a sip of her wine.

"Can I finish my toast?" Jamie asked, laughing. "Liv, there is no one I can imagine who is more perfect for my big brother than you. Thank you for helping him remember that it's okay to smile every once in a while, and for keeping him out of the tabloids!" Jamie raised his glass. "To Daemon and Liv."

Noah slid his hand onto Callie's knee as he raised his glass to toast the happy couple, the small point of contact rioting through her. Every part of her awareness centered on the heat of his touch, the fullness in her ass.

"That's my cue." Noah squeezed her knee and stood up. "It's my turn to embarrass my little sister, I suppose," he said with a wicked grin.

She couldn't help but think about the way that grin felt against her skin. *Now is not the time*, she told herself. Even still, she squeezed her thighs together at the image, barely containing another gasp when the move also increased the pressure of the plug.

"Noah, play nice," Mrs. Van Aller said, but even she was smiling.

"Livi, when you told me you were getting married, my first thought was that no one could be good enough for you. And while I maintain that my initial instinct was correct, if anyone was ever going to come close, it would be Daemon."

Callie watched Liv, cuddled beneath Daemon's arm and leaning back against him, so secure in their love. So blissful it was like a visible aura around her. Callie was happy for her friend, over the moon that Liv had found her forever person, and yet she couldn't help but wonder if that would ever happen for her. Would she ever have that kind of love, the kind she read about in her romance novels? The kind she wanted with Noah?

"I also promised you that I would take care of your something old and something new. First, the something new." Noah reached into his jacket pocket and produced a small green plastic army man.

Liv laughed, joy bubbling up and spilling over.

"For those of you who don't know, I've been giving Livi these little army men since we were kids. To help her be brave. I don't think you'll need any extra courage to walk down the aisle tomorrow, little sister, but just in case." He handed her the army man. "Daemon, it's your job now to make sure Liv has what she needs. And if you want a recommendation for where to buy those things in bulk, I've got you covered."

He glanced back at Callie, the affection in his eyes taking her breath away. *It isn't real,* she told herself. *It's only temporary. Isn't it?*

Before she could go too far down that rabbit hole, Noah returned his hand to his jacket pocket, this time removing it clenched tightly around something she couldn't see.

"And for your something old," he said to Liv, his voice tight in a way Callie wasn't sure she'd ever heard before. He stared at his hand for a long moment before opening it and holding a ring up for everyone to see. It was a simple gold band, nothing flashy or remarkable about it.

"Oh, Noah." Mrs. Van Aller's voice caught as she pressed her hand to her chest.

"You didn't get a chance to know Dad for very long," Noah said, never taking his eyes from Liv, "but my God, Livi, he'd be so proud of you. He was fascinated by airplanes and history. He loved Sondheim and gardening and no one on this planet made pancakes as good as his. But more than anything, he loved his family, and he was so damn happy to have a little girl."

Noah lowered his head, gathering himself as a single tear rolled down his cheek. He blinked hard, shaking his head slightly, and looked back up to meet Liv's watery smile. In all the years they'd known each other, Callie had never seen Noah cry. He rolled the ring over in his fingers, as though he was loathe to let it go even as his words gave it away.

"You were the light of his life, for the few years you had together. And I know he's here now and he'd want you to have this."

Liv sprang to her feet, throwing her arms around Noah's neck and half crying, half laughing against his chest. He held her against him with one hand, placing the ring into the palm of his sister's hand and closing her fingers around it. He held her closed hand against his chest, and with his other hand, he reached back towards Callie, capturing her hand in his and squeezing. Like he needed to know she was there, like he was inviting her into this sacred moment. Callie squeezed back and pressed a kiss to his knuckles.

"I'll keep it safe for you until you get married," Liv said as she pulled away with a glance at Callie before leaning back into Daemon who now stood behind her.

Noah squeezed Callie's hand again and she fought back her own tears. Maybe Noah would get married someday, but it wouldn't be to her. He'd been very clear that all he had to offer her was another few days together at best. Hoping for more was asking for heartbreak. But the way he gripped her hand begged her to hope.

He dropped back into the seat beside her and looked at

her with so much emotion in his eyes that she was afraid to hear what he might say, what words he might speak as her fake boyfriend that she'd want to believe for real. So she pressed her hand to his face and kissed him before he could speak. The kiss was tame compared to the ones they'd shared behind closed doors, but it was full of all the things she would never say to him, all the things she'd always want him to say to her. When they pulled away, he cupped her face, using his thumb to wipe away an errant tear still lingering on her cheek.

It was almost too much, this tender, raw side of him so overfull with emotion and love that she would never share. She looked away, laying her palm high up on his thigh, gripping his leg through his dress pants. He tried to catch her eye again, but she kept her focus on her hand, digging her nails into his leg.

It's just pretend, she told herself. *Only the sex is real.*
She needed to remember that this onslaught of emotion was temporary, an extension of their charade. The way he thickened behind the placket of his pants, the cool metal shifting within her as she moved—those were the only thing she could count on. Those were the only things they'd promised each other.

Chapter Twenty

Callie was quiet through most of dinner. She didn't even hum when the server placed a thick slice of cheesecake in front of her. She hadn't hummed since the rehearsal had started, and her silence was setting off all kinds of alarm bells in Noah's head. Callie was never silent. She laughed and sighed and hummed—a cacophony of sound that Noah had grown accustomed to over the last week. More than that, he missed the music, the soundtrack she supplied for the time they spent together.

She hardly said a word through dessert and her smile seemed forced as they said goodnight to their families. *I asked too much of her with the plug.* It was hours since they'd left the hotel room, a long time for someone who wasn't used to this kind of play. What if he'd caused her physical pain? The idea made him sick to his stomach.

The elevator doors closed behind them, sealing them off from the others, and Callie pulled her hand from his, leaning against the wall of the elevator and blowing out an exhausted breath.

"I pushed you too hard," he said, shoving his hands in his pockets and avoiding her eyes as a familiar tendril of guilt twisted in his stomach.

"What?"

He shook his head. "You're uncomfortable. I shouldn't have asked you to wear—"

"I'm not uncomfortable."

"You're not?" He met her eyes, hunting for the lie.

"No." She flashed a sad sort of grin.

"Then what's wrong?" Noah leaned his shoulder against the wall so he could face her, but he kept his hands in his pockets, afraid that if he touched her, he wouldn't be able to stop. And something was definitely wrong. His Callie was never quiet for so long. *Not yours, not really.*

She dropped her head back against the wall, closing her eyes as though she were tired of the conversation. "It's stupid."

"It's not."

"You don't even know what it is."

"I know it's not stupid."

She turned her face towards him, searching his eyes. Her lips parted as if she were about to speak, but the elevator chimed and the doors opened on their floor.

They walked to their room in silence, a silence that now felt thick and suffocating, isolating. He took off his shoes, a watchful eye trained on Callie as she slipped off her own shoes and unwound the bun at the top of her head. Noah came up behind her and took her hair in his hands, working his fingers through the strands to release the braid. As he worked, her shoulders softened, tension melting away beneath his hands.

"Do you ever get lonely?" she asked.

His hands paused for a moment, his heart clenching in his chest at her soft question. "All the time."

"I think I've been afraid to admit it to myself, but I want what Liv and Daemon have. What Liam and Min have." She blew out a slow breath, her voice growing softer. "And I don't think I'll ever have it."

He closed his eyes, his hands wrapping around Callie's waist and pulling her back against him, her body tight to his. He pressed his lips to her shoulder and breathed in the scent of her, that tendril of guilt from the elevator growing into a thick vine, wrapping around his lungs and squeezing. "Callie—"

"You don't have to say anything. I know what this is, Noah."

But did she? Did *he*? He'd never felt like this before—like she was some vital part of himself that existed outside of his body, a part that he'd gotten so very good at pretending didn't exist. But standing there with her in his arms, he didn't want to pretend anymore.

"I just..." She sighed, turning in his arms to face him. "I don't want to be lonely tonight."

He swallowed down the words he was dying to say—words like *I won't let you be lonely,* and *I want the same things you want,* and *I think I love you.* Words it wouldn't be fair to say. They'd agreed to this time together, to a lie that had somehow begun to feel more real than anything else in his life, and in a few days it would all be over. Even the thought of that impending deadline pressed on the landmine in his chest, reminding him just how easily she could blow up his life and leave him with nothing but rubble and ash.

Noah kissed her, a slow brush of his lips against hers, like he could deactivate the explosive beneath his skin if he moved slowly enough. Callie wound her hands around his neck, pulling his face down to hers and deepening the kiss, gentleness giving way to urgency, to hunger and need. He kissed her as though it could make up for the things he wouldn't say, as though a kiss alone could scour away the old hurts and give them a new start. She pulled his bottom lip between her teeth, and he growled at the sting, fumbling with the tie of her dress.

Her dress fell open, and he pushed the fabric down off her shoulders, leaving her bare except for her cotton panties. Noah allowed himself a minute to take her in, to let his gaze linger on the swell of her belly, the curve of her waist, the tight furls of her nipples. Taking her breasts in his hands, he kissed her again, plumping and caressing her until she shivered beneath his touch.

"You are so beautiful," he groaned against her lips. "Tell me what you want, Calico."

"Take off your clothes," she whispered.

He was more than happy to oblige, sparks skittering along his skin under her hungry gaze as he unbuttoned his shirt and tossed it aside. He worked his belt open, his cock straining against his zipper before he'd even gotten his pants unbuttoned. How could he not be hard as stone with Callie looking at him like he was a fantasy come to life? His pants and boxer briefs hit the floor and Callie sucked in an audible breath, her eyes locked on his cock. As she watched, he gave himself a firm stroke, drawing it out just to enjoy the sensation of her eyes on him.

"Come here," he said, his voice rough and low.

Callie came to him, her eyes flicking back and forth between his gaze and where he continued to stroke himself in long, lazy movements. When she was close enough, he wrapped her in his arms and tossed her onto the bed. She landed on the mattress with a yelp of surprise that turned to breathless laughter, the sparkle returning to her eyes. He settled himself over her, kissing her until he could hardly breathe and grinding his erection against her cotton-covered mound.

When was the last time he'd enjoyed kissing so much? He could kiss Callie all day, rock against her like they were teenagers, and never be bored. There was so much to discover, so many little reactions to learn.

"Noah," she whined, shifting her hips beneath him.

He grinned against her lips. "Something you need, love?"

She huffed out a frustrated breath, pressing her pelvis against him in a wordless plea. He chuckled and dragged his lips over her neck, down the slope of her breast, pausing to softly bite her nipple, before settling between her thighs and dragging her panties down her legs. He lifted her legs over his shoulders, tracing her folds with a single finger. His finger dropped lower, gently pressing on the jeweled end of the toy in her back entrance.

"Fuck, I like you wearing my plug."

She canted her hips into his touch. "So do I."

"Yeah?" He pressed against the toy a little harder.

"Yeah."

He dropped his mouth to her clit, working her until she arched and moaned beneath him, each little whimper making him harder. He could live his life between her thighs, getting high off the taste of her, the throaty cries that grew louder the faster he licked her. She came on his tongue, her hips rocking against his face, her pleasure thick on his lips as her thighs quivered. When she fell back against the bed, he reached for the small shopping bag he'd returned with earlier, producing a package of condoms.

Callie stilled his hand. "I'm okay without... If you are."

He blinked, struggling to process her half sentence. "You don't want to use a condom?"

She blushed, the pink glow spreading over her cheeks and chest. "I'm on the pill and I haven't been with anyone since I was last tested."

"Me either. But… I've never done this without a condom."

"I haven't either. I just thought… We don't have to," she hurried to say, "If you don't want to."

Noah captured her lips with his, kissing her soundly, his heart swelling with the enormity of her trust. He pressed his forehead to hers. "Of course, I want to, love. Tell me again. Tell me what you want. I need to hear you say the words."

She nipped at his lower lip, a mischievous tilt to her smile. "I want you to fuck me bare."

He groaned, his mouth crashing over hers as the box of condoms fell from his hands. Noah slid a hand between them, his fingers sliding through her wet slit just as her hand closed around the base of his cock. She pumped her hand over his erection, gathering the precum that leaked from his tip and spreading it along the distended length. He focused on slowing the pounding of his heart even as he rocked into her touch, loving her tight grip around him. He throbbed into that grip, growing so hard it was almost painful.

"You're going to let me inside you like this?" he growled, two fingers sinking into her. "With nothing between us?"

"Yes," she gasped.

"You going to let me come inside you too, sweet girl?" He curled his fingers until he found the spot that made her gasp, and then he did it again.

"Yes." The thought of gliding into her bare, of pumping deep inside her pussy and then watching his release leak out of her was almost enough to make him come on the spot.

"Fuck, Callie." He added a third finger, the heel of his hand pressing against her clit as he fucked her fist. "I can't wait to make a mess of this pussy."

"Do it already," she challenged, a smile in her voice.

Noah growled. He had to be inside her now. The need to fuck her was so strong he was shaking as he pinned her arms above her head with one hand and guided his cock to her entrance with his other. He pressed against her opening, sucking in a breath as the tip slid into the tight clench of her channel. He strained to go slow, working himself in by degrees. He gave a few experimental thrusts, short and shallow, giving her time to adjust to the way he stretched her.

She whimpered, her hands above her head flexing and clenching. "More."

He slid in an inch further, her heat clasped around his length and sparks shooting down his spine in the telltale sign of an impending orgasm. He fought against it, determined not to come before he was even all the way inside her.

"Noah," she breathed, "please."

"What do you need, love?" He dragged her earlobe between his teeth, nearly losing all ability to think when her pussy contracted around him in response.

"I need you deep." She strained against his hold on her hands, arching her back to get closer.

He crushed his mouth to hers and drove into her, burying himself to the hilt. She gasped into the kiss and he swallowed the sound, focusing on kissing her and not on the impossible heat, the mind-bending clutch of her pussy.

"Fuck, you feel so good," he groaned into her neck.

"So do you."

He was lost to her. Nothing existed outside of this moment, this woman, this sense that it was always supposed to be like this. He released her hands, tangling one hand in her hair and returning the other to her breast. How had he gone so many years without knowing the feel of her? Like she was inside him as much as he was inside her, like she was below and above and all around him. How had he never known that sex could be like this, more than just flesh meeting flesh? That it could turn his entire being into nothing but nerve endings, at once raw and soothed, body and breath and this feeling like he was drunk on her—on *them*.

Callie rolled them so she was on top, her thighs on either side of his hips, and began to move in rhythmic undulations. He watched in awe as she rode him, mesmerized by the swing of her breasts, the flush in her cheeks. Noah sat up beneath her, unable to keep his lips from her skin. Glancing over her shoulder, he caught sight of their reflection in the mirror opposite the bed and drew in a harsh breath.

"What is it?" she asked.

He watched in the mirror as she rode him, that jeweled plug winking in and out of view between her cheeks. "Look at you," he breathed, mesmerized by the image.

Callie glanced over her shoulder, her breath hitching when she saw their reflection. When she turned back to him, her smile was so bright it nearly knocked him flat. He wanted to make her smile that way all the time—forever. The word ripped through him, his chest tightening, and he waited for the panic to hit. But it didn't.

She swung off of him and he couldn't help the huffed breath of protest at the loss of her. She guided him to sit at the edge of the bed, and when she had arranged him exactly as she wanted, she turned so her back was to his front and sank back down onto his lap, impaling herself once again on his cock. He dropped his head to her shoulder, overcome by the sensation of being taken inside her at this new angle.

"Look at *us*," she said as she rode him, reaching back to wrap a hand behind his neck.

Together they watched themselves in the mirror, each lift of his hips sending shockwaves through her soft flesh, treating him to a delicious view of her breasts and hips. It was obscene and he never wanted to look away. He skated a hand over her belly, making a V with his fingers to pull back her puffy lower lips, more fully revealing the place where he disappeared inside her body.

"You take my cock so well," he crooned into her ear. "Look at how you open for me."

Her head fell back against his shoulder, but that wouldn't do. He needed her to see how well they fit together, needed her to acknowledge that they were a perfect match. He needed to know if she was as affected by this knowledge as he was.

"Watch, sweet girl. Watch my cock stretch your pussy."

She moaned, but lifted her head to watch with him.

Her breathing came faster and the intermittent fluttering around his cock gave away that she was close. He stroked a finger over her clit, cursing when she contracted around him in response.

"Oh God. I'm gonna come," she breathed, bouncing in time with the movements of his finger on her clit.

"That's right. Come for me. I want you to watch yourself come on my cock." She cursed and bounced faster. He drove into her harder as he chased his own release. Her thighs began to shake, her eyes closing. "Watch," he commanded through gritted teeth as his rhythm became erratic.

The first clench of her orgasm was like a vise, squeezing him so impossibly hard he could hardly move. As the waves of her climax rolled through her, he gave himself over to his own, his cock jerking as he pumped into her. She slammed her hips down onto him, crying out his name as she milked him dry. Through it all, they held each other's gaze in the mirror, watching as they were overtaken with pleasure.

The last pulses of their orgasms subsided and she leaned

back against his chest, skin misted with sweat, thighs sticky with cum. He wrapped his arms around her and pulled her down onto the bed beside him. He gently removed the plug from her ass, a contented sigh escaping her lips. She rolled into his arms, her head pressed to his chest and their legs tangling.

He knew they should wash up, but he closed his eyes and ran his fingers through her hair instead, clutching her against him. His heart raced and his skin buzzed and he couldn't reconcile the feeling of being split open, all raw sinew and tender skin, with the sense of rightness that pounded through his blood. Like all those vulnerable places that she'd torn open needed to be broken apart, like scar tissue, before they could be mended. Like being with her was stitching him together in ways he hadn't known he needed.

Callie turned her head and planted a soft kiss to the center of his chest before nuzzling against him again and drifting off to sleep. His throat was too tight, his mind a tangle of fuzzy afterglow that insisted he tell her that he wanted more than the next few days—he wanted everything. Even in his sex drunk haze he knew better than to make promises he was in no position to keep, so he gathered her closer and breathed in the citrus and rain scent of her, grounding himself with the feel of her skin against his as he gave himself over to sleep as well.

Chapter Twenty-one

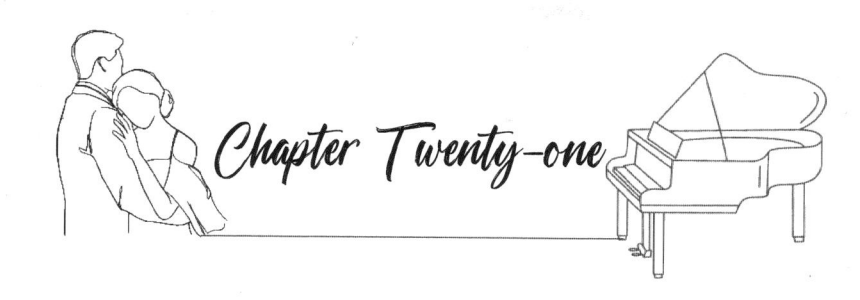

"Calico."

She woke to the sandpaper slide of Noah's stubble as he planted kisses on her neck and shoulders. But she didn't want to wake up. She wanted more time. She wriggled back against him, pulling his arms tighter around her and grumbled in protest.

He laughed, his breath hot on her skin. "It's time to get up, love. Liv will be expecting you soon for whatever primping women do before a wedding."

She chuckled. "Feminine secrets. I'd be excommunicated for telling."

He tickled her side, sending an unexpected jolt through her and she yelped in surprise. "No secrets," he said in her ear.

She turned in his arms, wrapping her own around him and holding him close, their legs tangling. She didn't want any secrets from him—imagined or otherwise.

"I owe you an apology," she said.

His eyes widened in surprise. "For what?"

Why is this so hard? She tucked her head beneath his chin, burrowing into the cocoon of his arms as she spoke into his chest.

"For ghosting you after my twenty-first birthday party." He went rigid in her arms, unnaturally still, but she pressed on. "I never told you what happened."

"I know what happened." She looked up at him, wondering what exactly he thought he knew. He met her gaze, his brow drawing low, highlighting the crinkles at the edge of his eyes. "Your mom told me."

It was her turn to be surprised. "My mom?"

"At the hospital."

She pulled away, needing to see his face, because what he'd just said made no sense. "You—the hospital?"

He took a deep breath, his jaw clenching. "Liv called me when you were admitted."

She closed her eyes. Of course, Liv would have called him. Liv had been halfway across the country at the time, unable to come herself, so she'd sent her big brother to take care of her best friend. It made perfect sense, except...

"You never visited me in the hospital."

He rolled away from her, sitting up on the bed and running his hands through his hair. She gathered the blanket around herself against the sudden chill.

"Liv called and I went straight to the hospital. I don't think I even said goodbye to her before I hung up. They wouldn't let me in to see you because I wasn't family. Best friend's older brother doesn't count apparently," he said with a sad smile. She reached for him, pressing her palm to his face. He held his own hand over hers, keeping her touch against his cheek. "Your mom found me arguing with a nurse in the lobby. When she told me what happened—" He closed his eyes. "It was my fault, Callie."

"What are you talking about?"

He pulled her hand away from his face, holding it in his lap and focusing his attention there. "Your mom said you were sick. Really sick. That they didn't know what was wrong yet, but that it likely started because you'd had too much to drink. If I'd done a better job of looking after you, if I hadn't kept buying you rounds—"

"Noah, look at me."

He shook his head, focusing on her hand. She scooted closer to him, until their knees were touching. Her stomach twisted in a knot of nausea.

"It wasn't your fault. I didn't get fibromyalgia because I had too much to drink. My mother—" She blinked back the stinging in her nose, the anger rising like bile at the back of her throat. "She was wrong."

With a shuddering breath, he finally raised glassy eyes to meet her gaze and her heart swelled. All these years he'd thought he'd caused her illness? All these years he'd stayed away...

"Shit, Noah, even a Google search could tell you that you don't get fibro from drinking."

He chuckled then, but there was no humor in it. "Would you believe me if I told you I never looked it up?"

"Oh." She stared at him, trying to reconcile this information with the Noah she knew. He was meticulous, knew every rule, left no stone unturned. He hadn't even bothered to look up her diagnosis? Had he cared so little about her?

His mouth twisted in disgust. "Liv told me how much pain you were in. I knew that if I started looking into it, I wouldn't be able to stop until I knew all the details. I couldn't handle knowing the details and not being able to help."

Oh. It wasn't that he'd cared too little. It was that he'd cared too much?

"It was pretty clear you weren't going to answer my calls, so it seemed unlikely that you were even going to tell me what happened. I figured you'd changed your mind about us."

"No," she said, squeezing his hand. "I never changed my mind." She needed him to know it all, to understand all the things she'd never been able to tell him before. "The morning after that party was the first time I couldn't feel my legs." He sucked in a breath, but she continued on. If she stopped now, she'd never get it all out. "It came and went, but it scared me enough that I went back to my mom's for the rest of the weekend. I'd forgotten she was out of town. By the time I got back to Jersey, my back had started to seize up. I thought I'd pinched a nerve, that I could sleep it off. When you called—"

"I don't care about the phone calls," he said, his voice tortured.

"I do. When you called, I was afraid that if I answered I'd ask you to come help me."

"I wish you had." He leaned his forehead against hers and gripped the back of her neck like he needed to reassure himself she was there. "I would have come."

"I know. But I didn't want you to." He recoiled, hurt flashing in his eyes. "I didn't want you to have to be my big brother. I wanted you to be the guy I was falling for, and that wasn't someone I wanted to see me like that."

He took her face in his hands, pressing a kiss to her lips. "I hate that you were alone."

"I should have answered. I'm sorry."

"I should have known something was wrong when you didn't answer. I should have come looking for you."

"You did," she said, still trying to reconcile everything she thought she knew about the last six years with the knowledge that he had gone to the hospital.

"Not soon enough."

She chuckled through the tears clogging her throat. "What? You should have searched the tristate area because I declined a few calls?"

"Yes," he growled. "I should have been there."

"Overbearing," she whispered, the ghost of a smile on her lips.

"What happened next?"

She shrugged, the story still sending a shiver of embarrassment through her even after all this time. "I waited too long to get help. By the time my mom got home, I needed to go to the hospital. I was dehydrated and over the counter painkillers weren't helping anymore. They ran a million tests, but no one knew what was wrong. So, they kept me for a couple of days, got my pain under control, and then sent me home. The doctors couldn't tell me what it was for another six months. There is no test for fibromyalgia, and no cure. Just ways to manage the symptoms."

"Your mom said—"

"My mother was wrong. There was no one thing that brought on that flare, Noah. My doctors think it was a perfect storm. You probably don't remember, but I was in a car accident earlier in the year."

"I remember."

"That's when the pain started, but I just thought it was left over from the crash. And I didn't make time for physical therapy—I was overscheduled and barely sleeping as it was. They're not really sure what causes fibromyalgia, but some of it may be genetic, and any kind of physical trauma or stress can bring on the first flare. I'm sure having too much to drink at that party didn't help, but neither did the intense cardio class I took that morning. Or the stress of taking too many classes and working part time. You did not do this to me. No one did this to me. It just…is."

Noah pulled her against his chest, holding her tighter than was comfortable. She nestled her head beneath his chin and breathed in his sage and leather scent, planting a kiss on the dip in his clavicle.

"I'm sorry I wasn't there," he whispered into her hair.

"I'm sorry I didn't let you be."

Noah hadn't intended to shower with Callie that morning—she needed to get to the bridal suite to get ready for the wedding and he needed to spend some time going over his new score sketches before he met his uncle and Wolf for brunch—but as he stood at the vanity brushing his teeth, she climbed into the shower with a saucy glance over her shoulder. "Don't wiggle your ass at me," he said around his toothbrush.

"You love it," she laughed.

And he did. He loved everything about her.

Fuck. I love her.

How the hell had he let that happen? He waited for the twist in his gut and the feeling like he had ants crawling all over his skin to demand that he sprint from the room and never again think about doing something as reckless as loving this woman. This woman with her novelty purses and incessant humming, her tarot cards and a smile like spring. He waited for the dread to come as he watched her in the mirror and rinsed the toothpaste from his mouth, finding instead a warm glow spreading in his chest, like Christmas morning in front of the fire, or a hot shower on a cold morning. How had he lived thirty-five years without knowing about the glow?

She turned on the shower, the spray splashing over her skin. "Join me?"

He stripped so quickly he nearly fell over getting out of his pants, but he didn't care—her laughter was intoxicating. He'd make a fool of himself again and again if it made her smile. He stood behind her, doing his best to keep his growing erection from poking her in the back. They didn't have time to fuck, not that his dick gave a shit about schedules.

When she reached for her shampoo, he stilled her hand. "Can I?" he asked, waiting for the moment she'd bristle, tell him she could take care of herself. She glanced at him with a shy nod, tilting her head back towards him and the glow in his chest grew.

He took his time, massaging the shampoo through her silken tresses, carefully rinsing every trace of suds from her hair. It was one of the most erotic moments of his life—topped only by when he'd shaved her legs a few days earlier, but he hadn't known he'd loved her then, even if he suspected he had. Funny how that tiny word made everything look different.

The last of the soap swirled down the drain and she leaned back against his chest, the ripe peach of her ass pressing deliciously against his groin as they stood under the shower's spray. He wrapped his arms around her, banding them across her waist just high enough that his thumb could sweep along the underside of her breast. She sighed happily, wriggling against him. His cock kicked at the friction.

He nipped her earlobe in warning. "If you keep that up, you're going to make us both late."

"Promise?"

He groaned into her neck, breathing her in as he dropped one hand between her thighs. She made room for him immediately, releasing another one of those happy sighs when his fingers skated over her swollen folds.

He hesitated, keeping his touch light. "You'd tell me if you needed me to stop, right? If you were too sore?"

She pressed her own hand over his to keep his touch between her legs, reaching back to cup his neck with her other. "I would tell you," she promised. The pressure in his chest relaxed. He trailed his lips over the column of her throat, admiring the long line of her body, all softness and curves. "Can I tell you a secret?"

"Anything." He drew lazy circles around her clit, angling himself behind her so his cock was cradled by her ass. He rocked against her experimentally, fire shooting down his spine when she ground back against him.

"Orgasms help."

"Now I know you're just telling me what I want to hear," he chuckled, increasing the pressure on that little bud of bliss.

"It's true. Releases endorphins, which are natural pain killers."

"Calico, are you telling me that the best way to help you when you're in pain is to fuck you?"

"Not exactly." She laughed, a breathless sound that went straight to his cock. "If I'm in a lot of pain, it won't help and the exertion could make things worse. But if it's mild—just soreness, a headache—God, that feels good." She broke off, dropping her head back against his shoulder, moving her hips so they rocked against both his hand at her clit and his cock between her cheeks.

She was so fucking perfect. How had ever thought he could have her in his bed and not fall in love with her? The idea seemed insane to him now.

"If it's mild...?" he prompted, dipping two fingers inside her, fucking her slowly with his fingers.

"Why do you think I own so many sex toys?" she asked with a laugh.

"You don't have that many." He added a third finger, pumping faster now, loving the way she moved beneath his touch, how responsive she was.

"You haven't seen my full collection."

"Hmm. Will you show me sometime?" He rocked his pelvis against her harder and imagined what other toys she might have, all the ways he would use them to make her feel good.

"Yes," she gasped.

"Are you close, love?" He knew the answer—her pussy was contracting around his fingers, her hips moving faster as she chased her release—but he wanted to hear her say it.

"Yes. Noah, please."

"Please what?" he asked, biting her shoulder gently.

"Please fuck me." She reached behind herself, digging her nails into his thigh and bending forward at the waist, offering herself to him. "I need your cock inside me."

He cursed, pulling away from her just long enough to line up the swollen head of his cock with her entrance. He moved his fingers to her clit as he plunged himself into her heat, cursing as he filled her. At this angle, she was unbelievably tight.

"Fuck, that's good," she groaned.

He pumped into her. The wet slap of their hips meeting resounded in the shower as he worked her clit harder. Her thighs shook, her ass quivering against him as he fucked her, and white spots danced in front of his eyes as he neared his own orgasm.

"Please make me come," she begged. He grinned,

working her harder, rubbing her clit exactly the way she liked. "Come with me. Oh, God, please."

Her legs shook and her breath shuddered as her climax moved through her. He held her tighter, savoring the feel of her trembling in his arms. A second later he followed her over the edge, lightning flying along his nerve endings as he pumped his release into her. He bit back the three words that pounded through his blood and threatened to break loose, instead roaring her name as he gave himself over to the pleasure.

He came back to himself slowly, those unspoken words echoing in his head as he washed his cum from between her legs and wrapped her in a fluffy towel. She hesitated in the doorway to their bedroom, her eyes narrowing as she searched his face. "Noah..."

"Yeah?" *Say it,* he silently begged. *Say you feel it too.*

The tension in her eyes melted away, replaced by a little smirk he wanted to kiss off her face. "Totally worth being late."

He smiled back, tamping down the disappointment. What had he expected? He'd explicitly told her they had no future—a few days and nothing more. Even if she felt the way he did, could he really expect her to say it? Not when he was the one who had put a deadline on their arrangement. If someone was going to say it first, it would have to be him.

He swallowed around the lump in his throat. "You better go before I get ideas about round two."

She laughed, dropping her towel as she disappeared into the bedroom, leaving him with the image of her plump ass as she walked away. *I love you*, he whispered in his head.

He would tell her for real. Just not yet. Not with the smell of their sex hanging in the air, and not on Liv's wedding day.

When we get back to New York. I'll tell her when we get home.

Chapter Twenty-two

Wolf MacMillan was a mountain of a man—tall, broad-shouldered, barrel-chested with a carefully styled shock of silver hair. When Noah was a boy and Wolf would visit his father, he always had peppermint hard candies in the pockets of his ubiquitous blazers. "So he can freshen his breath before he meets important people," his father had told him. Wolf had worked with former presidents, celebrities doing work for the UN, heads of major international organizations—and if he hadn't worked with them, he'd likely sat next to them at a dinner party somewhere along the line. Noah had always loved Wolf's stories—which actress insisted on sparkling water even when she visited war-torn parts of the world to deliver rice and baby formula, which Hollywood bigwig had testified in front of Congress with lipstick still on his collar from his State House bathroom tryst with a Senate intern, which former first lady made the best Sunday dinner (and who didn't even know how to turn on the oven).

That morning, sitting across the small table tucked in the corner of The Barclay's restaurant, was the first time Noah wasn't completely delighted to see his father's childhood friend. Despite the delicious meal they'd just shared, he could still taste the bitter resentment at the back of his tongue at having to prove his character to this man who had been there to witness the first time he rode a bicycle without training wheels. As if their lifelong acquaintance wasn't sufficient. As if his music didn't stand on its own merits.

"Your uncle tells me you've got yourself a girl," Wolf said with a glance at Uncle Stu.

Noah hated that phrase. It implied Callie was an item on a grocery list, something to acquire and not someone to win, someone to cherish. He took a sip of his coffee and nodded tightly. "She's the maid of honor. You'll meet her at the wedding."

Wolf raised a snowy eyebrow. "Is it serious?"

He nodded, swallowing around the realization that, for the first time, it wasn't a lie. He was serious about Callie, even if she didn't know it yet. "Yes, sir. She's...everything."

The suspicion cleared from Wolf's face, replaced by something that might be relief. "Excellent news. I'm glad to hear it. So, there will be no more newspaper articles."

Noah wasn't sure if it was a question or a command.

"Student newspaper," he corrected. "And while you should know better than anyone that you can't control the press—" Wolf chuckled "—I doubt my students will find my love life newsworthy."

"Good. We can't have anyone associated with the project who might cause trouble for the senator. She has too many important causes to discuss to have the damn vultures circling because of her staff's indiscretions."

"Is the documentary's composer considered part of the senator's staff?" Noah asked.

Wolf laughed, sharing a look with his uncle that spoke volumes about how naïve Noah's question had been. "Yes.

Undeniable

The senator has hired me to do a job for her, so anyone I hire is, by extension, working for her as well." Noah nodded. "Your girl understands you'll need to be on the road with us for three months at minimum?"

"At minimum?" Noah glanced between Wolf and his uncle. "I was under the impression that filming wrapped after the election, and I'd be completing my work from my studio in New York."

"If she loses. But if she's re-elected, we'll follow her through her first ninety-days in office."

Ninety days? That would be six months all together. His mind rebelled at the idea. Three months had felt doable, though he knew it would be hard—but six months? Could he really ask Callie to wait for him for six months? And what if he went away for half a year only to return and find the passion between them had cooled? They were just getting started, just discovering this new facet to their relationship. He'd be leaving before they'd even scratched the surface.

"I wasn't aware the outcome of the election could alter the timeline," he said slowly, hoping the practiced calm of his voice hid the nausea building in his gut and the sudden need to find Callie and hold her.

"Is that a problem?" Wolf asked, narrowing his eyes.

"I only submitted for a one-semester sabbatical," Noah replied, grasping at straws. "I don't have the seniority yet to take a whole year off."

Wolf waved away the objection. "I'm sure Stu can pull some strings. Think of the good press for the university when one of their own is associated with such a high-profile film."

Uncle Stu nodded. "It won't be a problem."

Noah considered his uncle. The man had always been a

force in Noah's life, even before his father died. He'd been the one to teach him the importance of following the rules, had ingrained the lesson to always play by the book deep into Noah's psyche before he even understood that there were others who thrived by coloring outside the lines. Yet at a word from Wolf, he would bend his beloved rules.

"That's settled then," Wolf said, setting down his coffee cup with more force than was necessary. "You'll need to compose most of the score as we film so we can keep to a tight post-production schedule. It's very important that the music capture the energy of the senator's campaign, the electricity in the room, as it were. But play me these new pieces you've been working on."

Noah agreed and made his way to the piano in the corner of the room, thankful for the bit of physical distance. He took his seat on the bench, lifted the lid from the keys, and dug in his bag for the pad of manuscript paper containing his latest sketches. Snippets of melodies that felt vaguely presidential or inspirational. Melodies designed to rouse pride and patriotism. He flipped through the pad, pausing when he found the loose sheet tucked amongst the pages containing his latest notation of one of Callie's songs. A melody so fraught with longing that if he closed his eyes he could picture the color of it, the texture of the orchestration.

"Everything alright?" Uncle Stu called, the unquestioned authority of his voice dashing away the image in Noah's mind.

He placed his manuscript paper on the piano and began playing. The theme was technically flawless and, when fully orchestrated with brass and percussion sections, would underscore Senator Thorne's leadership. He'd watched hours of YouTube videos of her speeches, learning the rhythm of her delivery, the inflection in her tone, and he'd written a theme that called upon the deeply ingrained

Undeniable

"American sound" honed by Copland while also matching her rhetorical style. When played beneath footage of one of her campaign stops, it would highlight the areas she naturally emphasized when speaking.

Noah was proud of the work, knew that it was fit for textbook analysis, and yet the music left him cold. He longed to turn the page and instead play Callie's piece, a melody that grabbed you by the throat and twisted in your gut—the kind of song that, even if you forgot the exact notes, you always remembered how it made you feel. Once upon a time Noah had written songs like that. He'd even written them with Callie, side by side at the piano in his mother's living room, improvising songs as he taught her the emotion of each chord, the shape and flavor of them. What he wouldn't give to write like that again.

Wolf gave an approving nod as Noah's hands fell away from the keys. "We'll finalize your security credentials right away. You should have clearance within a few days. Then we'll fly you out and the real fun will begin."

Noah knew he should say something, express gratitude or ask follow-up questions, but his mouth had gone dry and he couldn't form the words. It was all moving too fast. He couldn't leave Callie in a few days—*but that was the plan all along.*

Uncle Stu laughed, the sound a bit too forced to be jovial. "You've rendered the boy speechless."

Wolf chuckled skeptically. "If you'll excuse me, I'll go get the ball rolling. I'll see you both at this shindig in a few hours."

Noah watched Wolf leave the room, his mouth opening and closing uselessly as he thought of all the reasons he could give for not taking the job, not moving across the country for six months. Who would water his houseplants and bring in his mail? Who would teach his classes, coach his students? Who would clean out his mother's gutters? Would he have to miss Liv's opening night on Broadway? And what if Callie had a flare up and needed him? What if he needed her?

"Congratulations," Uncle Stu said, suddenly at his side.

A jolt of horror punched Noah in the stomach. "Uncle Stu—"

The older man held up a hand, shaking his head. "Sleep on it. You don't want to make a rash decision here, son. If the senator is re-elected, this documentary will be everywhere. Don't throw away this opportunity because of some woman."

"She's not *some woman.*"

"Humor me. Give it a day or two to settle." Uncle Stu clapped him on the back. "Now get out of here. I'm sure you're wanted elsewhere."

Noah deposited his things in his hotel room and retrieved his suit from the closet. He resolved to put the job out of his mind. Liv was getting married in just a few hours—that was where his focus needed to be.

The other groomsmen were already in Jamie's hotel room, which had been turned into Daemon's headquarters for the day, a half-empty bottle of whiskey on the table in the corner. Daemon and Patti sat in armchairs in one corner of the room, while Jamie and Liam sat on the edge of the bed. A cheer went up when Noah entered the room.

"What'd I miss?" he asked.

Liam thrust a plastic cup of amber-colored liquor into his hands. "You've got some catching up to do."

Noah took an overlarge sip, wincing against the burn of it down his throat. As the heat settled in his belly, his shoulders relaxed, tension melting from his limbs.

"Did you get the job?" Liam asked at his side, his voice low.

Undeniable

Noah focused on the whiskey in his cup, avoiding Liam's eyes. "Yeah. I got it."

"What are you whispering about over there?" Jamie called from his place sprawled against the headboard of the king-size bed.

"I got offered a job," Noah said, the words burning as much as the alcohol had.

"Congratulations!" Pattie said, raising her glass in toast.

"What's the catch?" Daemon asked, his eyes narrowing.

"No catch. It's a good job."

Daemon huffed out a laugh. "You're as bad of a liar as your sister." Noah locked eyes with his brother-in-law-to-be, who seemed to consider him for a beat too long, his brow drawn low.

"Alright, boys, that's our cue," Pattie said, getting to her feet. "Jamie and Liam, come help me find something decent to eat so we can soak up all this whiskey before we stumble down the aisle."

"I know just the place," Jamie said, sliding on his shoes. "The diner down the road makes great burgers."

Liam shot Noah a questioning glance, but he gave him a quick nod. If his brother-in-law wanted a minute alone, that was fine by him. Pattie followed Liam and Jamie from the room, throwing a wink at Daemon and Noah before closing the door behind them.

"What's the catch?" Daemon repeated when they were alone.

"Three months on the road. Maybe six." Noah sank onto the chair opposite Daemon. "How did you do it? The whole long-distance thing?"

Daemon took a slow sip of his drink, his eyes surveying Noah as if he were trying to decipher some riddle scrawled on his face. "It's not easy," he said at last. "You've got to make

245

phone calls a priority. Texting when there's no other option. Liv and I made a deal to never go more than two weeks without seeing each other, even if it was only for twenty-four hours. It's a lot of red eye flights and never knowing where you left your toothbrush. But it beats the alternative."

Noah took another sip. Would he fly back and forth every two weeks to see Callie? In a heartbeat. Daemon was right; it beat the alternative, but it still wouldn't be enough. He still couldn't guarantee he'd be there if she had a flare up.

"You want my advice?" Daemon asked. "Don't do it if you don't have to. I've seen the distance break more couples than I can count. You and Callie are the real deal."

"We haven't been together that long," Noah said, not entirely sure why he was fighting Daemon on that particular point.

"You two have been dancing around each other for as long as I've known you." Noah's eyes snapped to Daemon's, who grinned like Noah's shock was amusing. "The first Christmas I spent with your family, at the cabin in the Berkshires, I told Liv that you and Callie were going to end up together."

Noah remembered that trip—the way Callie's cheeks had turned red when they went sledding, how she emptied half a bag of marshmallows in each cup of hot chocolate, the nights he barely slept knowing she was just on the other side of the wall from him.

Daemon shrugged. "Even then it was obvious. You love her."

It wasn't a question and somehow having Daemon say it like that, like it was fact, plain and simple, untangled a few of the knots in Noah's stomach. He nodded.

"Then you'll figure it out."

Chapter Twenty-three

The feminine secret about primping before a wedding? It was a lot of sitting around and waiting. And mimosas. Lots of mimosas.

The hair stylist arrived with hot gossip about Raine Winters, a pop star Daemon briefly had a fling with a few years back—before he met Liv—and her bridezilla demands for her wedding to former boy band member Hunter Keating. Apparently, the stylist was a devoted fan of the reality TV show documenting the couple's road to the altar, and she delighted in sharing the details as Liv, Min, and Callie sipped their drinks.

"Aren't you going to that wedding?" Callie asked. The stylist's hands paused for a fraction of a section, her eyes going wide before she got herself back under control and slid another bobby pin into place.

Liv shrugged. "We're not sure yet. It's one of the things our managers are trying to negotiate with the new production, but they're not super willing to give both of their leads a weekend off only a month after opening."

"Wouldn't it be weird to go to your husband's ex-girlfriend's wedding?" Min asked.

"Nah. Despite her public persona, Raine's a total sweetheart and she and Daem didn't even really date. Besides, it was a million years ago. We met Raine and Hunter for drinks while we were in London. Speaking of which," Liv said, holding out her empty champagne flute with a little shimmy.

Callie shook her head and refilled Liv's glass with yet another mimosa. Callie was still working on her first glass of plain orange juice and had already lost count of how many of the bubbly drinks Liv had knocked back. By the time the hair stylist finished Liv's elaborate updo and said goodbye, the bride was well on her way to tipsy.

"I'm getting married today!" she squealed for at least the third time.

Callie laughed, clinking her glass against Liv's. "You better slow down, babe, if you don't want to be sloppy when you walk down the aisle."

"Fine, *Mom*," Liv said with an exaggerated eye roll, unable to hide her smile.

"Speaking of—how did you manage to finagle a mother-free morning?" Callie asked.

"I sent them for massages. Lord knows they both need to chill out."

"Genius."

"What should we do until the makeup artist gets here?" Liv asked.

"What about a tarot reading?" Min suggested.

"I don't know. Isn't that bad luck, like tempting fate or something to get a reading on your wedding day? What if it says something awful?" Liv asked, moving to the small grouping of sofas in the corner of the bridal suite and taking a seat opposite Callie.

"First off, it wouldn't say anything awful. The cards have

been giving nothing but green lights since before you were even dating," Callie said, ticking her points off on her fingers as she went. "Second of all, even if for some insane reason they did say something not great, do you really think I'd tell you? On your wedding day?"

Liv gasped theatrically. "You'd lie to me about what the cards say?"

"A maid of honor does what she has to do. But third of all, I don't think you need the cards today. You know Daemon is your guy."

"I do."

"And you want to live happily ever after and have lots of hot sex and adorable babies."

"I do want that. At least the first part. Not one hundred percent sold on the tiny humans part yet."

Callie smiled. "Then you don't need a reading. You make your own fate, babe."

Liv grinned, a twinkle of mischief in her eye. "Then we're agreed. No reading for me. Just one for you."

"Why would I need a reading?"

"Because something's different." Liv cocked her head to the side and narrowed her eyes as she examined Callie. "Shit. My brother didn't propose last night, did he?"

Callie nearly choked on her own tongue. "No!"

"Oh my God, he did!" Liv sat up on her knees, her eyes wide. "I guess at least he didn't do it at the reception."

Min glanced between the two of them, like she was watching a train go off the tracks and wasn't sure how to help. "I don't think Noah would do that."

"He didn't. He absolutely did not propose."

Liv sank back down onto the couch. "Then what is it? Is it a sex thing?" she asked, wrinkling her nose. "I know we tell each other everything, but if my brother does some weird sex thing, I do not want to know."

"There's no weird sex thing!" She should have had a mimosa after all.

"Maybe Callie doesn't want to talk about it," Min offered.

"If he fucked it up already, I'll kill him." Liv pounded a fist into her hand in a way that Callie was sure her friend had meant to appear threatening but was really just comical.

Callie laughed. "Will you let me talk? He didn't fuck anything up."

"Then what is it?" Min asked.

Callie looked between her friends. If she could find a way to talk about the tangle of dread and elation in her gut, would she be able to make sense of it all? "It's... complicated."

"Men always are," Min said as she deftly swapped Liv's mimosa for a champagne flute of plain orange juice.

"I guess I'm just nervous."

"About?" Liv prompted.

"What if he goes on the road with this documentary and...forgets about me?" She winced, hating how needy she sounded.

Liv held out her arms to Callie, gesturing for her to sit next to her on the couch. Callie joined her best friend and let Liv pull her against her side into a hug, Liv's head resting on top of Callie's. "He's not going to forget about you. He's finally gotten his head out of his own ass long enough to realize how much he cares about you. That doesn't go away because of a little distance. Trust me."

"Long distance is hard. And Noah's never wanted any kind of relationship before," Callie continued.

"So what? He wants one now, and when Noah decides he's doing something, he doesn't hold back. Remember that summer he thought frosted tips were cool?"

Callie barked out a laugh. "Oh, God, I almost forgot about that. To be fair, frosted tips were cool back then."

Liv shot her a skeptical look. "For a hot second. The point is, Noah goes all in once he's made up his mind to do something. And he's decided he's doing you… Shit. Not like that. I mean, maybe like that? I think I've had too much to drink," Liv groaned, dissolving into giggles.

"What I think Liv is trying to say is, Noah might be new to committing to relationships, but he's not new to committing to the things he cares about, including questionable hair styles, apparently. And he very clearly cares about you," Min clarified.

Callie squeezed Min's hand. It wasn't hard to see why Liam had fallen for Min, or how she'd so easily become a part of their extended family.

"Should we ask the cards?" Liv asked.

As much as Callie wanted to refuse, she knew she'd feel better after a reading. *Unless they say something you don't want to know.* She dug her deck out of her bag and began to shuffle, letting the repetitive motion settle her stomach, and focused her thoughts on Noah. Her eyes drifted closed as she shuffled, an image of him coming to mind, mischief and heat in his eyes as he'd climbed into the shower after her that morning. She flipped the first card.

Ace of wands.

Liv stifled a laugh. "That's clearly a penis, right?"

Callie grinned, seeing the familiar image of a single wooden staff through her friend's eyes. It was the most phallic card in the deck. "In some interpretations it signifies sex. But in others it's about new beginnings and creativity."

She flipped the second card, frowning at the image of the blindfolded woman: two of swords.

"It *is* a kinky sex thing!" Liv exclaimed triumphantly, her finger stabbing at the card. "Swords crossing!"

"That's your brother you're talking about," Min reminded her.

"It's not a sex thing." Callie's serious tone seemed to calm Min and Liv's laughter. "It's a stalemate. Confusion and indecision."

"Well, that makes sense. You're confused," Min said, but even Callie could tell that Min didn't really believe her own reassurance.

"One more," Liv said, urging Callie to flip the final card.

The Tower. Callie drew in a sharp breath and Min winced at the picture of a crumbling turret, people plunging from it into a lightning storm.

"Now hold on," Liv said, sounding more sober than she had all morning. "I've gotten this one before and you said it's not always bad. Something about big changes, right?"

Callie forced herself to breathe. "That's true. The Tower means your life is going to change dramatically, but it doesn't indicate whether that change is good or bad."

"Okay," Min said, ever the peacemaker. "So, you're having lots of sex—kinky or otherwise—and now you're confused, and your life is going to change. That's not a terrible reading."

"Not a great one either," Callie said.

"I think it is," Liv insisted. "This doesn't tell you anything you didn't already know. Just that there are big decisions to be made."

Callie gathered the cards, securing them with their rubber band and returning them to her bag. She knew her friends were right; there was nothing inherently negative about the reading. But she couldn't help the niggling suspicion that the big decisions about to change her life weren't going to be hers to make.

Chapter Twenty-four

Liv was a beautiful bride, as Callie had known she would be. It was true what people said: happiness could make a woman glow. Callie wondered if she was glowing, too, when she locked eyes with Noah across the aisle at the ceremony. He was always handsome, but his green tie made his eyes seem even more verdant than usual. His hair had been combed back so not a strand was out of place. She itched to run her fingers through it and muss him up just a bit. When he looked at her, his gaze running appreciatively over the length of the slinky emerald bridesmaid dress clinging to her curves, she thought she might float away from the sheer joy of it.

She wasn't sure when it had stopped being pretend, but somewhere along the way, their lie had become the truth. It was a heady thing to finally have the affection of the one person she'd always wanted, and to realize it was so much more than she could have imagined. She'd loved Noah her whole life, but she'd had no idea how being *in love* with him would color everything around her. And she was nearly certain he loved her, too. She'd even thought for a moment that morning that he might say so.

Still, as she watched him bow his head, caught the purse of his lips as he fought not to cry while Pattie crooned *Not While I'm Around* to the assembled guests—it had been Liv and Noah's father's favorite song—she couldn't help but think of the Tower. Sondheim's lyrics rang out across the lush lawn of The Barclay and Callie wondered when the lightning would strike.

That question niggled at the back of her mind as she took Noah's arm and processed back down the aisle at the end of the ceremony. They reached the small room of The Barclay where the bridal party was assembling before the reception, and Callie pulled him into her arms.

"I've got you," she murmured against his temple, threading her fingers through his hair, as much to comfort him as to reassure herself. She had him...but could she keep him?

He tucked his face into her neck and wrapped his arms tighter around her.

"I've got you," she repeated.

"I know."

Most of the reception was a blur, but Noah held her hand through it all: through every toast and passed hors d'oeuvre, and especially when yet another family member he hadn't seen in ages commented on how much he looked like his father.

"Noah!" Uncle Stu bellowed, beckoning Noah over to where he and Wolf stood at the bar at the edge of the tent.

"I'll be right back," Noah said, squeezing Callie's hand and leaving her as he went to the two men. She felt the loss of his hand as though all the warmth of that August night left with him.

Her mother's voice at her side startled her. "I owe you an apology."

Undeniable

"That would be a first," she said. "What for?"

"He clearly cares about you very much," she said, tilting her chin towards Noah, where he stood sharing a drink with his uncle and Wolf. The men were all smiling, Wolf shaking Noah's hand. *He got the job.* Pride burst in her chest, a smile spreading across her lips.

"I think he does."

"I shouldn't have implied... I'm still concerned that he's not ready to settle down, but..." Something in her mother's voice, a hesitation she couldn't ever remember hearing from her mother, pulled Callie's attention back to their conversation. "I've made an appointment with a realtor. Just to talk. I'm not sure I'm ready to move, but...maybe it's time."

Callie should have been elated. This was what she wanted. As she watched Noah celebrating his new position, one that would take him across the country for the next several months—and would surely lead to even more opportunities that would take him even farther away—she couldn't help but feel lonely, though. For all the times she and her mother didn't see eye-to-eye, there was no denying that she had been the regular fixture in Callie's life, and she would miss her when she left. But she also refused to be the reason her mother didn't find her own happiness. Her mother had talked about moving back to Ohio to live near Aunt Shirley since Callie was a little girl. Despite her own growing sense of loss, she was so happy that her mother was finally doing something for herself.

"I know I can be too hard on you, and you are far more capable than I've given you credit for. But you're my little girl. I don't want you to hate me for leaving—"

"I won't hate you." Callie took her mother's hands in hers, running her fingers over the weathered skin, the veins and wrinkles that had become more prominent in recent years.

"My sister certainly never forgave me for moving away," she said, more to herself than to Callie.

"Mom, it's time. You need to do something for yourself for a change."

"After your father left... It's just been the two of us for so long. I hope you can see that everything I've ever done has been to take care of you."

Callie searched her mom's face, so much older than she remembered it. The lines around her mouth had deepened from years of frowning and Callie's heart ached as she allowed herself to consider, perhaps for the first time, how much heartbreak had touched her mother's life. Had she ever seen so much emotion in her mother's eyes? The way resolve and regret swirled together was mesmerizing, like clouds parting and coming together, providing brief glimpses of the demons that haunted her mother.

"I know, Mom."

"And I can't promise to stop worrying about you. I know you don't need a partner to be okay, and it's obvious you and Noah have something, but I can't help it, Calandria. I just want you to be alright."

"I think it's time we both tried for more than just alright. Maybe it's time we both tried to be happy."

Her mother blinked, the emotion draining from her eyes and a careful calm returning to her expression. She flashed a quick smile, but there was no warmth in it, and squeezed Callie's hands before wandering off into the crowd. Callie watched her go, wondering at the things she and her mother had never shared, all the pain they'd concealed from each other.

Callie wound her way through the crowd towards Noah. As she neared, bits of his conversation with his uncle and Wolf reached her ears.

"I got word from Senator Thorne this morning. This is no longer a re-election campaign," Wolf said. "It's a vice presidential bid."

Noah glanced between the two men at his side. "I don't understand."

Uncle Stu laughed. "Look at him! The boy's in shock."

"Congressman Carmichael has announced Senator Thorne as his running mate. We're documenting a presidential campaign."

A presidential campaign was a whole other level of high profile. Whether or not Carmichael and Thorne were elected, scoring a documentary following the campaign of the first openly LGBTQ vice presidential nominee would skyrocket Noah's career. This would allow him to compose full-time. He could finally leave academia. It was everything he'd ever wanted.

She should be ecstatic for him, and yet she couldn't help the stab of loss, sharp and serrated. She had started to believe that it might be possible to find a way back to the music with him, that they'd have long days spent side by side at the piano again, him playing the songs they'd dreamt up together. Now he would go on the road, leaving her behind, to live his dream. A dream that didn't include a chronically ill girlfriend who couldn't travel the world with him, who couldn't even play the music she heard in her head. There was no room for her in this reality. She was going to lose him, and the music with him.

"Get ready, son," Uncle Stu said. "Your life is about to change."

Callie saw a flash of lightning behind her eyes, felt the ground sway beneath her, and turned and melted back into the crowd before anyone could see her plummet from the tower.

Noah stayed with his uncle and Wolf until he finished his drink, hardly hearing most of their excited chatter. This was it. The break he'd been waiting for that could finally take him out of academia and get him back to focusing on writing his own music. Why then wasn't he as excited as he should be?

As Liv and Daemon took the floor for their first dance, Noah found Callie slumped in a white folding chair at their table, stretching her neck from side to side. Even tired and sore, she was still the most beautiful thing he'd ever seen. Could he really go six months without her?

Noah sat beside her and tapped his knee, determined to focus on the problems he could solve rather than the ones he had no answers for.

She raised an eyebrow. "What is that supposed to mean?"

"Give me your feet," he said.

Slowly she lifted her legs until her feet rested on his thigh. He undid the ankle strap of her heels, doing his best to hide the surge of dismay at the red, swollen skin beneath the buckles. He ran his thumb over that abused skin before pulling the shoes from her feet and setting them aside. She sighed in relief, sinking deeper into her chair and letting him pull her feet closer as he began gently massaging them.

"You shouldn't have worn the heels," he said, unable to help himself.

"Everyone was wearing heels," she replied with a slight shrug, as if that made it okay that her feet were swollen. "I'm not putting those things back on, though."

"Good."

The DJ called over the speakers for the rest of the wedding party to join Liv and Daemon on the dance floor, but Noah held Callie's feet firmly on his lap.

"Dance with me, Noah."

He wanted to protest that she needed to rest, that she needed to be careful not to overdo it—but there was a melancholy in her tone that made his heart clench in his chest, so he let her pull her feet from his grasp, took her hand, and led her onto the dance floor.

By the time the band played the second verse of *The Way You Look Tonight,* he'd already forgotten about the other couples dancing around them. All that mattered was Callie, the slide of her dress beneath his hands, the heat of her pressed against him, the citrus and rain scent of her hair. He would adjust the plan, take Daemon's advice and make sure they never went more than two weeks without seeing each other, fly back and forth as many times as it took—whatever he needed to do to keep holding her. He'd make this film and then he'd come home and make her his forever.

Noah pressed his lips to her ear and softly sang to her, doing his best not to think about how fragile his plan was, how easily he could lose her.

Callie pulled out of his arms, turning away from him and hiding her face. "I need a minute," she said, her voice shaky, before she damn near ran from the tent.

Noah watched as she ran barefoot across the lawn and down the steps that led to the beach. He could feel the other guests' eyes on him, his sister's concerned frown boring into him from across the dance floor. With a muttered curse, he took off after Callie.

He found her standing on the edge of the ocean, the waves lapping at her bare toes, dampening the hem of her dress. The wind caught the few loose tendrils of hair around her face, lifting them in a frenzied dance. He approached slowly, picking his way across the rocks until they gave way to sand. The waves roared, their crash rivaled only by the blood pounding through his veins.

"My mom called a realtor," Callie said, not turning to meet his eyes. "She's really going to move."

A bright burst of triumph shot through his chest, immediately followed by the profound sense that he was missing something. This was what Callie wanted. Why then did she look like she was about to cry?

"I thought that's what you wanted," he said.

"It is." Callie glanced over her shoulder at him with a sad smile.

"Then what's wrong?" he asked, stepping closer, his shoes sinking into the damp sand.

Callie looked back out at the ocean. "She's all I have. She's the only one who's always there. Dad and Camille are always traveling—do you know he didn't even remember my birthday this year? Or last. And Liv's so busy between work and Daemon."

"You have me."

"Do I?"

"Yes." He took her shoulders in his hands and turned her to face him, the sadness in her eyes slashing across his skin. "Of course, you do."

"Even after tonight?"

He swallowed hard. He wanted to say yes, to reassure her. But he'd be going on the road with the documentary in just a few short days and he'd be gone for at least three months, maybe more. Even if he came home every couple of weeks, it wasn't the same. How could he promise to be there for her when he was getting ready to leave?

"I got the job," he said, the words bitter on his tongue.

"I know. I overheard. A presidential campaign. Congratulations," she said with a soft smile.

He didn't care about that right now. "I leave in a few days. If they win—I don't know how long I'll be on the road."

"This film is going to be huge for you. I'm happy for you."

"We can make this work," he said, taking her hands. "I know long distance is hard, but Liv and Daemon made it work."

She huffed out a disbelieving laugh. "Two days ago you were saying this was only until you left for the campaign. Now you want to try a long distance relationship? You've never even wanted a girlfriend before."

"That's not true."

"What's not true?"

"I've wanted a girlfriend before. I wanted you. I *want* you."

She shook her head, her gaze fixed on their interlocked hands. "Long distance destroys relationships. Liv and Daemon are the exception, not the rule."

"Fuck the rules," he growled. "We'll figure it out. I'll come back to visit every few weeks."

"No. You have to focus on your work, Noah. You can't be flying back and forth all the time."

She pulled away from him again, but he couldn't let her go. Not until she understood how badly he wanted to be the person who was there for her, how much she meant to him. He tugged on her hand, turning her back around to face him.

"So what? We just don't see each other? For months?" He shook his head, running his fingers through his hair. "Tell me what to do," he said, desperation creeping into his voice.

"I can't."

"Ask me not to go."

Her eyes widened, and her lips parted, a surprised huff

escaping. "I can't," she repeated.

"You can," he insisted, his fingers digging into her arms. "Ask me to stay with you."

"No," she whispered, the sound lost in the wind.

She took his face in her hands, her fingers stroking over the stubble along his jaw, and he squeezed his eyes shut. No matter how hard he'd tried to avoid it, he was going to hurt her. And she was going to hurt him. He'd spent the last twenty years trying to avoid losing another person he loved and yet he wouldn't have done anything differently over the last week, even knowing it led here.

"Why not?" he asked.

"Because you're the only one of us who can do the things we always talked about doing. And I love you too much to ask you to give that up for me."

Her words tore through him, shredding him from the inside out and making his knees weak. It was so much worse than he'd expected. Knowing the music had been her dream, too, one that was taken away from her. Knowing she loved him back, and it still wasn't enough. He should tell her he loved her, that he had always loved her...

"I'll tell Wolf I'm not going. There will be other projects."

"Not like this one."

"Dammit, Callie, I'm not ready for this to end."

"Maybe it's just not our time," she said. "I can't be the reason you don't live your dream. I can't be someone who holds you back."

"Don't do this."

"One of us has to." She stepped away from him. "The job was the goal. You got what you wanted. This was always supposed to end, Noah. It was never supposed to be real."

"It was always real and you know it."

She took a deep breath and another step away from him.

Undeniable

He was losing her. She was disappearing right in front of his eyes and he didn't know how to stop it. Why couldn't he stop it?

"I have one more night," he said, raising his voice over the waves and the wind.

"What?"

"You promised me one more night. You're still mine until we get back to New York."

"Noah—"

"Please, Callie."

She searched his eyes and he hoped she could see all the things he couldn't bring himself to say. He needed this last night. It wasn't enough—it would never be enough—but maybe it would be sufficient to convince her to give him another night. And another. He'd spend every day convincing her to give him one more night if that's what it took.

Finally, after what seemed like an eternity, she nodded. He held out his hand to her and she took it, letting him lead her back up to the reception where they danced every song as if they were the only people in the room, clinging to each other until the very last note had died away.

Chapter Twenty-five

"What are we doing here?" Callie asked as Noah led her into the deserted hotel restaurant. The room was dark, the chairs stacked on top of the tables sending long shadows across the floor.

Callie's feet ached and her lower back was tight in a way that meant she'd have difficulty walking properly tomorrow, but she hadn't wanted to leave the reception. They'd danced until her legs burned, and when she could no longer dance, she'd sat wrapped in his arms. She needed to hold him close enough that the memory would last after he'd left.

When he kissed her hair and stroked her arm, she told herself that he would come back to her; when the film was complete, he would come home, and they could start again. But she wasn't sure if she believed it. After all, he'd only agreed to this arrangement in the first place because there was a deadline. As much as it hurt to say goodbye now, it would hurt so much more if they stayed together and he one day looked at her with regret.

"I need to show you something," he said, flipping a light switch at the edge of the room. A small spotlight lit up above the baby grand piano.

Normally Callie would be excited to hear Noah play, but just then she wasn't sure she could handle it. The music that had brought them together all those years ago was now taking him away from her. And she was emotionally and physically wrung out. They only had a few hours left and she didn't want to waste a second.

"Noah, I'm tired."

He guided her to a wingback chair at the edge of the makeshift stage and directed her to sit. "Just give me a minute."

She sighed and sank into the chair, letting the fabric bolster her sore muscles. Noah took a seat on the piano bench, the light glinting off the chestnut highlights in his hair, sharpening the angles of his jaw and cheekbones with harsh shadows. He raised the lid on the keyboard and lay his hands on the keys, hesitating for just a moment as he shot her a glance from beneath his long eyelashes.

"It's a work in progress," he said. "Just something I've been playing with."

She nodded, determined to be supportive no matter how tired and sad she was.

His fingers drifted over the keys, caressing them in a fluid dance that he always made look so effortless. As he played, he cast furtive glances her way, his eyes soft, those faint laugh lines at the edges crinkling.

It took a minute for her to recognize the melody, the gentle sway of the pitches buoyed by a tinkling accompaniment. Like floating. Like falling.

Her mouth dropped open as he played for her, her breathing coming faster, and tears forming in the corners of her eyes. His hands moved faster, seamlessly transitioning into a second theme, the two melodies combining and overlapping. Like waves crashing onto the shore, continuous, relentless. Cleansing.

She slid onto the bench beside him, needing to see each depression of the keys beneath his fingers. Somehow the songs that had played in her head for so long were now reverberating throughout this darkened space, blending with the moonlight until none of it felt real. She'd never thought she'd get to hear these melodies aloud, to see the notes hanging in the air as he wove the music—her music—around them.

The last note rang out in the empty room. Noah lifted his hands from the keys and slid his foot off the pedal. They sat for a moment, both staring at the gleaming white and polished black of the keyboard.

"How?" she asked.

"You're always humming." He glanced at her with a sheepish smile. "I wrote it down for you."

"I can't play it."

"Maybe not. But you can still write." He caught her chin between his thumb and forefinger, turning her attention from the silent piano to him. "Those things we said we would do someday? You can still do them, Callie."

"You wrote my song," she marveled. "Why?"

"Because I love you."

She searched his eyes, the familiar flecks of gold and shades of green, and she knew he meant it. She pressed her lips to his, wanting to taste the words, to consume them so they became a part of her. The kiss turned urgent, bruising need and stinging bites as she climbed into his lap. The silk of her dress bunched around her hips as she straddled Noah on the piano bench in her quest to get closer, to savor every last second she had with him.

His hand slid from her chin to bracket her throat, his thumb pressing to the pulse point there, and he controlled the kiss, tilting her head until he had her at the angle he wanted. His other hand slid up her thigh, holding her tight against the bulge of his erection. She loved when he was like this, commanding and in full control of her body without saying a word. She rocked against him, shuddering as the hard length of him ground against her through the thin fabric of her panties.

"I need you," she whimpered against his mouth. She wasn't sure what she meant—she needed him to fuck her? To come back for her? *Both.*

The hand around her throat slid down between her breasts and over her rib cage, gripping her around the waist and lifting her until she was sitting on the edge of the piano lid. Her bare feet rested on the keyboard, the instrument clanging as her toes slid across the keys. Noah stood between her spread thighs, his hips holding her open as he devoured her mouth, his tongue stroking hers.

With a firm press of his hand on her breastbone, he eased her back until she was lying flat across the lid of the piano. He pushed the slinky material of her dress up over her hips before he hooked her panties with his index fingers and dragged them down her legs. Cool air hit her wet center and she bucked her hips in an effort to get closer to him, the movement striking another discordant tone on the piano.

"What did I tell you about this pussy, love?" Noah rumbled as his stubbled cheek dragged over the sensitive skin of her inner thighs.

She wiggled her hips, trying to get him closer to where she wanted him. "It's yours."

"That's right." He ghosted a finger over her slit, his touch so feather light she wasn't sure if she imagined it. "This pussy is mine. To lick and play with and fuck and care for."

There was that finger again, passing deeper, just barely parting her puffy lower lips. "And you're trying to take it away from me," he growled.

"Noah," she whined. She was too lust drunk for a serious conversation, too needy to go another round with him about the inevitable.

"So you leave me with no choice." He plunged two fingers deep inside her, and she gasped at the sudden intrusion. "I'll have to remind you who you belong to."

And then his tongue was on her clit, masterfully stoking her pleasure higher. She dug her hand into his hair as her thighs began to shake, but he pulled away and slowed the stroke of his fingers on her inner walls. He blew a cool stream of air over her swollen sex and her thighs fell even further apart. An invitation, a plea for more.

"Say it," he commanded, his voice so hard that she could almost mistake the steel of his tone for a lack of emotion. But she knew better. It wasn't a lack of anything, but a tidal wave barely held at bay.

"I'm yours," she panted.

"That's fucking right." He bowed his head again, flicking her clit with his tongue. "No matter where you are, or where I am. You've been mine for six fucking years, Calandria Cole. You'll always be mine."

His words reverberated through her head but she could barely parse them she was so desperate for his mouth on her. "Noah, please," she begged.

"I take care of what's mine, love."

He closed his lips around her clit again and worked her towards an orgasm that stole her breath and sent electricity down her legs. Her back arched off the hard wood of the piano lid, her toes digging into the keys as she rode his mouth. As her climax retreated, he began mercilessly licking her again. "Another," he grunted, fucking her with his fingers and tongue until she came a second time.

When he stood up, his chin was wet with her release, his eyes wild. He gripped her hips and pulled her closer to him, her ass sliding off the edge of the piano. She reached out and grabbed the sides of the instrument to steady herself as the clatter of his belt falling against the polished parquet floor echoed through the room. Before she'd even registered the source of the sound, he thrust into her, filling her in one smooth stroke, using his grip on her hips to leverage himself deeper.

"Oh, God," she cried out as he drove into her again and again.

"You can send me away, Calico, but you'll never stop being mine." His hips pistoned faster, his cock driving directly into that sensitive spot on her front walls. "I love you," he growled, the words almost angry.

"I love you," she gasped.

He curled himself over her, his teeth closing around her nipple through the fabric of her dress. He tongued her through the silk as she wrapped her legs around his hips, holding him so tightly that his thrusts slowed to deep rolls of his hips, his pelvis grinding against her clit with each undulation.

She wrapped her arms around him, curling herself around him as her stomach contracted and her pussy grasped at the solid length of him within her. She came with a cry, the pleasure bordering on pain, a sharp, stinging bliss that made her tremble in his arms. With a roar, he pumped his own release into her, his cock kicking within her as heat rushed between her thighs.

He pulled out and rearranged her dress down over her thighs, and then helped her to sit upright on the piano. Once she was sitting again, he stepped away, but she caught him by the collar of his shirt, drawing him back towards her. He avoided her eyes, his hands stroking over the silk covering her thighs, concealing the mess he'd made of her.

"Look at me," she said. He swallowed hard, his Adam's apple bobbing in his throat, before he finally glanced up and met her eyes. The depth of feeling there stole her breath, the hurt and frustration and love all tangled together. "Noah—"

"It's late," he said, looking away again as he held out his hand to help her slide off the piano. "We should get some sleep."

Chapter Twenty-six

Noah hardly slept. Every time he nodded off, he startled awake, sure that Callie was gone. He'd tuck her back against his body, bury his face in her hair, and will himself to sleep, but his thoughts raced as he tried to come up with a way to keep her.

As the sun peeked through the gauzy curtains in the morning, Callie turned in his arms and he tightened his grip on her. The sweep of her nose across his chest ripped open the old wound there. Funny, he'd always thought it would be something monumental to finally set off the landmine she'd planted beneath his skin all those years ago, something bombastic enough to justify the devastation it would bring. He'd never expected it to be the flutter of her eyelashes against his skin.

His throat tightened and he closed his eyes, determined to etch the feel of her into his body.

"I'm coming back for you, Calico," he said, his voice hoarse.

"You don't have to say that." She kissed his chest and, Christ, how her lips burned.

"I'm coming back for you," he repeated. "There is no part of me that does not belong to you. You have my whole heart." He caught her hand and held it to his chest. Could she feel the crater she'd left there, the place that would remain empty until she was his once and for all?

She ran her finger over his heart in an x-shape. "I'll keep it safe for you, then, until you come back for it."

He kissed her, a lingering slide of lips and tongues as though he could make the moment last if he moved slowly enough. When kissing was no longer enough, he slid into her welcoming heat and made love to her. Noah had never understood before why someone would choose such a sentimental turn of phrase to describe something so physical, but there in the hotel bed they'd shared all week with the distant waves crashing outside their window, he understood. This was more than pleasure, more than pain, more than the ephemeral joining of bodies. This was spirit and breath and the stuff of stars.

They were late to Livi's farewell brunch, but he didn't care. The out-of-town guests gathered on The Barclay's back patio to toast the newlyweds one more time didn't seem to notice when he and Callie joined them, their hands clasped together tightly. He lifted their joined hands to his lips and pressed a kiss to her knuckles.

At the front of the assembled crowd, in front of a table piled high with croissants and muffins, Noah's mother tapped a butter knife against her glass. A silk scarf in a floral pattern tied around her neck fluttered in the breeze off the ocean. "Hush, now. It's time for the bride's mother to have her say," she said, her eyes sparkling with humor.

"No more embarrassing stories, Mom," Liv said.

"Lots more embarrassing stories!" someone called from the crowd, the response met with scattered laughter.

"No, I have something serious to say," his mother said. She smiled softly at Liv, then scanned the crowd. "Is your brother here yet?"

"I'm here," he said, pulling Callie with him to the front of the group.

"Ah, wonderful. I'm afraid you all must forgive me for I'm about to be terribly sentimental."

It was then that Noah noticed the folded square of paper in his mother's free hand, the creases soft and fragile from repeated folding and unfolding, the paper stained in places. His breath caught in his chest and he swayed on his feet with the shock of it. *She's going to read it now? Here?* He'd been waiting to know what was on that piece of paper for the last twenty years; he wasn't prepared to find out in front of all these people, most of whom he barely knew.

"What's wrong?" Callie asked, but he didn't have words to explain.

His mother unfolded the paper and Noah caught Liv's eye across the space, knowing instantly that she, too, recognized the paper. Liv pushed through the crowd until she was at his side, wrapping herself against him and letting him pull her close with his free arm. He held tight to Callie's hand on his other side, and hardly noticed when Daemon took up his post beside Liv. The four of them faced his mother, waiting, and he let himself be buoyed by two of the people who meant the most to him in the world on either side of him, holding him up, letting him hold them.

"When my Jerry got sick, we didn't know how much time he'd have, and we made all these grand plans. He was going to finally score a full-length film. We were going to take you kids to Paris. He wanted to fill a journal with letters to you both, with the stories he wouldn't get to tell you over dinner, and the bits of wisdom he wanted to pass on." She bowed her head to collect herself and Noah closed his eyes, surprised to find his eyelashes were already wet.

"He never did do any of those things. But he wrote this," she said, holding up the paper, "and he told me I'd know when the time was right to read it to you."

She carefully unfolded the paper and took a shaky breath before meeting Noah's eyes, then Liv's. With a nod, she turned back to the paper and began to read:

Olivia and Noah,

Once, a very long time ago, I thought I would like to be an airplane pilot. I even took lessons and earned my license to fly small planes. Ask your mother sometime about the day I flew us to Martha's Vineyard for lunch.

After your mother found out she was pregnant with you, Noah, I decided it was time to stop flying. I had never been afraid to fly, but I suppose I had never had anything so great to lose before.

It has been years since I sat in a cockpit, but what I wouldn't give to take you two into the sky and make one more good landing on a half-moon night on a well-lit runway. An airport at night, viewed from the approach path, is one of the most beautiful sights I've ever seen. There are lights everywhere and they all have a purpose. It's the pilot's job to keep them all lined up and the proper colors. Any deviation from the proper approach and things change color or perspective. It's like falling slowly into a Christmas tree where you know every light and every ornament by name.

It's the intersection of beauty and order, adrenaline and calm. I hope you build yourself a life that balances each of those things. Order is tedious without beauty, and you will grow weary of the calm without the moments of adrenaline.

Do things that scare you; you cannot know the joy of landing without the fear of falling.

Never shy away from an adventure, especially when it comes in the form of someone you love. Choosing love is always the right decision.

You, my family, have been my greatest adventure.

Now it is time for you to fly. Say hi to the stars for me.

Love, Dad

Before their mother had finished refolding the paper, Liv flung herself into her arms. Noah wanted to join them, but his feet were rooted to the spot. Through the blur of tears, he could almost imagine his father was standing at his mother's side.

"Noah," Callie urged at his side.

Her voice shook him from his trance. He blinked to clear his vision and joined his mother and sister, but he kept one hand firmly grasping Callie's. His father's words infused his blood, weaving themselves into his muscles and sinew. His mother had read the letter, but he'd heard the sentences in his father's own voice, the deep timbre of it flowing through him like water returning to a dry riverbed.

All this time he'd thought he understood about love, about loss. How had he been so wrong?

The drive back to New York was over too quickly, with Callie silently lamenting every mile that brought them closer to the end. There was no traffic, and Noah was still lost in thought, the ghost of his father's words flickering in his eyes like some kind of mirage. Callie turned up the music on her road trip playlist and watched the exit signs on the highway fly by.

Noah turned his Toyota into the driveway of Callie's condo and helped her bring her bags in, but he didn't venture further than a few steps beyond the front door.

"When do you leave?" she asked him. Wolf had caught him as they'd left The Barclay, rattling off instructions, but Callie had already been in the car. She'd watched through the passenger side window as Noah shook Wolf's hand, a vacant look on his face.

"The day after tomorrow. The senator is going to join Congressman Carmichael for an appearance in New Hampshire. I'll join the rest of the film crew there."

Callie stepped closer, wrapping her arms around his waist and leaning her forehead on his chest, afraid to meet his eyes. He enveloped her in his sage and leather scent, resting his chin on the top of her head.

"I meant what I said, Calico. Every word."

"Me too."

"I'll call you." He pressed his lips to her temple.

"I'll answer," she promised.

And then he was gone.

Callie went about the business of unpacking, refusing to crumble under the crushing weight of letting him go. As she loaded the laundry into the machine and measured out the soap, she told herself there was no point in wondering if she'd made the right choice. In two days, he'd be in New Hampshire, living his dream, and she would go back to work at the library.

She added the shiny metal plug he'd bought her to the gift bag with her lingerie, the tags still on, and put it carefully at the back of her closet where it couldn't ambush

Undeniable

her with memories of the best week of her life. A girl had to be prepared for that kind of walk down memory lane, defenses in place, so she wouldn't be tempted to change her mind, to tell him that yes, she wanted to be his girlfriend, distance be damned. As his father had written, this was Noah's time to fly, and she refused to clip his wings.

It was the book that finally broke her from her trance. From the bottom of her suitcase, the glossy red cover with its gold script stared back at her. She clutched it to her chest and slid to the floor beside her bed, leaning against her bedside table, and cried the kind of wracking sobs that left her throat raw and her cheeks red for hours after the last tear had fallen.

In the middle of the night, Callie sat bolt upright in bed and flipped on the light on her bedside table. She fumbled through the top drawer of the table, tossing aside vibrators and half-used tubes of lip balm until she found a small sheet music manuscript book at the very bottom. With a fervor she hadn't felt in years, she scribbled out the melody for the final movement of her unfinished sonata.

When she was done, she flipped back to the front of the book, humming through the first two movements, running her fingers over the faded marks and hurried notes in the margins, things she jotted down during those phone calls with Noah all those years ago. Things like, "feel the current" and "explore the edges of emotion" alongside his more technical pointers on rhythm and meter. When she'd dropped music as her second major, she'd never thought to finish the piece, but she also hadn't been able to part with it. She added new notes as she went, scribbling additional bars of music in the margins and hearing the music in her mind as she did. Images of the last week flitted past her eyes like a movie played on an old projector as she worked.

She'd still need to tweak the modulation in the second movement, and the final cadence was still eluding her, but she knew she'd find it. It was like she'd been hearing these melodies at the back of her mind all her life, low like the distant crash of the waves from their hotel room in Aster Bay, a song so ever-present she'd almost forgotten it was there. But now it was roaring through her, like the music was in her very bloodstream. Ignoring it now would be like trying to silence the ocean.

It wasn't technically perfect but, for the first time, it captured the feeling she'd been unable to invoke all those years ago—which, she supposed, made sense. After all, she didn't know what it was to wake up in Noah's arms until a week ago. She'd had no idea how much more she could love him; not the infatuation she'd mistaken for love as a teenager, but this bone deep realization that her heart would always search for him. How could she put emotion like that on the page when she hadn't felt it yet, when she hadn't known how wonderful it would be to have him love her in return? Or how badly she'd wish she didn't have to let him go?

Chapter Twenty-seven

Noah sat at the back of yet another hotel ballroom listening to Senator Thorne give the same speech for the ninth time in two days. He scrubbed his hand over his face to cover his yawn and checked his phone for the hundredth time. Not that he expected Callie to have called or texted, but he couldn't help but hope.

He'd called her twice in the last week, and both calls had been painfully awkward. She'd told him about the Fall Into Reading costume party she was planning at the library and he'd complained about the shitty continental breakfasts put out for the campaign staff and film crew. And after that, there had been nothing left to say that hadn't already been said as they both avoided yet another rehash of their circumstances. She refused to "be a distraction" and he refused to even entertain the idea that it was over, so they were locked in a stalemate that tore at his heart like a physical ache all the damn time.

When he wasn't obsessing about Callie, he was replaying his father's letter over and over.

Do things that scare you.
Never shy away from an adventure.

"I'm trying, Dad," he mumbled to himself. But he was also a man of his word, someone who prided himself on being dependable, true to his commitments. If he could just get a few minutes with the senator, he knew he could find a way to be both. But he was running out of time.

His phone rang and he startled, the heavy metal version of ABBA's *Take A Chance* drawing glares from across the room. He quickly silenced the phone as a campaign aide shot him a dirty look. Holding up the phone with a grimace, Noah gestured to the doors behind him, practically sprinting for the exit. Outside on the sidewalk, he answered.

"Did you change my ringtone?" he asked.

Liv laughed on the other end of the phone. "That was all Daemon. Pay back, big brother. Are you really just hearing it now? He did that at least a week ago."

"My phone's been on vibrate."

"Sorry it's taken me so long to call you back. This rehearsal schedule is intense. I'm on my ten-minute break so I don't have long."

Noah paced the sidewalk, running his fingers through his hair, and blew out a slow breath. "I need to tell you something and I need you to get over it really fast so we can move past the you being mad part and get to the you helping me fix it part."

"What did you do to Callie?" she asked, her voice steel.

Noah stopped. "I didn't—How did you—" He took a deep breath, exhaling hard, and started again. "Callie and I were never dating."

"What are you talking about?"

"We made it up so Mrs. Cole would get off her back about settling down and Wolf would see that I wasn't a risk to the senator's campaign." He closed his eyes and waited for the screaming to start. When it didn't, he pulled his phone away from his ear to make sure they hadn't been disconnected. "Livi? You there?"

"Of all the *stupid*—What were you thinking?" Liv shouted.

He winced. "I know."

His phone dinged as Liv switched their call over to video chat. He accepted the change and gritted his teeth, waiting for the barrage to continue. Instead, he was met with Liv's narrowed eyes and furrowed brow, her head cocked to the side.

"You're not that good of a liar," she said.

"I'm not," he agreed.

"And Callie's even worse than you are. So what the hell is going on, Noah?"

"It was a lie," he started again, "and then...it wasn't. We weren't dating when we got to your wedding."

"But you are now?"

He shook his head. "I don't know.

"This is the most frustrating conversation I've ever had—and I married a man who counts his macros but refuses to eat lettuce!"

Noah leaned against the brick façade of the hotel. "I fell in love with her."

Liv rolled her eyes. "Obviously. She's fabulous."

"And I want to be with her, but she's gotten it in her head that if we're together right now then she's somehow going to cost me this job and I don't even give a shit about the job anymore, Livi, I just... I love her."

"Then quit the job! It's ludicrous that Wolf wants you to tour the damn country with the campaign anyway. Doesn't he know you can compose from anywhere?"

Noah smiled. "You're not mad?"

"Oh, I'm *so* mad, but I only have six more minutes before I have to be back in rehearsal and apparently you need my help to un-fuck this situation, so I'm tabling the mad part until I have more time to yell at you properly."

He chuckled. "I appreciate that."

"Are you going to quit?"

"I can't. I agreed to do this film. And even if I hadn't, Callie will just think she'd cost me my dream if I quit now."

"But that wouldn't be true," Liv said, a mischievous smile crossing her face, "because she's your dream now. Right?"

"Something like that. But you know how she gets when she thinks someone is—"

"Making her a priority? Yeah, we've had many a conversation about that particular hang up. Shit, I'm probably violating some kind of friendship code by telling you that."

He grinned. "Look, I have a plan, but I need your help."

"Name it."

That night, as Noah was texting Liv the final details for his plan, his phone buzzed with a new incoming message. Callie had sent him a series of pictures of a score. The images were dim but even with the poor lighting he recognized Callie's slanted notation.

He hummed the piece through, the emotion in each note slicing through him like glass, shredding the last vestiges of his restraint with each turn. Then he went back to the first image and hummed it again, the familiar phrases punctuated by new cadences and capped off with a third movement that, to his knowledge, had never existed before. Her sonata. She'd finished it.

He felt like he was floating, his limbs fuzzy. He knew he shouldn't assign any deeper meaning to it, but he couldn't help himself. Surely it meant something that she'd finished this piece after all these years, that she'd sent it to him. Fuck, it meant *everything*.

She answered on the second ring.

"You finished it," he said.

"I did," she said.

"I'm so proud of you, love. It's...fuck, it's beautiful." He was met with silence on the other end of the phone. "Talk to me, Callie," he pleaded.

"I'd forgotten how much I missed composing. Or I wouldn't let myself remember. Either way."

"The music will always find its way back to you." He squeezed his eyes shut. *I'm coming, love. Just wait for me.*

Even though he wanted to, he couldn't make her promises. There were still things to arrange, and she was still too skittish, too determined to sacrifice her own happiness—and his. But he'd not only heard his father's words, he'd carved them into his heart, and he was done letting fear keep them apart.

"I don't want to keep you from your work," she said. He hated how she tried to push him away even now, even with her music playing through his mind.

"It's almost midnight. I wasn't working."

"Oh. Then I should let you get some sleep."

"Callie," he began, swallowing down the lump in his throat. "We're gonna figure it out. *I'm* gonna figure it out. Just trust me, okay?" Silence. "Callie?"

"Mmhmm. I'm nodding."

He chuckled.

"Noah?"

"Yeah, love?"

"I miss you."

He closed his eyes, the words like a balm over the tender places that ached for her. "God, Callie, you have no idea."

Chapter Twenty-eight

Liv dropped into the seat across from Callie in the little diner, draping her messenger bag across the back of the chair with one hand as she hailed a server with another. "Sorry, sorry, I got on a local train instead of an express."

"What'll you have?" the waitress asked as she poured Liv a cup of coffee.

"Two eggs over easy, rye toast, side of sausage and a fruit cup," Liv rattled off.

The waitress turned to Callie. "I'll have what she's having," Callie said.

Liv took a long sip of her coffee, her eyes drifting closed, and sighed contentedly. "Thanks for coming into the city this morning, Cal. I have rehearsal in a few hours and I really wanted to see you."

Callie stirred another sugar packet into her tea. "What's wrong, babe?"

Liv placed the mug on the table but kept her hands wrapped around it. "Why would something be wrong?" she asked, her voice too high.

"Noah told you," Callie said, shaking her head. "I guess I should be impressed that it took him this long."

"What are you talking about?"

"You're an awful liar, Liv."

Liv dropped the wide eyes and pursed her lips. "Unlike you, apparently!"

Callie winced. "I'm sorry. We wanted to tell you but, you know... You're an awful liar." She focused on her tea, watching the warm liquid swirl in the white China mug. "How is he?"

"You haven't talked to him?"

"Not in a day or two. I mean, we've been texting a bit but..." She broke off with a shrug.

"Okay, well that won't do," Liv said, scooting her chair closer. "Look, if you want to make long distance work—"

"No, we're not doing that. It was all pretend, Liv. We're not together."

"Oh, please. Now who's the awful liar?" Liv paused as the server returned with their orders, nodding politely to her in thanks, before she continued. "I know my brother, Cal, and I know you, and there was nothing fake about what I saw between you two this past week."

An impossible flame of hope flickered in Callie's chest. She'd been doing her best over the last few days to snuff it out, but no matter how many times she told herself their connection was purely circumstantial, that by the time he came home from the campaign he would have moved on, that stubborn flame refused to be put out. And now her best friend was fanning the fire.

"He needs to focus on his work—"

"And what about what *you* need?"

Callie closed her eyes. She would not cry over breakfast in some hole-in-the-wall diner. She'd made a conscious decision to let Noah go, to release him from whatever sense of obligation he felt towards her so she would never have to look in his eyes and know he regretted choosing her. It had been the right decision, even if it felt like a kick in the gut every time she thought about the way his hair had moved in the breeze on the beach, the tightness of his voice as he offered to give it all up for her. As if she ever would have let him.

When she opened her eyes again, Liv was watching her with her head cocked to the side in that way she did when she was puzzling something over.

"I'm alright, babe. Just don't tell my mom, okay? If she knew we lied she'd never go through with selling the house and moving away."

"I see." Liv stabbed the corner of her toast into the runny yolk of her eggs with far more aggression than was called for. "Your mom gets to move to Ohio, and Noah gets to compose his film score—and what do you get, Cal?"

She opened her mouth to respond but found she had no answer.

"What do your cards say about this, huh? Have they yelled at you yet?"

"The cards don't yell," Callie said in a small voice.

"Okay, then I guess I'll have to do it. You are arranging your life so that everyone is happy except you."

"That's not—He wouldn't be happy, Liv. Not for long. Not when he realized what he'd given up for me."

"First of all, that's crap. He didn't have to give up anything. From what Noah says, he was willing to try long distance and you're the one who said no."

Callie sat back in the chair. How did Liv really not understand? "I—"

"I'm not finished," Liv said. "Second of all, even if he did have to choose between you and the job, that's his choice to make. You don't get to decide what's best for him. Isn't that exactly what you're always complaining about other people doing to you?"

Well, shit, she has a point.

"And third of all, when are you going to realize that loving you is not a sacrifice?" Liv reached across the table and squeezed Callie's hand, her eyes softening. "You are not a consolation prize. You're the whole damn jackpot, Cal. It took my stupid brother far too long to realize that, and now that he has, you're going to throw it away?"

Liv reached up and wiped away a tear streaming down Callie's cheek. She hadn't even realized she was crying.

"I love him," she said.

Liv rolled her eyes. "Yeah. I know. And he loves you, too, you big dummy."

Callie dropped her head into her hands. "God, I've made such a mess of it."

"Yeah, but lucky for you, I'm here to help." Liv speared a grape with her fork and popped it into her mouth.

Callie shook her head. It was impossible. "He's gone for the next three months—or six."

"We'll see," Liv said with the smile of a child who'd snooped and discovered their Christmas presents.

"What does that mean?"

Liv shrugged, her smile widening.

"Babe, come on. What do you know?"

"Nope!" Liv mimed zipping her lips and throwing away the key. "I'm sworn to secrecy."

"Senator Thorne, thank you so much for meeting with me," Noah said as he shook the older woman's hand.

Senator Thorne was shorter than he'd thought she would be, probably only five foot six despite her patent leather pumps, her statuesque appearance an optical illusion created by the pinstripe pantsuits she favored. Her black hair was cropped short, making her features appear more severe and her blue eyes seem larger. Despite having been on the campaign trail with the senator and Wolf's film crew for the last week, this was the first time he was speaking to the woman directly.

"Of course," the senator said, gesturing for Noah to take a seat in the wingback chair opposite her.

The small seating area in the senator's suite, which was also serving as headquarters for the campaign's week in New Hampshire, was cluttered with lawn signs and stacks of flyers proudly proclaiming the first LGBTQ+ vice presidential candidate.

"Please, call me Laura," the senator said. "I understand you have something on your mind."

"Yes, ma'am."

"Laura. Please," she insisted.

"Laura," he relented with a smile.

"Oh! Thank you for allowing us to use your piece for the new commercial. When Wolf played it for me, I just knew that was the one."

A television commercial featuring the senator and her wife walking hand-in-hand through a farmer's market had been shot the day Noah arrived and would begin airing next week. The senator had requested to use one of Noah's score fragments from his application package as the background music. He warmed under her praise, but he was too nervous about his request to really enjoy it.

"Tell me. How did you make it sound so much like…me?"

"Actually, that's what I wanted to talk to you about." Noah scooted forward on the chair so he was sitting on the very edge of the seat, his elbows braced on his knees. "I watched hours of your speeches on the internet. I could probably recite a few from memory at this point."

"Not the old 'A library in every city' one I hope," she said with a laugh.

He nodded, smiling. He'd played that one for Callie a few times. He was pretty sure it was the reason Callie was planning to vote for the Carmichael-Thorne ticket in November.

"That one and many others. I especially liked your speech about better protections for workers with invisible disabilities."

She sat back in her chair, crossing her legs. "I'm glad someone did. The crowd wasn't too fond of that particular idea that day."

"I watched the videos, studied the rhythm of your speech, the pattern of your gait. When you pause and when you rush ahead. You have this habit of elongating the last syllable of a word if you want to really emphasize it."

She laughed again. "Yes, I'm aware. It drives my communications team batty."

"But it's you," he said. "It's the unique sound of Senator Laura Thorne. That's what I wrote into the music."

She smiled. "Wolf wasn't lying about you. You are quite the impressive young man."

"Thank you."

"So what can I do for you, Noah?"

He released a breath. Now or never.

"I'm honored that you and Wolf chose me to write the score for this documentary. It is a dream come true in so many ways."

"But...?" she prompted.

"But I'd like to write the rest of the score the same way I've written everything else so far. From my home studio. I'll study the footage Wolf sends me so it's just like I was in the room. But my best work is not done on the road, ma'am. I can't give this score the full attention it deserves when my heart wants to be someplace else."

He waited for her to respond, maintaining eye contact as she considered his request. His heart pounded in his chest and he thought he might be sick if she made him wait much longer.

"Who are they?" she asked, a twinkle in her eye.

He smiled, some of the tension leaving his shoulders. "Her name's Callie. She's a librarian, actually, and a composer, too. And I can't be without her for the next three months. Not if you want something other than sappy, depressed love songs," he added with a self-deprecating smile.

She looked thoughtful. "Wolf seems to think it's necessary for you to be on location with the crew."

"I know. But I think I've proven that's not true. Wolf's process might work for some but not for me."

"Hmm," she hummed. "Do you know the only thing I have ever regretted about my career?" He shook his head. "It's not the late nights or the long hours or the seemingly endless battles to fight. It's never the times I spent working. It's always the times I didn't spend with my wife."

She considered him again, that keen eye assessing him.

"I'll make you a deal. Two days a month on the campaign trail—just our biggest and most important appearances. And the rest of the time you write from home." He could hardly contain the joy bursting within him, fresh hope bubbling up for the first time since he'd walked out of Callie's condo a week ago. She stood, and he did the same.

"If you can continue to produce music like what you've sent me so far, then I don't care where you do it from."

He shook her hand more vigorously than was necessary, but he was too excited to care. "Thank you."

She winked at him, a knowing smile on her face. "Go on. My scheduler will be in touch, and I'll see you in Iowa."

He thanked the senator again and practically floated back to his hotel room. Part one of his plan was complete. Now he just had to hope Liv came through with part two.

I'm coming for you, Calico.

Chapter Twenty-nine

Callie was running late. She'd been planning the Fall Into Reading costume party at the library for the last four months and now she was going to miss half the damn thing because the stupid zipper on her stupid costume was stuck. That's what she got for ordering a cheap pre-made costume from a discount Halloween store rather than putting together an outfit from thrift store finds like she usually did. But it didn't matter now. The zipper wasn't budging and there was no way the dress was going to fit over her head. She tore through her closet for something—anything—that would work. She couldn't go to her own costume party without a costume.

At the back of her closet she found a dress she hadn't worn in years—a faux-brocade dress with a full skirt and a low, ruffled neckline. In the center of the chest, a long-forgotten sticker had practically fused with the fabric: *Hello, My name is: Bernadette Farthingworth.* She fingered the lace at the neckline, remembering the last time she'd worn this particular dress. It would have to do. She was out of time and she couldn't very well wear the only other costume in her closet (a sexy Daphne costume from *Scooby*

Doo) to a work event.

By the time she pulled up to the library, the parking lot was full and golden light spilled from the tall windows across the pavement. She rushed up the front steps, practically running right into a group of teenagers in wizard robes on their way out.

The main hall of the library was packed with people of all ages. Children squealed with delight in one corner as they posed with giant cardboard cut-outs of superheroes and perused picture books and comics. Teenagers, too cool to show their enjoyment, congregated around the snack table, but Callie noted that most of them had a book or two tucked under their arms. At the far end of the room, adults browsed a selection of books, all discarded from the library's collection, wrapped in brown paper with a teaser quote lovingly written on the outside beneath a sign that declared: "Blind Date with a Book." Best of all, the boxes by the entrance collecting gently used books for donation to local senior centers and schools were overflowing.

"Hey, Callie! This is amazing!" her co-worker Kristin said as she pulled Callie in for a hug. "Where did you find a life-sized Frankenstein?"

Kristin gestured to a room just off the main hall that had been decorated like a haunted house, an homage to horror. Each reading room was decked out to represent a different genre. The sci-fi room featured a giant UFO hanging from the ceiling; the mystery room looked like the inside of a film noir detective's office; and the romance room had been turned into a regency-era ballroom.

"That little thrift shop next to the diner," Callie said. "He had a life-sized Dracula, too, but some teenager bought it before I got there."

"Okay, and how did you pull this off," Kristin said,

Undeniable

pointing to the ceiling of the main hall. "I can barely get IT to update my antivirus."

Callie glanced overhead, not sure what Kristin meant, and was met with a ceiling covered in stars. She gasped, turning around in circles to take it all in. The entire ceiling of the great hall had been transformed into a night sky, stars twinkling and a shooting star occasionally floating across the room. You could hardly see the drop ceiling tiles through the projected image.

"I didn't," she stammered. "I don't know..."

She was so focused on the impossible image on the ceiling that she almost missed the buzz of her phone in her leggings pocket. With a glance to be sure no one was looking at her, she reached beneath her skirt and extracted the phone, her heart stopping when she saw it was a text message from Noah.

The photo was dim and from an odd angle but it was unmistakably a photo of a cluster of stars, edited to have a circle drawn around them.

Noah: I found a pelican.

Callie laughed as she typed out her reply.

Callie: There aren't any pelican constellations.

Noah: Not with that attitude.

Another photo. Equally fuzzy, with a similar circle drawn around a different cluster.

Noah: What about this one? I think it's a giraffe.

Another photo. This time, there was a hint of something in the lower corner that she couldn't quite make out, but it looked awfully familiar.

Noah: Okay maybe the last one wasn't a giraffe, but this is clearly a castle.

Callie: Where are you?

Awareness prickled at the back of her neck, that pesky hope sending tingles down her spine. *No. He can't be.*

Noah: Look up.

Callie looked up as the image on the ceiling began to change. Slowly, glowing lines began to connect the stars into pictures, like some kind of giant connect-the-dot puzzle. First, a castle with turrets and streaming banners. Then a teddy bear and a pelican. Next, a rose, a suspension bridge, an elephant. Finally, a snowman and a ladybug. All around her, people had grown quiet as they watched the changing shapes on the ceiling.

She clasped her hand over her mouth as she took in each of the fake constellations.

"I think that one's supposed to be a piano."

She jumped at the sound of his voice at her ear, whirling around to find him so close they were practically touching. A sob escaped her lips and she flung herself into his arms. He wrapped himself around her, pressing one hand to the back of her head and his lips to her temple.

"How are you here?" She nuzzled into his neck, struggling to believe he was really there. "How did you do all this?"

"I called in reinforcements." When she gave him a

questioning look, he said, "Liv has some lighting designer friends."

She was surprised to know her best friend had been able to keep the surprise a secret, but she was so glad she had.

"You're supposed to be in New Hampshire," she said, running her hands over his chest.

"I'm supposed to be here. With you."

She pulled away to meet his eyes, worry beginning to pull at her. He ran his thumb over the crease between her brows. "I figured it out."

"Noah, you can't walk away from the film." She shook her head, the cold dread of having to let him go sinking through her bones all over again. How was she supposed to let him go again?

"I'm not," he said.

"I don't understand."

"I talked with the senator. She's agreed to let me work on the score remotely, as long as I join the campaign for two days each month."

It was too much to hope for. "What about Wolf? I thought—"

"The senator outranks Wolf. I'm sure he's not too happy with me for going around him." He cradled her face in his hands and looked at her with such tenderness she thought she might cry. "But you are the most important thing in my life, Calico."

He pressed his forehead to hers. Her fingers dug into his back and she squeezed her eyes shut, her breath shuddering.

"What is it, love?" he asked, his nose sliding against hers.

"I'm just so scared, Noah," she whispered.

"Of what?"

"What if you change your mind?"

"I won't."

"What if you wake up one day and realize I'm holding you back?"

He dug his hands into her hair. "That will never happen."

"You can't know that." She wanted him so badly, and she wanted to believe she could be enough for him, but she had years of experience proving that she wasn't.

"I will rearrange the stars for you every day if I have to. Whatever it takes to prove to you that you are worth it."

"This is crazy," she said, even as she dug her hands into his shirt and pulled him closer. "You are completely changing your life for me after only a few weeks."

"I spent six years trying to convince myself that I didn't love you, but the way I feel about you is undeniable." He pulled back to look in her eyes, his thumbs sweeping away the tears that formed at the corners of her eyes. "Do you trust me?"

"I trust you."

"Then that's all you have to do. Trust that I know what I want. You are my adventure, Callie. And I'm scared, too. But I think my dad was right. You can't have the joy without the fear, and I'm tired of letting the fear win. Please take this leap with me." The corners of his eyes crinkled, the warmth in his gaze washing over her. She nodded, her head bobbing in his hands.

"Okay," she said, a smile stretching across her face. She could do this. *They* could do this.

"I love you, Calandria Cole."

"I love you," she whispered.

"Kiss him already!" Callie and Noah turned to see Kristin watching them with a wide grin.

Noah dropped his head and chuckled, but when he looked back up at her, her heart stopped. *He loves me.* The edge of his mouth tipped up in a lazy grin, a sparkle in his eyes.

Undeniable

His lips brushed against hers too lightly, and that just wouldn't do. She dug her hands into his hair and pressed her mouth to his, melting into his touch. He nipped at her lower lip just as the catcalling began. They pulled apart to see half the gathered crowd clapping and staring, hollering their approval. She blushed and buried her face in his chest, rocked by his laughter.

She pressed her lips to his ear, murmuring so only he could hear. "Do you want to stay awhile longer, or can I take you home now and make you mine?"

He grinned, and heat flooded her veins. "Don't you know by now, sweet girl? I've always been yours."

Epilogue

One Year Later

"I can't believe I just walked a red carpet!" Callie trilled.

She squeezed Noah's hand and bounced on the balls of her feet as they moved into the theater where *Thorne in Their Side*, the completed documentary on Senator Thorne's vice-presidential bid, would premiere. The senator and Congressman Carmichael hadn't won the election, but she had been re-elected to serve another term in the Senate, and Noah wouldn't be surprised if she made the short list of presidential candidates in the next election.

He bent his head to whisper in her ear. "I can't believe you just walked a red carpet while wearing my plug."

Her cheeks darkened to the prettiest blush and he nipped at her earlobe. "Behave," she scolded, but her hooded eyes demanded he do anything but.

"Never," he said with a smirk.

"Noah!" Senator Thorne's voice rang out through the crowd.

Reluctantly, Noah tore his gaze away from his wife. "Senator, so good to see you."

The senator took his hand with a knowing smile. "Laura, please." She turned to Callie, extending her hand. "And you must be Callie. I've heard so much about you."

"It's wonderful to meet you. I've been following the coverage of your work to expand funding for public libraries."

"I'm so glad. It will make our next project together even easier," the senator said. "If you'll excuse me, I'm being summoned. Noah, my scheduler will be in touch." She tilted her head towards a young woman with a clipboard who was trying—not so subtly—to flag down the senator, then disappeared into the crowd.

"Next project?" Callie asked.

"I'll tell you about it later." Noah ushered her into a mostly empty aisle of seats towards the back of the theater.

Through most of the film, Noah kept his hands to himself, though his fingers itched with the need to touch her. If he was honest, he was always desperate to touch her—from the moment he woke in the morning to the second he fell asleep with her wrapped in his arms. Marrying her had only intensified the need. There was something about calling her "wife" while he made love to her that drove him out of his damn mind.

Towards the end of the documentary, she began squirming at his side. Lust pounded through his veins knowing the jeweled toy beneath her clothes was preparing her for all the filthy things he'd do to her later. He slid his hand into her lap, through the folds of fabric of her wrap dress. She glanced around, but no one was paying any attention to them, and widened her legs slightly to give him better access. *Sweet girl.* He moved his hand higher on the silky skin of her legs, his eyes flying to hers when his fingers brushed against the curls at the apex of her thighs.

He leaned closer, his lips pressed to her ear when he

whispered, "No panties?"

She shook her head, biting her lip with that mischievous glint in her eye that he loved so much. He hummed in approval, stroking over her lightly.

"What were you hoping would happen, love?"

"I don't know what you mean," she demurred.

"Oh, I think you do. Coming out with me tonight with a bare pussy, wearing my plug." He dragged his knuckle through her folds, pressing against her clit until she sucked in a sharp breath.

"Let's get out of here," she whispered.

"Not yet."

She grunted in frustration and shifted her own hand higher on his thigh, her thumb brushing against the growing bulge in his dress pants. His cock pulsed in reaction—as she, no doubt, had known it would. But two could play that game. He slid two fingers inside her, stifling his own groan at how wet and ready she was, but he didn't move them, content just to feel the clutch of her hot channel.

"Noah, please."

"Patience, love. I want to see the credits."

She huffed and he bit the inside of his cheeks to keep from laughing. She was adorable when she was frustrated—and it would make it all the more delicious when he made it up to her later.

A few moments later the music swelled and the credits began to roll. Callie squirmed impatiently in her seat, seeking friction against his unmoving fingers.

"Just watch, Calico."

He knew the moment she saw it. She sat upright in her chair, the move dislodging his fingers from within her, and gasped. The hand that had been on his thigh flew to her mouth. There on the screen, for only a second, it read:

Cara Dion

Composers: Noah Van Aller and Calandria Van Aller.

She turned to him, her eyes wide.

"You helped me write damn near half the score, love. That music is as much yours as it is mine."

She kissed him, hard and fierce, her fingers tugging at his hair. He was done waiting. He took her hand, and led her out of the darkened theater, ignoring the questioning glances from those they passed on the way out. She raced to keep up with his long stride as he led her through the lobby and out onto the sidewalk.

"I can't wait to get you back to the hotel. I have a whole evening planned for us, love. An entire night of worshiping my wife's pussy, and a whole bag of new toys for you to try." He scraped his teeth along the column of her throat to hide his smile.

Her eyes lit up and she arched her neck to give him better access. "You always take such good care of me."

"Always will."

He was half tempted to drop to his knees right there on the street and lick her until she came on his face, to drink down her pleasure. Instead, he broke away from her and hailed the nearest cab to take them back to the hotel and the evening he had planned for them. Once in the cab, barreling down the crowded streets of Manhattan, she slid her hand back up his thigh.

"Now who's misbehaving?" He bit back a groan as she palmed his cock through the fabric of his pants.

She slowed the movement of her hand. "What's this new project with Senator Thorne?"

"You want to talk about this now?" he asked with a meaningful glance at her hand wrapped around his erection.

"Might as well. Nothing more to be done until we're back at the hotel."

"Don't tempt me," he huffed.

"Okay," she said, pulling her hand away. He caught it with a growl and dragged it back to his crotch, pressing her hand against him. She laughed, her eyes sparkling. "Tell me."

"Senator Thorne wants to do a docuseries featuring small town libraries across the country and the work they do in the community."

"That's incredible."

His eyes flared as she squeezed his cock harder. He should have known better than to tease her in public; Callie always gave as good as she got.

"She wants us to score it. And she'd like your help as a consultant on the project."

Her hand stilled. "Are you serious?"

He caught her chin with his thumb and forefinger, bringing her lips to his. "Mmhmm."

"But you're supposed to go back to the university in the fall. You've already had more sabbatical time than—"

"I already spoke to my uncle. If we do this, I'll resign from the university." He scanned her face, taking in the flush high on her cheeks, her wide, sparkling eyes. "What do you think, Calico?"

"Let's do it."

He kissed her, his tongue sweeping over the seam of her lips. "Fuck, I love you," he groaned against her mouth. "When we get back to that hotel, I want you naked. No clothes for the next twenty-four hours."

She smiled, the curve of her lips pressed to his. "Overbearing."

The End

Also by Cara Dion

Love Song Series
Irreplaceable

Indiscreet

Undeniable

Aster Bay
Whisking It All

Visit my website to learn more and download free bonus content:

Acknowledgments

There are many people who helped bring Noah and Callie's story to life, and who have supported me as I pursue this dream of being an author.

First, my husband. Thank you for always supporting me, for taking our son so I can write, for making this work a priority for our family. It means more to me than I can say.

Second, my mother and stepfather, who were the first to read a physical copy of *Indiscreet* in public and have been a source of never-ending encouragement and enthusiasm. I would be lost without you both.

I am incredibly lucky to have a large family who is always in my corner (and, in some cases, handing out copies of my books to their friends). I have also been blessed with amazing friends who have been cheering me on since this was all just a "what if." Thank you to Megan, Phil, Ann, John, Mindy, Alysa, and Devon.

No writer creates in a vaccuum and I am infinitely grateful for the friends I have made in this industry who read early drafts of Noah and Callie, brainstormed with me when I couldn't find my way through the story, offered advice, and saw the potential for these two before I did. Ginny B. Moore, Liz Alden, and Maria Secoy—thank you.

And finally, to each and every person who has read one of my books, talked about them on social media, written a review, or recommended them to their friends: thank you. I will forever be grateful to be a part of the romance community.

About the Author

Cara Dion writes steamy, contemporary romance, often with a forbidden or age gap relationship.

Cara has always had an overactive imagination and spent much of her teenage years watching 80s and 90s romcoms with her aunt. She read her first romance when a friend snuck one of their mother's Harlequins into their Catholic school and passed it around like contraband, but she didn't return to romancelandia until the pandemic.

She has been an English teacher, professional musician, and nonprofit administrator. When she's not reading or writing romance, Cara loves cooking, Broadway musicals, and all things Disney.

Cara lives in a small town in New England with her husband, son, and two very demanding cats.

Follow Cara on Instagram at caradion.author and contact her at cara@caradion.com.